IT WAS ALL HAPPENING AGAIN.

Would they catch the murderer this time? Or would there be other deaths?

Jenny had been away at college last year; now she was beginning to understand how the residents of Pine Valley must have felt that first winter after the murder of the two women. The tensing of her stomach muscles, the dull throbbing behind her eyes—unlike the taut alertness with its surge of adrenalin that is triggered by a sudden unexpected threat, this fear would go on until the murderer was caught.

Suddenly the anonymous message she had received took on even more sinister meanings. *For your own good, you must leave town.* For her own good? Was this a warning that she was marked for murder?

Shadow of the Tamaracks

SARA NORTH

PLAYBOY PRESS
PAPERBACKS

SHADOW OF THE TAMARACKS

Copyright © 1979 by Sara North

Cover illustration by Walter Popp: Copyright © 1979 by Playboy

All rights reserved. No part of this book may be reproduced, stored in a retrieval system or transmitted in any form by an electronic, mechanical, photocopying, recording means or otherwise without prior written permission of the author.

Published simultaneously in the United States and Canada by Playboy Press, Chicago, Illinois Printed in the United States of America. Library of Congress Catalog Card Number: 79-83962. First edition.

This book is available at quantity discounts for promotional and industrial use. For further information, write our sales promotion agency: Ventura Associates, 40 East 49th Street, New York, New York 10017.

ISBN: 0-872-16553-1

First printing October 1979.

Prologue

Winter crept near, hurling its gusty warning out of the cobalt sky, across the sheer, brooding faces of the mountains, into the little valley town.

These "shining mountains" bred tough, independent men who met the harsh land head-on, who did not acknowledge the possibility of defeat. Consequently, to the loggers in the camps on the town's perimeter, the wind only heralded several frigid months to be challenged and overcome with the aid of insulated clothing and power saws.

Beyond the logging camps, the great mountains endured, having heaved and trembled through four ice ages. When the last glacier receded, millions of years ago, these mountains were ripped and torn and finally thrust upward from the earth's surface. Now their snow-covered peaks ringed the town, ageless sentinels, infinitely patient, seeming to hold the valley in a secret circle of foreboding.

In the town little movement could be seen, only an occasional car or bundled-up pedestrian on the main street. There, a sense of dark enchantment vibrated on the wind. And the town waited, the terror of more than a year past, when a murderer had stalked the valley, hidden now beneath the surface of placid lives. The town waited for the gripping fear to return and the suspicion of lifelong friends and neighbors to stir to life again. For when the ice and snow pelted the valley, driving into high drifts and glass-hard surfaces, when blasting cold flew on the shrieking wind, the town was isolated, shut away from the outside world, shut in with fear.

The murderer had never been caught.

One

Jenny Curtiss stood at the window of the Pine Valley Library and gazed out at the gray November afternoon, which lay like a shroud on the cobbled streets and old brick storefronts of the town. On the west side of Main Street, facing the library, no customers entered or left Banner's Department Store, the Four Seasons Dress Shop, the variety store or the dry cleaner's. This section of Main Street had been virtually deserted since the temperature dropped sharply about noon and the wind began to blow out of the north with a fierce intensity that made it necessary to lean into it to remain upright.

Jenny hated days like this. They made her feel lonely, cut off from other people by an invisible barrier that could not be easily breached. Even for the two hours that afternoon when the high-school research class filled the library, keeping her busy with their questions, she had felt somehow detached from it all, as if she were standing outside her own body and watching what transpired from a distance.

It was on such rare occasions that she wished fleetingly for wider, though undefined, vistas; but this desire was always vague and out of focus. She had long since decided that she was one of those people upon whom the weather had an undue effect, that her mood at such times was some sort of genetic quirk that had survived from the days when her ancestors lived in caves and looked upon the elements as messages from the gods.

A sudden gust whipped a discarded candy wrapper past the window and sent it spinning wildly down the street. Inside the tight, square library building, the wind sounded like the anguished moaning of some wild animal. Jenny shivered and pulled her heavy cardigan sweater closer about her.

She turned away from the window and quickly began taking books from the library cart and sliding them into

7

the proper shelf sections. It was almost four, quitting time.

Jenny had been the town librarian for six months now, after two years at the University of Montana in Missoula, where she had taken library-science courses. At twenty, she was the youngest librarian Pine Valley had ever had, even younger than Leah had been when she was in charge. Young people usually preferred to leave such small towns for the bustle and opportunities found only in larger cities. But whatever inclination Jenny had had in that direction, she had managed to stifle it. She was an only child, and her parents doted on her; her leaving would be nearly unbearable for them. Jenny was all they had, now that Leah was dead.

As always, when memories of her mother's younger sister came to mind, she forced them away. Memories of Leah were too painful. Pale, lovely Leah who had left the house one summer evening sixteen months ago and been brutally murdered.

But somehow life went on. Jenny's life at home with her parents, a job that she enjoyed, frequent contact with lifelong friends, occasional dates with Tom Irving, who worked as a printer in her father's newspaper office —all made for a satisfactory existence. It was rare these days that she allowed her imagination free rein to conjure up the tall, dark, mysterious stranger of her high-school dreams, her knight in shining armor who would one day appear from out of the mist beyond the mountains to sweep her away to happiness. Jenny's hand lingered on the plastic-covered spine of a book as her lips twisted in a wry smile. Such dreams were for school-girls. Grown women knew that one hardly ever ran into a knight in the Rocky Mountains of Montana.

When the cart was empty, she glanced at the round-faced wall clock. It was ten minutes past four. She aligned the small, bright-colored chairs around the low tables in the children's section, picked up the few books left on the long oak tables in the reference corner and returned them to the shelves, scooped up the pencils scattered across her desk, dropping them into the center drawer, and covered her typewriter. Then she went into the back room, where her camel's-hair coat with the plaid-lined hood hung on the rack.

She took a quick look at herself in the small mirror hanging in one corner. Heavily lashed eyes that were either blue or green, depending on the color of the clothing she wore—they were green now because of her green sweater—tawny hair that curled under just above her shoulders, a nose a trifle too short, a mouth that was wide with a generous bottom lip that she often caught between her teeth when she was thoughtful or worried. She was no great beauty, but she might pass as pretty.

She turned away from her reflection, put on her coat, and left the library, locking the door behind her. She walked down Main Street toward her father's newspaper office, leaning into the wind, shivering at its sharp, cutting edge.

She passed the Sears catalog store, where the woman sitting behind the order counter waved to her, and then the furniture store, where the display had been changed since the previous day. Now a blue velvet pit, soft with matching chairs and footstools, filled the window. The display created a warm, bright oasis that seemed to beckon her in out of the cold.

She hurried past, continuing down the street, struggling against the wind to keep her hood in place, and her gaze was drawn upward to the mountains. It was impossible to turn in any direction in Pine Valley without seeing them. They rose all around the town, tier after tier of them, snow-capped and awesome in their stark majesty. Forecasters were predicting an early winter. Already there had been several light snowfalls. By Christmas, four weeks away, the mountains would likely be completely covered with snow, and Pine Valley would have settled down to wait out the long, frigid months until spring. Even now there was a trace of frost in the air. They could very well have the first big snow of the season tonight.

A bell attached to the door tinkled as Jenny entered the office of the *Pine Valley Journal*. Mazie Jones, an energetic brunette in her late twenties who had worked at the newspaper office for five years, was typing at the desk. Mazie was short and might have been described, in a earlier day, as "pleasingly plump." Her shining cap of thick, dark curls haloed a round face dominated by large brown eyes. She had a cheerful personality and, under the press of a deadline, became jumpy with nervous energy. Yet Jenny occasionally had sensed unhappiness under Mazie's breezy, joking exterior.

Mazie gave Jenny a harried glance and chomped vigorously on her chewing gum. "Hi, Jen," she said, never missing a beat on the typewriter or the gum. "Your dad's in back."

"No, he's not." Gerald Curtiss's tall, slender form emerged from the pressroom. Jenny noticed that her father's shoulders seemed to have taken on a perpetual slump, and a few silver stands shone in his sandy hair. Upon her return from the university, she had seen her parents with fresh eyes and suddenly had become aware that they were no longer young, causing a wave of sadness to envelop her.

"Hi, honey," Gerald said. "How was your day?"

"Thrilling!" Jenny answered with mock enthusiasm. "Hattie Sterling called and commissioned me to find six or seven bloody mysteries that she and her sister haven't read. Now, *that* will take some doing."

Mazie paused in her typing and swung her head around. "You'd think they'd have had enough horror to last a lifetime."

Mazie's blunt statement surprised Jenny. For some months now, all of Pine Valley's residents had avoided speaking of the murders, as if ignoring the subject would make it go away. Recently Jenny had been angered by the seeming conspiracy of silence, feeling that open discussion of the deaths might bring to light a clue to the murderer. At the moment, however, she was in no mood to pursue the subject; so she changed it abruptly.

"Later, Miss Black brought in her high-school research class, but the kids definitely were not interested."

Her father gave her a thin smile, as if he understood her desire to switch the topic of conversation. "The little devils preferred making out behind the bookshelves, eh?"

"Right. And after that Mr. Elledge raked me over the coals because he claims I sent him an overdue notice for a book he never checked out. Well"—she threw out her hands—"it was like that all day, just one madcap adventure after another."

Her father chuckled, his blue eyes twinkling with an indulgent look reserved for his only child. "You ought to change jobs with Mazie here if you hanker for a little more excitement."

Mazie's gum popped. "Anytime."

Gerald's expression sobered. "Doc Weaver called a minute ago to ask me to print a request for blood donors in this week's paper. I thought I'd run by the hospital and give a pint before going home. You game?"

"Sure," Jenny agreed. "How about you, Mazie?"

Mazie did not take her eyes from the paper she was typing. "Come on, Jen. You know I faint at the sight of blood. Especially my own."

Gerald laughed and got his overcoat from his small, untidy office. "Let's go, Jenny."

In the car he said, "Doc gave me some bad news when he called. Harold Highbridge had a stroke today."

"Oh, no, Dad! How bad is it?"

"Doc says it's too early to tell, but it looks like Harold might be paralyzed on one side."

"Poor man."

"And poor Sarah. Luke gone for more than a year, and now this. I wonder if Luke's refusal to come home brought it on. Ah, poor Sarah."

"Yes," Jenny replied, disturbed by the expression on his thin, faintly freckled face. She always felt a little uneasy when her father spoke of Sarah Highbridge, because of things that had happened long before she was born. But small-town people remember such things and talk about them for generations. Sarah Highbridge and Jenny's father were once engaged. They were desperately in love, or so the stories went, but then something happened. They quarreled, and Sarah left Jenny's father, practically at the altar, and married Harold Highbridge, son of the town's wealthiest family, who evidently had always loved Sarah, too. The Highbridges had made their fortune in the lumber business, which was still Pine Valley's biggest industry.

Sometime after Sarah's marriage, Jenny's father married her mother, Doreen. Even though both parents loved

her totally, she had often sensed something missing in
their marriage—some spark of passion that ought to
have been there. They were fond of each other, but
Jenny had always suspected that Sarah Highbridge still
had her father's heart. However, perhaps she was too
sensitive to nuances in other people's tone or manner and
too inclined to read secret motives into ordinary actions.
Maybe the idea of her father's harboring an unrequited
love simply appealed to her imagination.

A gust of wind hit them broadside, causing the car to
shudder. Her father's face was set and heavy, all the
liveliness gone.

"Surely now Luke will come home," he said.

Jenny could not think of a suitable reply to that, and
a heavy silence fell. His words had conjured up dark
eyes, a lean, tan face, tousled black hair, and a tall
strong body—an image that sent a disturbing chill
through Jenny. How was it possible, she wondered, that
she could see Luke Highbridge so vividly after more
than a year? And how was it possible to be both at-
tracted and repelled by the same memory? A shiver ran
down her spine, and she chewed her bottom lip as she
turned her attention to the passing scene.

The hospital was in the southeast corner of town. They
took Main Street south and Bridge Street east, crossing
over the bridge spanning the Blackfoot River. Bridge
Street was a wide, birch-lined avenue with modest frame
houses, the majority of which were occupied by mill-
workers. The Highbridge Corporation owned some of
the houses and rented them to employees. Others were
privately owned, and these could usually be identified
because they were neater and in better repair. The
owners had bought the houses from the corporation,
which at one time had owned all the houses on this
street. Recently the corporation again had been selling
the houses to individuals, a few at a time, with employees being given first priority and the corporation holding
the mortgages and carrying the notes.

At the time the first houses were sold, an article in the
Pine Valley Journal had quoted Harold Highbridge as
saying that, with the plywood plant and the new paper
mill, the corporation had expanded to the point where

dealing in rental houses was no longer in keeping with the overall direction of the organization. It was not clear exactly what he had meant by that, but it was well known that since the employees had organized into a union several years ago, the old paternal-type services provided by the corporation, such as company houses and company stores, had been dispensed with one by one, usually as a result of union demands to improve them.

During the same period of time, numerous safety regulations had been instituted at the mills and pollution-control devices installed. It was said that Luke Highbridge, during his short tenure as his father's assistant, had been responsible for most of these innovations, as well as for the computer that now handled the more repetitive and boring tasks in the sawmill.

Looking at her father, Jenny asked, "Do you really think Luke would dare come back?"

"Why shouldn't he?" her father said sharply. He was obviously aware of the implication in her question. "Luke was never officially accused of anything."

"Not officially, no."

Gerald frowned. "Be fair, honey. There was never any proof."

"I know, Dad, but haven't you had doubts about Luke? We all had them."

"Doubt is not knowledge." Gerald sighed heavily. "If only Leah had lived, she could have told us."

"Or that other girl. I still get chills when I think about poor Mary Steed. She was only seventeen, Dad." Jenny's voice was a husky whisper. "Seventeen and unmarried and pregnant by Luke Highbridge."

"She *said* Luke was the father."

"And died shortly thereafter. Aunt Leah, too, because she knew who killed Mary."

"That is mere supposition, my dear. We don't know that the two murders were connected." There was a stubborn note in her father's voice that made Jenny feel impatient.

"Oh, Dad, what other reason could anyone have had for killing Leah?" She had an abrupt, painful memory of her aunt sitting in the old swing in the backyard, as

Jenny had often seen her. An open book lay forgotten on Leah's knees. Her dark-blond hair cascaded down her back, and her green eyes gazed dreamily up at the mountains, glazed with some unfathomable emotion. Leah had looked like a young girl, but, then, she had always seemed younger than her years, her moods shifting frequently, like a child's.

Once when Jenny had found her like that, she had asked, "What are you thinking about, Leah?"

Her aunt had turned to look at her, green eyes focusing slowly, as if she had come back from a far distance. Then she had smiled wistfully and made room on the swing for Jenny to sit beside her. "I was wondering if reincarnation could possibly be true, and hoping it might be."

Jenny, who was fourteen or fifteen at the time, had stared at her aunt in shocked surprise. "You mean you'd like to come back to earth again as a dog or a cow or something?"

Leah's tinkling laugh had pealed out. "Not exactly, sweetie, but I'd like to have the opportunity to live my life over. Oh, you can't understand that, not yet. You're too young. Wait until you're older, and then you might know how I feel." She had hugged Jenny then, and when she spoke again, her voice shook a little. "Actually, I hope you never understand. I hope you find some handsome, devoted, settled young man to marry, someone who'll adore you above all else so that you won't ever regret loving him."

Jenny had known Leah was thinking about Gideon Garfield, the young actor with whom she had run away at seventeen and who had later deserted her in New York City. With all the confidence of youth, Jenny had declared, "I'll *never* allow any man to break my heart. I mean to make certain of the man before I fall in love."

Leah had laughed at that. "Impetuous little Jenny! Your emotions are too headlong to demand guarantees, I'm afraid. And, besides, I'm not sure we can ever know another person that well."

As if he were reading her mind, Jenny's father said thoughtfully, "We never know what is going on in another person's life, not even those who live in the same house with us. Not really. Someone could have had another reason for killing Leah." The regretful note in his voice reminded Jenny of Leah's mood that afternoon when she'd spoken about reincarnation.

She studied his profile. "What a strange thing to say."

He glanced at her and smiled. "I wasn't implying anything, just pointing out that Leah could have had a secret enemy. Not that I think she really did."

"One thing is clear," Jenny said. "Since Luke left, there have been no more mysterious deaths. And now— if he comes back—"

"Don't borrow trouble, Jenny. We don't know anything for a certainty. No one was ever able to prove a thing against Luke, even though plenty did try."

"But it fits! There was motive and opportunity." She was aware that her words sounded harsh and judgmental. Were they an attempt to exorcise that seductive image from her mind? But it did fit. Mary Steed, working as a maid for the Highbridges, had turned up pregnant. She had told the Highbridges' housekeeper, Beth, that Luke was the father of her child. Two days later, she was found in the woods above the Highbridge house, her skull crushed by a large rock. Leah had befriended the murdered girl, in the same way that she took in abandoned animals and tried to find them homes. Jenny's cat, Beast, for example, a small scrap of matted gray fur stretched over a bony, starving body. Gerald had taken one look at the animal and asked Leah, "Where did you find that pitiful-looking beast?" unwittingly giving the cat his name. And then, as usual, Jenny's mother had taken over the day-to-day job of nursing the cat back to health. That was often the way with Leah's sympathetic impulses. She was quick to offer help, but it was the practical Doreen who usually saw Leah's projects through. Still, if Leah had suspected that Mary was pregnant, she would have been determined to help the girl.

It was believed that Leah had gone up to the Highbridge house to see Mary on the afternoon Mary died. One vein of speculation had it that, upon discovering Mary had gone out for a walk, Leah had followed her into the woods and caught sight of the murderer leaving the scene. Leah had found Mary's body and called the sheriff. When the sheriff questioned Leah, however, she said she had seen no one. But Jenny could still remember the dark circles around Leah's eyes the following morning, as if she had not slept at all. That same evening, Leah's body was found in the woods. Like Mary, she had been felled from behind by a heavy stone.

Jenny had tried many times to recall everything Leah had said on the last day of her life, hoping some word or phrase might point to the murderer. But Leah had said very little. She had seemed distracted and unresponsive to others in the family. Whatever had worried her during the night had evidently not been resolved. Was it only that she couldn't erase the memory of finding Mary's dead body? Or had she seen the killer after all—or something that led her to believe she knew the killer's identity? But if that were the case, why had she lied to the sheriff? Even though Doreen usually avoided Sarah, the Highbridges were close friends of Leah. Had she been protecting them? Had she known Luke was the killer but been unable to bring herself to accuse him?

Leah had been a gentle person, incapable of willingly hurting anyone. She would have known that naming Luke as the murderer might well have destroyed Harold and Sarah. Jenny shook her head to clear away the confusion. This all had the ring of logic; yet there was still an element of doubt in her mind. Why would Luke have killed Mary when he could easily have paid her off? Unless she didn't want money. Unless she had threatened to go to his father. Somehow that did not seem enough of a reason for murder, particularly since Luke Highbridge had a rather wild reputation. Jenny doubted that Harold and Sarah would have been shocked to learn of his involvement with Mary Steed.

As far as anyone knew, Mary had told no one except the Highbridges' housekeeper, Beth, that Luke was the father of her child. But, at the time of Mary's death, Luke could not have known that she had told Beth. So perhaps, feeling that he must keep the secret, Luke had panicked and, in his agitation, killed Mary as his only way out.

With a rush of compassion, Jenny thought of Mary Steed. Mary had worked for the Curtisses for several weeks before she moved to the Highbridges. Jenny remembered her as a shy, naíve farm girl with a pert, uptilted nose and rosy cheeks. There had been a touching air of vulnerability about her. She was a year younger than Jenny but had quit high school after her junior year. They might even have become friends, if Mary hadn't wanted to go to the Highbridges. Because Luke was there, of course. Every girl in town had been in love with Luke at one time or another.

Jenny found herself blinking back tears as her father turned into the hospital parking lot. All of her senses were flooded with a stunning flash of insight. Luke Highbridge's image had merged with the dark, mysterious stranger of her teen-age dreams. When had it happened? Why had she never realized it before? She told herself as she got out of the car, grabbing her hood against the wind, that she was being silly. This drab November day had dampened her spirits. The conversation about the murders had darkened her imagination so that her thoughts had turned morbid. Luke Highbridge's image had come into her mind with such force only because of the conditions under which his name had entered the conversation. Yet why should it disturb her so?

With the wind at their backs, they walked toward the large front doors of the hospital. Entering the lobby, they saw Sarah Highbridge sitting alone on one of the tan vinyl-covered couches. She rose at the sight of them.

"Hello, Jenny, Gerry." As far as Jenny knew, Sarah was the only one who ever called her father Gerry.

Gerald took Sarah's slender, beautifully manicured hands in both his ink-stained ones. It seemed to Jenny that her father and the tall, auburn-haired woman leaned slightly toward each other. "We are so dreadfully sorry about Harold," he said. "What can we do?"

Sarah brushed her free hand across her forehead, pain in her gray eyes. "Just knowing we have friends like you and Doreen is a great comfort, Gerry. Doreen was here earlier. But you probably know that."

He shook his head. "We haven't been home yet."

"She brought flowers—though, of course, no one but family is allowed in Harold's room. She stayed and talked to me for a few minutes. So many friends have come—"

As she swayed forward, Gerald caught her and led her back to the couch.

"You're exhausted, Sarah. What good will you be to Harold if you collapse?"

"I know—I know. I must go home for a few hours. I've hired private nurses round the clock; he's being cared for. I just feel less anxious somehow when I'm here." She glanced at Jenny, suddenly remembering her presence, and managed the ghost of a smile. "If only," she said, her voice trembling, "Luke comes home soon."

"You've reached him, then?" Gerald asked.

"Yes. He's coming into Missoula on the earliest available flight. Pray we don't have so much snow that the buses are delayed. If we're lucky, he could be home by tomorrow afternoon."

Jenny wondered if *lucky* was the right word, then told herself the thought was unfair. Of course Sarah Highbridge adored her handsome son and wanted him by her side in the midst of this family tragedy. What mother wouldn't?

"Promise me, Sarah, you'll call me at the office if there's anything—anything at all—I can do." Jenny noticed he hadn't said to call him at home and wondered, with a flash of resentment, if it had been intentional.

"I will, Gerry."

"We're going back to the lab for a few minutes. The blood bank's low on blood," he told her.

Sarah gazed at him rather dazedly. "Oh, I didn't know. Perhaps I should—"

"*You* should go home and to bed immediately," Gerald said firmly.

"You're right," she agreed. "I'll go now, but I doubt I'll be able to sleep."

"Just lying down will help," Gerald said.

Sarah pulled on her mink coat. She squeezed Gerald's hand and kissed Jenny on the cheek. "Thank you, dears, for caring." They watched her straighten her shoulders and move purposefully toward the door, as if she'd been given a special surge of strength. Strength, Jenny realized, with an unworthy pang of jealousy, that she'd drawn from Gerald.

In the lab, Jenny's father explained to Marty Brubaker, the lab technician, why they'd come. Jenny watched the burly, blond-haired Marty as he prepared the vials for the blood samples. Marty looked more like a boxer or a logger than a lab technician. However, he was known to be perpetually even-tempered and soft-spoken, hardly the stuff of which boxers or loggers were made. But his friends had also caught a glimpse of something else in Marty, a suggestion of unplumbed depths that, in rare moments, flashed from his blue eyes. There was a hint of restlessness that perhaps explained his having worked at a variety of jobs over the past several years—from selling real estate to being a forest ranger. He had come to Pine Valley three years previously, looking for work, and had been hired by the hospital, which was desperately in need of lab workers, as an on-the-job trainee. He had attacked the job with dedication and an eagerness to learn, which had endeared him to the hospital's administration.

Jenny had come to know Marty well, because he'd been at the house to call for Leah frequently before her aunt's death. Marty and Leah had been dating rather steadily, and everyone had expected them to be married.

Marty pricked their fingers and deposited blood samples on glass slides, which he took to the microscope. "You're just about my most regular customer, Gerald. I don't really need to check you out again, but I will, because it's hospital regulations." He peered into the microscope, humming softly to himself. "You're the same type as Mr. Highbridge, which will be handy if he needs a transfusion."

"Is that likely?" Gerald asked.

Marty shrugged. "Not because of the stroke, but there are sometimes secondary problems. I'll go ahead and crossmatch his blood with yours just in case." He glanced up. "I don't think I have a card on you, Jenny."

"You don't," Jenny said. "This is my first time to give blood. You may not take it, though. Mother has always insisted that anyone as thin as I am is bound to be anemic."

Marty grinned and changed glass slides on the microscope stage. He studied Jenny's blood sample. "That's a common misconception. Can't ever tell, though. Some of the most robust-looking individuals are anemic. Conversely . . ." He stopped, concentrating on the blood sample before him. "Hey, your count's terrific, girl. Pretty rare type, too. AB-negative. You can bet we'll take your blood. If you don't mind, I'll put your card into my walking-blood-bank file."

"Sure," Jenny said. "Glad to help whenever I can. Gosh, a rare type, huh? My claim to fame. I've always been so ordinary."

"Ordinary?" Marty teased. "Why, I'll bet you're the only girl in town with that particular color of blue-green eyes."

"I always said she's the prettiest girl in Pine Valley," her father said fondly.

Jenny blushed. "Oh, sure. I'm a regular *femme fatale*."

"Ha!" said Marty. "Her beauty is exceeded only by her modesty. Lie down on that table, girl." With a flourish, he reached for a length of rubber tubing. "Now that I have you at my mercy, I will further weaken you by drawing a pint of blood."

Gerald raised light-colored brows. "Good thing the old man's here to keep an eye on things."

Jenny stretched out on the narrow table against the wall, and Marty fastened the tubing around her arm above the elbow. "Curses," he drawled good-naturedly. "Foiled again."

As he bent to insert the needle into her vein, Jenny steeled herself for the slight sting as the skin was broken, then watched him from beneath lowered lashes. He was not an especially good-looking man, but there was something extremely engaging about him, something in the quick, intense way he looked at you sometimes, as if he had caught a glimpse of your most secret thoughts. Jenny had the feeling that he would remain calm in all manner of dire crises. He was of medium height, and she knew from something Leah had said that he was in his mid-forties, a few years younger than her father. As he bent over her, she noticed that the skin across his high cheekbones was slightly pitted by a few scattered acne scars from adolescent years. His chin and jawline were square and prominent, giving his face a look of strength. He was dressed in a white, high-necked lab coat and gray corduroy trousers and seemed sure and deliberate of movement—as if he knew exactly what he was about.

Jenny had at first found it difficult to picture Marty with the mercurial, other-worldly Leah. Yet he might have been just the solid influence Leah had needed. But how, Jenny wondered, would a marriage between two such seemingly opposing personalties have worked out? Had Marty gotten over Leah yet? When he first came to town three years ago, before he started taking Leah out, he had dated Mazie Jones, who worked in the newspaper office. But if that relationship had been taken up again, Jenny hadn't heard of it. As far as she knew, Marty hadn't been seeing anyone since Leah's death; yet he rarely spoke of her. But, then, he was the sort of man who wouldn't.

After the blood was drawn, Marty gave her a glass of orange juice and insisted that she lie still for ten minutes. He took her father down the hall to the snack bar for a cup of coffee while she rested. When the men came back, she was allowed to get up, and her father took her place, while she went along the hall to the now-deserted lobby to wait.

The wind seemed to be rising. She stared at one of the huge plate-glass windows and imagined that it gave slightly with the wind. She leafed through an old magazine lying on the table in front of her, then tossed it aside.

Restlessly, she walked about the lobby, pausing to read the names of major contributors to the hospital, listed on a brass plaque. Harold Highbridge's name topped the list of people who had made it possible for the Pine Valley Hospital to be built fifteen years ago, since a government grant had covered only half the construction cost.

She moved away from the plaque and went to stand at the window. Winter days were short in Montana, and although it was only a little after five, full darkness had descended. Beyond the glass, the wind wailed through the blackness.

She thought about Harold Highbridge, lying critically ill in his room down the hall. She thought about Sarah, with her thick, upswept auburn hair and the limpid gray eyes that had contained a lost expression earlier. And she thought about Luke aboard a jet, flying in from California. Would his return to Pine Valley herald a fresh outbreak of terror?

Two

The Curtisses lived in a residential area that had sprung up in the last ten years between Pine Valley's business district and the lower slopes of the mountain north of town. A single wide lane, Fir Street, climbed steeply toward the mountain, with streets running off on both sides at right angles. The Curtiss house, one of the first to be built in the development, was on Fir Street in the block farthest from the business district and nearest the mountain. It was a colonial two-storied red brick with white shutters and trim.

Doreen had done all of the first-floor rooms in Early American decor. The carpets were striped in varying widths of autumn colors—brown, beige, gold, and orange —and gave the impression of having been hand-braided. Most of the furniture was maple, well made and heavy. One wall in the den was of the same red brick as the exterior of the house, as was the fireplace, which had a raised hearth and bookshelves on either side of it. The small, rarely used living room was slightly more formal than the den, although still furnished with Early American pieces.

Upstairs were three bedrooms—Jenny's room, Leah's old room, and a guest room, which had been used briefly by Mary Steed when she worked for the Curtisses. Jenny and Leah had chosen the colors and furnishings for their own rooms, the only two in the house that were not Early American.

It was a comfortable house. On the whole, Jenny liked it and looked forward to returning there each afternoon. Several of the downstairs lights were on as Gerald's car pulled into the drive, and Jenny knew a wood fire would be blazing in the den fireplace. She felt a sudden urgent need to get inside, where there was warmth and light.

Doreen had dinner waiting for them in the dining room, off the den. They sat down to a spicy Mexican casserole, tossed green salad, and corn muffins. As her mother served their plates, Jenny was struck anew at how different Doreen was from the ethereal Leah. Doreen was taller, with a more substantial bone structure. Her light-brown hair was clipped short in a no-nonsense bob, and her hazel eyes never wandered off dreamily. She was dressed in a tailored green pantsuit and sensible crepe-soled leather shoes. Somehow, of the two sisters, Doreen had gotten all the practicality and strength necessary to face life squarely. Leah had been gay and lively on the surface, but underneath had lain an obscure fear of believing in her own competency. Doreen had understood this and had been there to pick up the pieces when Leah's life fell apart in New York City. When, after a few months, the young actor Gideon Garfield deserted Leah, she had been unable to accept the reality of the situation and had suffered a nervous breakdown. Doreen, already pregnant with Jenny, left Gerald in Pine Valley and went to New York to nurse her sister back to health. By the time Leah was sufficiently recovered to be removed from her doctor's care, Doreen's pregnancy had reached full term. So the sisters stayed on in New York until after Jenny was born.

Upon their return to Pine Valley, Doreen and Gerald took Leah into their home, where she found some measure of contentment. Enough so that Jenny had never heard Leah speak of leaving to find a place of her own. Leah was not the sort of woman who yearned for independence. Yet, oddly, she was the most untouchable person Jenny had ever known. Doreen, who was ten years older than Leah, had become a substitute mother to her, and Jenny had grown up thinking of Leah as a much older sister. It was Leah who played with her, who read to her and told her stories, while Doreen was busy managing the household.

Her mother's voice interrupted Jenny's reverie. "You two were late getting home this evening."

"We stopped at the hospital," Jenny explained.

Doreen's hazel eyes regarded her husband. "Was Sarah still there?"

He nodded. "She said you'd been by earlier, that you brought flowers. That was thoughtful of you, Doreen. Sarah appreciated it."

Jenny felt a tension between her parents, an undercurrent she'd sensed at other times when Sarah Highbridge's name entered the conversation.

"We've known the Highbridges all our lives, Gerald. They're our neighbors," Doreen said tersely. "Did you think I'd ignore Harold's illness?"

Jenny's father looked troubled, and his mouth thinned with irritation, but when he spoke there was a studied tolerance in his tone. "I didn't think anything of the kind, Doreen."

"Sarah and I may not be bosom friends," Doreen went on, unmollified, "but I *am* capable of feeling compassion for anyone whose husband has suffered a stroke. I went to the hospital as soon as I heard about Harold. Not that there was anything I could do."

"As Sarah told Jenny and me, it's a comfort just knowing people care," Gerald said as he buttered a corn muffin.

"I don't know that I helped her much." There was still the undertone of resentment in Doreen's words, but she was obviously making an effort to throw off whatever thoughts troubled her.

Gerald took a deep breath, as if the air in the dining room had become too thin all at once. "I spoke to her only briefly. I did manage to convince her she ought to go home and rest. This thing could drag on for days before the doctor knows the full extent of the damage. From what he told me on the phone, there will be some paralysis on one side. He can't say yet whether it will be permanent."

"Doc Weaver called to tell you of Harold's stroke? Did Sarah ask him to do that?" Doreen's voice was tight again.

"No, he called about something else. Naturally, Harold's stroke was on his mind, and he mentioned it."

"The Highbridges are expecting Luke home any day," Jenny put in, thinking to shift the focus of her parents' conversation.

Doreen looked faintly startled, as if she hadn't until then considered the possibility of Luke's return. "That was to be expected, of course," she said after a moment.

"Harold and Sarah will certainly try to talk him into staying."

"He may want to return to San Francisco now that he's been in business there for over a year," Jenny said.

"Harold told me only a couple of weeks ago that Luke's insurance agency out there is doing quite well. But Harold is confident the lumbering industry is in Luke's blood. He practically grew up in the logging camps and at the sawmill, working there after school and during vacations. Harold feels Luke eventually will come home to stay."

"He probably wouldn't have left in the first place if there hadn't been all that talk," Jenny ventured. "After all, he went into business with his father as soon as he graduated from college. Apparently he had planned to stay."

"He left on an angry impulse," Gerald said, "but he's had time to think things through."

"Well," Doreen insisted, "it's not as if anything has changed. There are those who still suspect him—"

"I hope no one in this family is among that number," Gerald said pointedly. "Luke Highbridge will always be disliked by some people. One born to wealth is inevitably the object of envy and resentment."

"Besides which," Doreen added, "he's the only one who had a motive for getting rid of Mary Steed. And his reputation didn't help matters, either."

"It's true," Gerald conceded, "that Luke sowed his share of wild oats."

"A little more than his share," said Doreen tartly. "I could name a dozen girls he was involved with during high school and college, and *they* were inevitably the ones who got hurt."

"That's all past history," Gerald insisted. "A boy's escapades. I'm certain he's changed. We all eventually have to grow up and accept things as they are. There comes a time when . . ." He broke off, but Jenny sensed his thoughts had wandered to something or someone besides Luke Highbridge. Perhaps he was thinking of the time, long ago, when he finally faced the truth that Sarah Highbridge was lost to him forever. But perhaps not, for the smile he turned on Doreen was affectionate. "I haven't lived with a practical woman all these years without learning that. People do change. Their interests and aspirations, the direction of their lives, nothing is static."

"You never step into the same river twice," Jenny said lightly, recalling an oft-repeated statement of her semantics professor.

"That sounded like Leah," Doreen said. In the light from the overhead chandelier, her hazel eyes seemed darker and full of pain. "Remember the outrageous things she used to say?"

"Aunt Leah was not like anyone else in the world," Jenny said. "She was beautiful and gay, and yet at times she could be so strange."

Gerald gave her a wry smile. "Dryads tend to be stranger than ordinary mortals. I always suspected that Leah lived in the woods and on the mountains when she was out of the house."

Jenny said, "And yet she didn't get those cryptic remarks of her from wild creatures. Many of them came from the books she read. I've run across several of her sayings at the library. There's a lot of time for reading on the job, and I suspect that suited Leah more than me, but at least I'm finding time for some of the books I always wanted to read. And often I come across a familiar line and realize that Leah had been there before me."

"Leah used to bring those books home and read half the night," Doreen mused.

"Obsessive reading can be a form of escape," Gerald said. "I think that was true in Leah's case. She didn't like this world very much."

"I'm not sure about that," Jenny told him. "Leah once said she'd like to be reincarnated so that she could live her life over again."

"I doubt," said Doreen with a sigh, "that she'd manage things any better the second time around. When she wasn't reading, she was daydreaming."

Gerald reflected, "Remember how she would look at you sometimes with that unfocused stare, as though she didn't see you clearly because she couldn't bear to look at anything too closely."

"But there were other times," Jenny said, "when I had the feeling that she could read my mind, that she understood me, when she wanted to, better than anyone else in the world."

Doreen's look was thoughtful. "I doubt that Leah fully understood anyone as normal as you are, honey."

Jenny wrinkled her nose. "For normal, read ordinary."

Gerald chuckled. "There you go again. I'm beginning to suspect you are fishing for compliments." He turned to Doreen. "She managed to get one or two out of Marty Brubaker today."

"Marty Brubaker?" Doreen looked puzzled.

"He took our blood," Jenny explained. "Actually, that was why we went to the hospital in the first place, to give blood."

"*You* gave a pint of blood?" Doreen asked. "But I always thought . . ."

"That I was anemic," Jenny finished. "I know. I told Marty that, but he said it's a common misconception that thin people are anemic. In fact, he said I have plenty of red and white corpuscles and all that sort of thing. Not only that, I have a pretty rare blood type; so I'm now a part of Marty's walking blood bank."

Doreen frowned. "I'm not sure I approve of that. It can't be healthy for you to give blood in the wintertime when you need to fight off colds and flu."

Jenny laughed. "Don't fuss, Mother. I feel fine. And one of these days I may be able to help a patient who needs my blood type."

Doreen shot Gerald a helpless look. "You shouldn't have allowed it, Gerald."

"Mother," said Jenny with a trace of impatience, "you're forgetting I'm a grown woman. It was my decision."

Gerald and Doreen exchanged an uneasy glance. Jenny realized her words were an unpleasant reminder that she was no longer a child. With this insight, her impatience vanished. "My goodness, what a fuss about nothing. But there's one thing I'm very happy about."

Both parents looked at her. "What's that, honey?" Gerald asked.

"Do you realize that we have talked about Leah more tonight than in the entire sixteen months since her death?

In a way it helps to keep her alive. She was really a very special person."

Doreen got up abruptly and began to clear the table. Jenny suspected her mother was fighting back tears. It was not easy for Doreen to show her feelings, and she usually tried to cover them up with some brisk activity.

Gerald put a hand over Jenny's on the tablecloth. "Yes, she was. I think we're all pretty lucky to have known her."

After a moment Gerald went into the den to sit beside the crackling fire and read a magazine. Jenny helped her mother clear the table. She felt a special closeness in her family circle that she attributed to the fact that they had, for the first time, been able to talk about Leah with more nostalgia than pain. When the kitchen had been put to rights, Jenny went upstairs to her bedroom.

A great ball of gray fur lay in the middle of her bed. Beast raised his head when Jenny opened the door and stared at her with haughty disdain, as though she were the intruder. But when she sat down on the bed and began to stroke his fur, his eyes became slits and he pushed against her hand, purring contentedly.

Jenny scratched behind his ears, murmuring, "Did you miss me today, Beast?"

His ears twitched, and his yellow eyes regarded her with a sort of detached interest. He got to his feet and stretched lazily, then leaped to the floor and moved silently toward the door.

"So you're angry with me for interrupting your nap, is that it? You're an insufferable snob, Beast!" Jenny went to open the door for him, and he moved swiftly out of the room, melting into the gray shadows in the hall.

Jenny's bedroom was a calming oasis of blue and white —white-sprigged wallpaper of pale blue with a darker-blue shag carpet and a quilted cotton spread on the white-and-gold French provincial bed. A narrow bench under the dormer window was covered with a blue floral print, and curtains were made of the same cotton fabric. Paintings of snow-clad mountains and deep-green forests looked down from the walls, and in one corner shelves held books, plants, framed photographs, and an assortment of keepsakes from Jenny's schooldays.

This evening, however, the room did not soothe her.

Some obscure restlessness would not let her lose herself in the soft music from the stereo or the make-believe world of a book. She sat on the window seat and stared into the thickening darkness. A flicker of light from the tree-shrouded Highbridge house—the Tamaracks—could be seen at the end of the street. The house, which faced the dead end of Fir Street, was named for the trees, plentiful in the area, from which it had been built. A western species of the larch tree, the tamarack was the only conifer to lose its needles in the fall. The Tamaracks' melancholy history had been the source of many an eerie tale passed among Jenny's school friends as they grew up in Pine Valley. She wondered if Sarah Highbridge was resting in the house now, or had she returned to the hospital? This would surely be a long, sleepless night for Sarah. Harold Highbridge was just fifty-two, young to be felled by a stroke. Was it possible that anger at Luke's refusal to come home had brought it on? Or did those old childhood tales contain an element of truth? Was it possible that the Tamaracks was contaminated by its morbid history, so that its very atmosphere infected those who lived there?

The ringing of the phone beside Jenny's bed shattered the silence, startling her. After a second ring, it stopped; one of her parents had answered downstairs. Then she heard her father calling her from the bottom of the stairs. She moved to her bed and sat down as she picked up the receiver.

"Hello."

"Jenny, it's Tom." The familiar deep voice brought the tall young man's image into the room with Jenny—the unruly red hair, the light-brown eyes with their flecks of gold, the serious expression that usually sat on the long face.

"Oh, hi," she said.

"I'm sorry I didn't get to speak to you when you came by the newspaper office this afternoon. I was elbow-deep in printer's ink. Mazie said you left with your father."

"We went out to the hospital," Jenny explained.

"I heard about Harold Highbridge. I'm sorry. I know the Highbridges are friends of your parents." They were more her father's friends than her mother's, but Jenny saw no reason to elaborate on that.

"We didn't get to see Harold, but we talked to Sarah.

She seemed drained. Dad convinced her to go home for a while. I think she'll be all right when Luke arrives."

There was a pause on the other end of the line. Then Tom said, "I guess he'll have to come home now." Tom had been a high-school classmate of Luke Highbridge, and his dislike of Luke came across in the terse tone of his voice. Jenny assumed that Tom's feelings were the natural reaction of a poor farm boy to the cocky, self-assured son of the town's wealthiest family. Whatever the reason, Tom held a deep antipathy for Luke Highbridge.

"Yes, Sarah said he'd be here in a day or two."

"Hopefully," said Tom curtly, "he won't have to stay long."

When Jenny did not respond, he went on. "I was wondering if you'd like to go out for dinner tomorrow night. If the snow that's forecast arrives, we probably won't be able to leave town, but I'll spring for steaks at the Copper Kettle."

Jenny tried to inject enthusiasm into her acceptance. Normally, she enjoyed her dates with Tom, and she knew that her lack of eagerness was due to the depression she'd been feeling most of the afternoon.

When she had hung up, she wandered into the white-and-blue bathroom adjoining her bedroom. She had shared this bath with her aunt when Leah was alive. A second door led into Leah's room. Jenny had been in there only two or three times since Leah's death. The bedroom gave her such an empty, sad feeling now, but, because she was restless, she opened the door and entered the room, switching on the overhead light.

Little had been changed since Leah's death. Doreen had packed most of Leah's clothes into boxes, which Gerald had carried to the attic. Otherwise, the room was as Leah had left it, pink roses everywhere—on the wallpaper and the bedspread and the padded chair cushions. The arched canopy that rested on the four-poster bed was a mass of sheer pink ruffles, as were the curtains. The shag carpet was thick and creamy white and the small, round table near one of the windows was spread with a white satin cloth trimmed with rows of pink ball fringe. A delicate pink-and-white china tea service sat on the table as if it awaited Leah's imminent return. It was an utterly feminine room, like Leah herself, and it evoked the memory of her so vividly that Jenny's heart constricted.

"Leah." She spoke softly in the heavy silence, her voice catching. "Who killed you?"

Slowly, she began to walk around the room, gazing at the tea service, the soft pink roses on all sides, the silver inlaid brush and comb that were perfectly aligned on the dressing table next to a spray bottle of White Shoulders, Leah's favorite cologne. An enlarged, framed color snapshot of Leah and Marty Brubaker sat in one corner. Jenny sat down at the dressing table and picked up the photograph, holding it up to the light. The picture had been taken at the town park a few weeks before Leah's death. It had been the first warm Sunday of spring. Leah had packed a picnic lunch for the two of them, and they had stayed all afternoon. Evidently they'd asked a passer-by to snap their picture.

They were smiling out of the photograph, Marty's stocky strength in sharp contrast to Leah's pale, delicately boned beauty. Marty's arm was around Leah's shoulders. He wore jeans and a yellow cotton shirt that was open at the neck, showing a thick mat of light-colored hair on his burly chest. Leah wore a tiered lavender skirt trimmed with wide bands of white lace and a drawstring blouse. Her long blond hair was tang'ed, as if the day had been windy, and her right hand touched the gold medallion hanging on the chain that she wore around her neck almost constantly.

Jenny returned the photograph to its corner, and her hands moved to open the miniature cedar chest that Leah had used as a jewelry case. A snarl of chains and a variety of necklaces lay in the bottom of the chest, all inexpensive costume jewelry. The medallion was probably the most expensive piece of jewelry Leah had owned. Jenny saw it in one corner of the chest and lifted it out, carefully untangling its chain from the others.

The medallion felt cold in her palm. She ran her fingertips over it, remembering how attached to it Leah had been. It was a smooth circle about two inches in diameter, with the crowned profile of Demeter, the Greek goddess of growing things, carved in *bas-relief*. A stalk of corn curved around the back and across the top of Demeter's head.

Leah had worn the medallion most of the time, even

sleeping with it on, for as long as Jenny could remember. When Jenny was a child, Leah had told her about Demeter, the goddess whose sorrow caused her to withhold her gifts from the earth, which turned into a frozen desert. While Demeter's unhappiness lasted, the green and flowering land was icebound and lifeless. But Demeter's mood swung from sorrow to joy regularly, and then she was sorry for the desolation she had brought about, and she made the fields once more rich with abundant fruit and the whole world bright with flowers and green leaves; thus spring came.

Leah had told her other stories of gods and goddesses. When Jenny had asked, "Why do you like Demeter the best?" Leah had said, "Because we are a lot alike, Demeter and I."

This had puzzled Jenny for some time, until she realized that Leah, too, experienced wide swings in mood. She could go from gaiety to depression in a moment, and often for no discernible reason.

Jenny unclasped the gold chain and fastened it around her neck. The smoothness of the gold circle felt cool in the hollow between her breasts. She would wear the medallion, she decided, in Leah's memory. Then, on second thought, she dropped the medallion out of sight beneath the neck of her green sweater. Seeing it might be painful for her parents.

She left the room quickly, switching off the light and closing the door behind her. She had a sudden longing to go walking, to feel the cold, cleansing wind in her face, as she had often done as a child with Leah. Darkness had settled outside, but the street was well lighted. Making a swift decision, she managed to descend the stairs without being heard.

Beast was sitting patiently beside the front door, waiting to be let out. Jenny put on her coat, pulling the hood snugly about her face; then she opened the door quietly and slipped out with Beast at her heels. She didn't want to try to explain this sudden desire to be outside alone on such a cold night. She would not be gone long and could probably return to the house without being missed.

Although it was not late, the street was as quiet as if Jenny were the only mortal within miles. The wind was piercing, and she pulled her scarf up over her chin, so that only her nose and eyes were exposed. Beast moved silently beside her.

In spite of the cold, she began to relax and feel the quiet and peace seeping into her restless mood. She decided to walk to the end of Fir Street before turning back.

The Tamaracks was set apart from the other houses on the street by twenty acres of land thickly overgrown with evergreens. Before the other houses had been built on this hillside, the Tamaracks had sat above the town alone in its splendid, wooded isolation.

Just as Jenny reached the street's dead end, Beast meowed mournfully and darted into the trees.

"Beast!" she called after him. "Come back here!"

She waited for several minutes, then called the cat again. When he did not appear, she followed him into the trees. As she entered the Highbridge property, the land began another steep rise and the trees on all sides cut off most of the light from the streetlamps behind her. But Jenny had walked this path many times as a child and knew her way through the shadows. The lane took a circuitous approach to the house, seeming to wander idly beneath the trees. She called Beast softly, feeling more and more impatient, but unwilling to leave the cat outside on such a cold night.

When she came into the clearing where the Tamaracks sat between two tall yard lamps, she stopped and looked around. There was no sight of Beast. She looked up at the house. Lights burned dimly in the living room and in one of the second-floor bedrooms. The garages were in back, so she couldn't tell whether Sarah's car was here or not, but it didn't matter. She did not intend to make her presence known.

The house had been built in the late 1800s by one of Montana's copper kings, Cyrus Storm, a man who had apparently had more money than architectural knowledge. Perhaps the house was what Cyrus Storm thought befitted a king, in spite of the fact that it followed no particular style or period. And somehow it suited the rustic scenery, with the rugged mountains rising behind it and the ancient trees crowding all around.

The Tamaracks was painted white, its numerous gables and turrets outlined with fluted copper trim. It appeared to have been sitting there for centuries, certainly much longer than a mere hundred years, as if it had grown out of the mountain that backed it up. Its windows were many-paned, some rectangular and some arched at the top. The house was three stories high with a round, towerlike structure on one corner that, Jenny knew, contained a circular staircase leading to the third floor. A broad, white-pillared porch swept across the front, two stories high, with wide steps leading up to an oversized front door framed by leaded glass panels on both sides. Some of the second-story bedrooms had narrow, railed balconies where the occupants could sit and enjoy the wildly beautiful scenery. The third story had been used by servants in Cyrus Storm's day, but now Beth Denton, the housekeeper, lived there alone. Since Mary Steed's death, a girl came in from the town by day to help the housekeeper but returned to her family at night.

The Tamaracks was large and rambling and by modern standards would have cost a fortune to build; in fact, it had cost Cyrus Storm a small fortune in the nineteenth century, for the millionaire had indulged his every whim, from fireplaces of marble or stone in every room to a bathroom lavish with imported Italian tile for each of the six second-story bedrooms.

A brooding atmosphere seemed to hover about the house, but Jenny shrugged off these feelings, realizing they were caused by her knowledge of the Tamaracks' history. Cyrus Storm's copper mine had played out, leaving him penniless, and the proud copper king shot his brains out in one of the second-story bedrooms. His wife, left alone in the house except for the servants, whom she soon had to release because she could no longer pay them, became a recluse. Eccentricity eventually turned into madness, and Marietta Storm had roamed the many rooms of her rustic castle night after night, searching for her dead husband, carrying a candle to light her way. She had stopped eating, either from lack of appetite or because her muddled mind simply forgot. Her decomposing body was found one day by a county official who had come to the house to inform her that the property was to be sold for nonpayment of taxes.

Harold Highbridge's grandfather, who was building a lumber empire in the area, bought the house. Down through the years there had been other tragic deaths connected with the Tamaracks. One of the first Highbridges' young children had accidentally hanged himself from an upstairs balcony while playing with a rope. A later Highbridge had fallen to his death from one of the treacherous high cliffs on the mountain behind the house. Mary Steed, a servant in the house, had been murdered. And now Harold Highbridge had suffered a paralyzing stroke.

Jenny shivered violently. It was little wonder that she imagined a dark foreboding enveloped the Tamaracks. Was it possible for a house to be haunted by the tragedies that had occurred within and around it? Was it possible that the very atmosphere pulsed with a dark enchantment that sometimes broke through the barrier of the past and touched those living in the present?

And yet Leah had loved this house. Jenny had sometimes thought that her aunt's friendship with Sarah Highbridge was carefully nourished so that Leah would have access to the Tamaracks. Leah had found only contentment and a much-needed sense of permanency here; but Leah was dead.

For one brief instant, Jenny experienced a sense of Leah's presence so strong that she whirled about, staring into the dark circle of trees behind her. It was as if whatever remained of Leah—spirit, soul, or only memory—cried out to her in that moment.

She felt the gold medallion, warm now from her body heat, pressing against her breast. More than ever before, she longed to unmask Leah's killer, to make him pay for taking the life of that fragile, gentle creature.

The house loomed ahead as though mocking her. Somehow she had to learn what had brought about Leah's death, whether Luke was responsible or someone else. She supposed that Leah would have said this was a headlong impulse. What did she hope to uncover that the sheriff had missed? How did she hope to accomplish what no one else had been able to do?

It seemed to her that the answer lay with Luke Highbridge. *And Luke Highbridge was coming home.*

Three

"Stay where you are!"

The harsh command shattered the night, jolting Jenny from her thoughts. A bulky shadow moved around the corner of the house. It was a man carrying a rifle. Too frightened to think clearly, Jenny whirled and ran into the trees.

A shot blasted out behind her as she raced down the path, dodging headlong through the trees, somehow finding the way in the darkness. A loud, angry voice shouted to her to stop, but she ran all the faster, her heart thudding furiously. When she reached the boundary of the Highbridge property and gained the street again, she had to slow down to a walk. Trying to catch her breath for renewed flight if necessary, she glanced behind her. But she did not see anyone or hear the sounds of pursuit or the voice that had called to her. She seemed to be safe on the lighted street. It was almost as if she had imagined that rifle shot.

She stopped and drew in several deep breaths to steady her nerves, and suddenly she remembered the wandering Beast. Well, let him come home when he was ready. That independent cat had almost gotten her shot. She realized now that the man who fired at her must have been Beau Gleason, the Highbridges' caretaker, who lived in the apartment over the garages behind the house. Technically, of course, she had been trespassing, but she should have identified herself instead of running. Her flight had probably convinced him she was a burglar or a vandal bent on mischief.

Why hadn't she identified herself? She had been too gripped with panic to think rationally, but there was another reason, too. She had never liked Beau Gleason. He was a surly, uncommunicative man whose black eyes, peering out of a battered, weather-beaten face, seemed to stare right through her. Gleason was an old logger. He still wore his white hair over his ears and had a full beard, as many of the loggers did. His right leg had been crushed by a falling tree several years ago, an injury which had resulted in a permanent limp. Since he was no longer able to work as a logger, and an unbending pride would not allow him to accept charity, Harold Highbridge had installed him at the Tamaracks as caretaker. As a result, he was fiercely loyal to the Highbridges. Jenny had little doubt that he would literally die for them if need be. Gleason was short and stockily built, and, in spite of his limp, one sensed in him an almost superhuman strength that seemed always to be coiled, waiting.

Had he recognized her? Even if he hadn't, would he actually shoot at a trespasser? Or had he merely shot above her head to frighten her?

When she reached her house, her father was standing on the front porch, looking toward the Highbridge property. Beast sat on the top step and peered down at her innocently.

"Jenny! What are you doing out here?" Gerald cried.

Somehow she managed to sound matter-of-fact. "I went for a walk."

Her father glanced up the street again. "I thought I heard a shot, but it's a little late for hunters. Did you hear it?"

"It—it could have been a car backfiring."

He seemed satisfied with this, and they went into the house together. Beast slipped silently past them and up the stairs as Doreen called to Jenny from the den, asking if she would like a piece of pie or a cup of tea. Jenny declined, saying she was tired.

Doreen came into the entry hall and looked at her worriedly. "What's wrong, Jenny? Your face is so flushed."

"Of course it's flushed," Jenny retorted more sharply than she intended. "It's cold outside." Then, seeing the hurt expression on her mother's face, she added, "Maybe I'll take a cup of tea upstairs with me."

"You go on up," Doreen insisted. "I'll bring the tea in a minute."

"You shouldn't be climbing stairs when it isn't necessary," Jenny protested. "It's probably not good for your heart."

"What nonsense!" Doreen said. "I haven't had one of those silly spells in months. Besides, it's not as if I ever had a genuine heart attack." She started toward the kitchen. "Now, you go on, and I'll bring your tea up shortly."

Knowing the futility of arguing with her mother, Jenny went up to her room. Beast was back in the middle of her bed, but this time he only opened one eye slightly and promptly went back to sleep.

Jenny sat down on the window seat, wriggling her feet out of her shoes. Why had she evaded her father's question about the rifle shot? First, she hadn't wanted to worry him. But, more than that, how would she explain skulking around the Tamaracks at night? Chasing a cat seemed a lame excuse. She wondered if Beau Gleason would report to the police that he's surprised a trespasser. Somehow she doubted it. She thought that Gleason would prefer dealing with intruders in his own way.

After a few moments her mother came in carrying a steaming mug of tea. "It's just the way you like it, a teaspoon of honey and a sprinkle of cinnamon."

Jenny accepted the mug, glad now that her mother had insisted on bringing it up. She was still chilled from her walk, and the good strong tea warmed her. "It's perfect," she said after a moment. "Thanks, Mother."

Doreen pulled out the dressing-table stool and sat down facing Jenny. Evidently Doreen had something on her mind, for she had never been one for cozy mother-daughter chats.

"Jenny," she said seriously, "that was no car backfiring, was it?"

Jenny could not keep up the fabrication in the face of her mother's steady, penetrating gaze. "No, Mother, it wasn't. But it was nothing important, and I didn't want to worry you and Dad. I wandered onto the Highbridge property in search of Beast, and evidently Beau Gleason thought I was a potential burglar and shot over my head."

"Shot!" Doreen's hazel eyes grew wide, then narrowed with indignation. "Beau Gleason! Why, how dare that crochety old cretin shoot at you! He shouldn't even be allowed to have a gun. I never have trusted that man. He's dangerous."

"I'm sure he didn't know who I was," Jenny said, "and I did run when he told me to stop."

"That's no excuse," Doreen said furiously. "He can't be allowed to go around shooting at people. I'll tell Sarah about this. Gleason is her responsibility."

"I'd rather you didn't mention it to anyone," Jenny said. "I feel silly enough already. I should have walked up to him and identified myself. Instead, I panicked."

"Well"—Doreen frowned—"I'll certainly speak to that man in private if the opportunity presents itself."

Jenny smiled, thinking that Doreen was acting like a tigress protecting her young. The one thing that could ruffle Doreen's usually calm manner was for someone to harm some member of her family. Jenny continued, "Sarah shouldn't have to cope with Beau Gleason just now, and let's not tell Dad, either. He has enough on his mind as it is."

Doreen's thin lips pressed together. "Harold's stroke, you mean. And, of course, he'll probably feel he has to provide a shoulder for Sarah to cry on." The words were bitter, communicating to Jenny a little of the doubt and jealousy her mother must have suffered over the years. It was this, rather than intentional cruelty, that made her say such things.

"Sarah won't need Dad. I'm sure Luke will give her plenty of support," Jenny said, trying to reassure her mother.

"Well, I can't feel that's all to the good. Luke's coming back, I mean."

"It was bound to happen sooner or later."

Doreen ran a hand through her short-cropped brown hair. "I don't like it."

Jenny sipped her tea without answering.

After a moment Doreen changed the subject. "You made me realize something tonight when you reminded me that you're a grown woman."

"I didn't mean—"

"No, no," Doreen interrupted. "You're right. I'm afraid your father and I tend to forget it, and that's not fair to you. I know you came back here to work because we wanted it."

"I like my job," Jenny assured her. "I'm able to use

my education, and I'm virtually my own boss. The members of the library board rarely object to my ideas for changing or adding to the library."

"But you could have made more money in a larger town," Doreen persisted. "And most girls want to be on their own before they marry."

As Jenny studied Doreen's plain, solemn face, she realized that this conversation must be costing her mother a great deal. In spite of Doreen's words, Jenny knew that both she and Gerald would suffer if Jenny moved away. She said lightly, "I have no burning desire to move into some lonely little apartment in a big city. I guess I'm like Leah in that. And it's not as if you and Dad have ever been especially overprotective. You've let me make most of my own decisions for a long time now."

"Just don't rush into anything," said Doreen worriedly, "with Tom Irving—or anyone—to prove that you're an adult."

This was the first time Doreen had ever said anything even remotely personal about Jenny's relationship with Tom, and Jenny was amazed that her mother seemed to think she might settle for a marriage, any marriage, to get away from home. "Mother, Tom and I have never even spoken of marriage. He's a good friend, that's all."

Doreen sighed. "There's that, too. Tom's a nice person, but he's not the right man for you. There are so few men your own age in Pine Valley." She leaned forward and spoke hurriedly, as if she must say what she had to say in a rush, before she lost her nerve. "I want you to know that if you'd like to take a job in Missoula or even farther away, it's a natural desire for a girl your age. Your father and I wouldn't try to stop you—we'd understand."

"That's very unselfish of you," Jenny said sincerely, "but at present I have no such plans. Please don't worry about it anymore." She held out her hand to her mother.

Doreen gazed at her for another moment, seemed about to say something else, then decided against it. She stood and took Jenny's hand for a brief moment and pressed it warmly. Then she moved toward the door. Jenny saw that once more her mother's usual cool, competent manner had returned. "Good night," Doreen said and closed the door softly behind her.

Jenny finished her tea, got up and went into the bathroom to run hot water into the tub. She wasn't sure what had prompted her mother's generous gesture. Was she afraid Beau Gleason actually had meant to harm Jenny tonight? Or was her fear more general and undefined, based on the knowledge that Luke Highbridge was coming home? Did Doreen, like others in the town, suspect that Luke had murdered Mary Steed and Leah? Did she perhaps harbor the apprehension that there might be more deaths after Luke's return? It was difficult to tell. Doreen was not a woman who confided in others. But she was sensible, and more likely she had simply been letting Jenny know that she and Gerald would understand if Jenny decided to strike out on her own.

Yet, for some crazy reason, Doreen's unexpected generosity made Jenny feel even more obligated to stay at home, for the present at least. For the first time, she admitted to herself that she had a perhaps irrational fear that her parents' love for her had given the marriage its only substance and form all these years, that should that form be removed, there would be nothing left between her parents to hold the marriage together.

After her bath, Jenny got into bed, disturbing Beast, who meowed grumpily and wandered across the room to the window seat, where he curled up and went back to sleep. Jenny fell asleep quickly, too. Her experience at the Highbridge house must have exhausted her enough to counteract her concern about her parents' relationship. It was much later when she awakened and lay listening to the wind sweeping the trees outside her window. The strength of the gale had grown steadily while she slept and now sounded as if a blizzard was in the making.

She moved her arm outside the covers and glanced at the luminous dial of her watch. Two in the morning. She curled back into the warmth of her bed, but after several minutes she was still wide awake, and she couldn't help wondering if the wind or some other sound had awakened her. She threw back the covers and fumbled for her velour robe, which lay across the foot of the bed. Tying the robe about her, she slipped her feet into scuffs and padded to the dormer window to see if the snow had started. Beast leaped from the window sea and paced back and forth across her feet, rubbing against her legs and making an occasional restless mewing sound.

In the stream of light from the yard lamp, she could see flakes of snow whirling thick in the wind, but the snow had just started, for the ground in large patches was still the brown color of dead grass. Then her heart lurched as she saw a movement in the shadows near the edge of the pale-yellow circle of light. A figure moved hesitantly nearer the light, and she saw that it was a man wearing a gray overcoat and a stocking cap pulled down on his head. She received a second shock when the man turned and she recognized her father. What was he doing down there at this time of night? At first he had seemed to be looking toward the trees surrounding the Highbridge house, and now he looked toward the street. His hands were plunged deep in his overcoat pockets, and he moved unsteadily. Was he sleepwalking? But Jenny had never known her father to sleepwalk. Suddenly she was seized with a sense of foreboding.

She grabbed her coat, slipping it on her the robe, and left her bedroom, moving silently along the hall and down the stairs in her quilted scuffs. A lamp in the den had been left burning, throwing an eerie light into the entry hall. She noticed, with a feeling of relief, that her parents' bedroom door was closed. No light could be seen under the door. Evidently her mother was sleeping.

Quietly, Jenny let herself out of the house and walked around to the side yard where she had seen her father. He was still there, gazing back toward the woods again. Her nearly bare feet felt as if they'd been plunged into a bucket of ice water.

She shivered and spoke softly. "Dad, are you all right?"

Gerald turned to look at her. His nose and cheeks were flaming from the frigid wind. He must have been outside for some time.

When he didn't answer, she said, "Come inside. It's too cold to be out here."

He seemed to hesitate a moment, then he came toward

her and followed her slowly back to the house and into the den, where orange-red coals still glowed in the fireplace. She stirred up the coals and laid a log from the wood box on top of the ashes. When she turned to her father, he had pulled the stocking cap off, and his sandy hair stood out in clumps. He was fumbling with the buttons of his overcoat, and for the first time Jenny caught the smell of whiskey on his breath. Her father had been drinking! Heavily, judging by his unsteadiness. This stunned her even more than finding him outside at two o'clock in the morning. Gerald had never been a solitary drinker. His limit was two drinks before dinner, and only on rare occasions. She shed her own coat, then helped him out of his overcoat, saying, "Sit down by the fire, Dad. I'm going to make you some coffee."

Without waiting for a reply, she went into the kitchen. She heard no sound from the den while she heated water for instant coffee. When she returned to the den, Gerald was sitting in one of the armchairs in front of the fireplace.

He looked up as she handed him the coffee. "You didn't need to go to so much trouble. You ought to be in bed."

He sounded almost cross, but his words, while slow, were quite distinctly spoken, and she was relieved that, at least, he was not so drunk that he couldn't think clearly. What could have brought this on? she wondered. The only even slightly unusual thing that had happened to her father today was learning of Harold Highbridge's stroke. And, of course, the visit to the hospital and finding Sarah so near collapse. But her father was a strong man. It would surely take more than either of those things to bring on a bout of solitary drinking in the wee hours of the morning.

Jenny took the other armchair and, after several moments of silence, asked, "Have you had any sleep at all?"

Gerald's blue eyes squinted as they rested on her face. "Some. Here in this chair. I've been too restless to go to bed."

"Would you like to talk about it?"

He made a sound that was half laugh and half jeer.

"What good would that do? Anyway, I don't know why I'm restless. I'm depressed tonight, I guess. Surely you've felt like that yourself sometime."

"Everyone has." But, Jenny was thinking, she had never felt the need to obliterate everything in an alcoholic haze.

"Are you worried about Harold—and Sarah?"

Gerald sipped the hot coffee and set the cup down near him on the brick hearth. In an absentminded gesture, he scratched at the tangled clumps of his hair and attempted to smooth out the strands with his fingers.

"I'm concerned about the Highbridges, naturally. But Harold is in good hands, and he has a strong constitution and will to live. He won't give up without a fight. And Sarah is strong, too, in her way."

"Then, it must be something else that's bothering you."

He took another sip of his coffee, and a wry smile curved his lips. "Lay it on old age. It's creeping up on me, and I don't like it. So tonight I fought back. Everyone's entitled to kick over the traces now and then." He placed the cup on the hearth again and sat back in the chair, staring into the flames that were beginning to curve around the log Jenny had fed them.

In the silence Jenny wondered if he was as unconcerned about Sarah as his words seemed to indicate. Had he felt compelled to go to her tonight out of a lifelong friendship or even a love that had never died and been properly buried? Would he have gone to her if Jenny had not appeared to thwart his plans?

"I realized something tonight," Gerald said heavily. "There comes a time when you're stuck on the road you've chosen. It's too late to try another route. Who was it said, 'Two roads diverged in a wood, and I—I took the one less traveled by, and that has made all the difference'?"

"Robert Frost," Jenny said quietly, wondering if he was becoming bored with the newspaper, perhaps regretting that he hadn't gone to work for a big city daily, where the challenges would have been greater.

The fire popped. "It's starting to snow," Gerald mused. "We could have a foot by tomorrow. We could be snowed in, and that might delay Luke's bus from Missoula." He sighed deeply, still staring into the fire. "I never really knew that boy. Who were his friends, do you know?"

"Tom Irving knew him," Jenny said, "although they weren't exactly friends."

"Well, maybe Luke didn't have any real friends here. Oh, there were a lot of girls, but they came and went. Kind of odd when you think about it."

"That Luke didn't have many friends?"

"No, that's not so strange. He was set apart from the other boys his age by wealth and family background. Maybe that's why he wanted to get away from here. No, I was thinking how odd it is that I watched Luke grow up and never really knew him; we can be acquainted with a person for years and not have the vaguest notion what is going on in his head."

Jenny realized that her father's depressed state of mind must have started much earlier in the day. On their way to the hospital that afternoon, he had said much the same thing, that you could never know what is going on in another person's life, even those who live in the same house with you. He had been thinking of Leah then. Maybe that was at the bottom of this—their conversation about Leah's death during the ride to the hospital and later at the dinner table.

Gerald continued to speak, as if to himself. "That little girl, Mary Steed. She always seemed so innocent. The picture of chastity, that girl. All rosy cheeks and demure blushes. Who would have guessed that she'd been carrying on an affair with the son and heir of the manor?" He laughed softly, humorously. "Who would have guessed? Or that, in seventeen short years, she could have made an enemy who hated her enough to kill her? And there was our sweet, fragile Leah, a wood sprite bringing home stray animals. Yet someone hated her enough to kill her, too." He shook his head forlornly, and his chin sank forward on his chest. "Incomprehensible, that. If any of us had had an inkling of such a possibility, we might have saved them. But nobody guessed. They were strangers to us." He looked at Jenny, and she was amazed to see his eyes swimming with unshed tears. "Ah, we are all strangers to each other." Gerald said sadly; then his heavy eyelids closed, and he began to snore softly.

Jenny got up and shook him gently. "Dad, lie down on the couch, and I'll bring a blanket. It's going to be cold in here when the fire goes out."

He struggled upright, twisting his head to stare up at her with watery, bloodshot eyes. "If only we knew how things would turn out, we'd do them differently, eh, Jenny girl?"

"Come over to the couch," she urged. "That's right. Lie down now, and I'll bring a blanket from upstairs. We'll tell Mother you fell asleep watching television."

Gerald stretched out on the couch, his feet hanging off one arm. He grunted something Jenny couldn't understand and closed his eyes, snoring again. She went upstairs and found a blanket, which she brought down and spread over his sleeping form. She removed his shoes, and he stirred, murmuring, "Shame we have to lie to Doreen. Honest woman. Always stands by her agreements. Ah, what tangled webs . . ." He drifted into a snore.

Jenny carried the cup he'd used into the kitchen. Thank goodness Doreen had slept through all this. She must have taken one of the mild sedative pills her doctor had prescribed for her when she'd had that flare-up with her heart a couple of years ago.

Then, satisfied that her father was as comfortable as she could make him, Jenny turned out the den light and felt her way up the stairs. Beast was not on her bed or on the padded window seat. She looked in the corners of her room, but the cat was not there. She left her bedroom door open in case he wanted to return during the night.

After she was back in bed with the lights out, she stared into the darkness. The wind continued to howl outside, and her father's words echoed in her head: *We are all strangers to each other.* There was a strong element of truth in that. Tonight, for instance, both her parents had surprised her. Her mother, by suggesting that Jenny might want to leave home; and Gerald, with his unprecedented drinking in the small hours of the morning. Both things were starkly out of character, and that troubled her more than the actions themselves. Was something going on in this house that she'd missed? It was not uncommon these days for couples to discover, when their children were grown, that they had grown apart, and often divorce was the outcome of that discovery. Is that what both her parents had been trying to tell her tonight, that they were contemplating divorce? Is that why Doreen had subtly suggested that perhaps the time had come for Jenny to be on her own? But her mother had not said that. She had merely wanted Jenny to know she and Gerald would understand should Jenny decide to go. Jenny was imagining the rest. And, even if it came to divorce, they would all three survive. Other people did, although, as different as her parents were in temperament and personality, Jenny could not imagine either of them without the other.

She yawned and decided that tomorrow both Gerald and Doreen would be themselves, and things would be all right again. Slowly the tension drained out of her. She relaxed and snuggled down under the blankets. It occurred to her that her parents might simply be reacting to the strain that the whole town had been under ever since the murder of the two women months ago. Once the murderer was exposed and removed from the town, they could all breathe easily again.

If only she could discover who the killer was. Who had seized a heavy rock and brought it down over Mary Steed's head and, later, Leah? Luke Highbridge? Possibly. And, after tonight, another name crept into Jenny's consciousness. Beau Gleason. He would do anything to protect the Highbridges, and if he had known that Mary was trying to force Luke to marry her . . . There must be a way to find the truth. There had to be.

She fell asleep finally, rousing once more before dawn only enough to be aware of the reverent hush left by the dying of the wind.

Four

She awakened to the lulling sound of the wind whispering around the mountains and a brilliant square of large snowflakes drifting outside the window opposite her bed. She got out of bed and went to stand at the window. Everything was covered with several inches of white powder, and the snow was continuing to fall thickly. Although the wind had dropped in the valley, higher on the mountains it would be a gale. The first big ski weekend of the season was approaching, and skiers would flock to the ski lodge on the mountain northeast of town. Ski trails had been cut through the trees when the lodge and a number of cabins were built by the Highbridge Corporation a few years ago on forest land owned by the company. Although the facilities had been built mainly for the benefit of company employees, they were open to nonemployees as well.

Jenny was not an expert skier, but, like most people in the area, she's had a few lessons and could handle herself adequately on the easier slopes. And she enjoyed the feeling of freedom she had found swooshing down a mountainside alone.

She dressed warmly in blue wool slacks, a long-sleeved cotton shirt, and a heavy sweater, making sure the medallion was tucked out of sight. Then she went downstairs to the kitchen, where Doreen, still in her robe, was sitting at the breakfast bar having a cup of coffee. Jenny poured herself a cup and sat down opposite her mother.

"What would you like for breakfast?" Doreen asked her with a wry smile. This was an old joke between them, since Jenny had the same thing every morning.

"I'll scramble my egg in a minute. I want to enjoy this coffee first." Jenny saw no evidence of her father's having eaten already, and she wondered if he was still asleep on the couch in the den. She hesitated to ask, however, since he might have gone to bed at some time before morning and her questions could cause Doreen to worry over something she would be better off not knowing. Her mother appeared rested, if a little preoccupied.

"Well," said Jenny after a moment, "winter had arrived. How much snow are we in for, do you know?"

"I was listening to the radio earlier," Doreen said. "They're forecasting eight to twelve inches by this afternoon."

Jenny made a face. "A perfect day to stay tucked in by the fire. However, duty calls. I don't suppose the street crew is out yet."

"I doubt it. Your father left early. He wouldn't even eat breakfast. Said he wasn't hungry."

Her tone gave Jenny no clue as to what she thought about this, although Doreen could hardly help noticing, as Jenny did, that it was very unlike Gerald to leave Jenny to traverse the slippery streets between the house and the library as best she could. Jenny had bought a secondhand compact car when she started working, but usually she rode to town with Gerald, using her own car mostly on weekends. Had her father felt too ashamed to face her this morning? Of course, today was Wednesday, the busiest day of the week at the newspaper office, since the *Journal* came out on Thursdays. Still, he ordinarily drove her to work on Wednesdays, the same as on other days.

She tried to keep the chagrin out of her voice as she said, "Dad left me to fend for myself, did he? I think I'll walk to town, then. I trust my feet much more than my driving skill on icy streets."

"Gerald didn't seem himself this morning," Doreen said. "He didn't sleep well, but, then, you know about that, don't you?"

Jenny looked at her in surprise.

Doreen met her gaze steadily. "I heard the two of you talking sometime during the night."

"We were both a little restless," Jenny said lightly. "I made coffee, and we sat by the fire. I think Dad was worried about Harold, but after drinking the coffee he dropped off to sleep on the couch. I covered him with a blanket and left him there. I'm sorry if we disturbed you."

Doreen got up and went to pour herself another cup of coffee. When she returned to the bar, she said, "I can always catch a nap during the day, unlike Gerald and you.

What bothers me is the way your father draws into himself. I've tried to tell him that if we talk about our troubles, it helps to put them into perspective."

"Then you think Dad *is* troubled about something?" Jenny asked.

"As I say, I don't know. He didn't confide in me. But if he will talk to you, that's better than keeping it inside."

She was not, Jenny realized, making idle conversation. She was probing lightly, curious about what Gerald had said to Jenny last night, and feeling more than a little left out. Jenny felt a rush of compassion for her mother.

"Dad seems to be a little depressed, that's all. He told me it's because he's growing older." She forced a laugh. "Maybe it's the male menopause."

"Nonsense," said Doreen curtly. "If such a thing exists, your father is the least likely man to fall prey to it. He hasn't a hysterical bone in his body."

"I agree with you," said Jenny quickly. "I'm sure he'll be fine this evening. Work's good medicine for the doldrums. And, speaking of work, I must be on my way."

"But you haven't had breakfast," Doreen protested.

Jenny finished her coffee. "I'll grab a doughnut at the drugstore later if I'm hungry. Now I'd better wrap up and hike to town."

She hurried to her bedroom, where she exchanged her suede shoes for fur-lined boots. Then she put on coat, scarf, and gloves and left the house, telling Doreen that she'd be home at the usual time but would be going out with Tom for dinner later.

The only thing that marred the virgin whiteness on all sides was the tire tracks in the street, which were already being smoothed over by falling snow. She made her way to the tracks and followed them down the hill toward town. Her boots crunched loudly in the crisp, quiet morning, and under her feet the snow was deepening. Now and then she stumbled into a drift alongside the curb, and the powdery snow fell inside her boots. She managed to keep her feet under her, nevertheless, laughing at her sometimes awkward attempts to do so. But it was only about a mile and a half to the business district, and when she reached Main Street, where the traffic was moving slowly, she made for the sidewalk, which already had been shoveled in a few spots by shopworkers. Most of them would renew the shoveling at intervals during the day as long as the snow came down.

Not many patrons came into the library during the morning, leaving Jenny time to catch up on the mailing of reminders for overdue books. Shortly before eleven, Doreen arrived, stamping snow from her boots on the thick mat at the door and massaging her cold nose with both hands. Jenny's first thought was that something must be wrong to bring Doreen out on a day like this, but her mother seemed in excellent spirits.

"Whew!" Doreen exclaimed. "The white stuff's still falling. I think somebody up there forgot to close the windows."

"Mother, what in the world are you doing traipsing around town in this?"

"Couldn't stay shut up in that empty house another minute with a wonderland outside my window. Besides, we were out of butter."

Jenny shook her head disbelievingly. "So you drove to town."

"Nothing of the kind. I walked. You don't think I'm nervy enough to drive on these streets, do you? I've got my butter here, and a few other things." She held out a large shopping bag. "And I stopped by the newspaper office."

So, Jenny thought, we come to the real reason for the trip. "Is Dad feeling okay?"

The question seemed to startle Doreen. "Fine, fine. Busy as a birddog, as usual. I offered to help fold papers, but they shooed me out of there. Said I was in the way. No one would ever guess Gerald and I ran that newspaper alone for several years after we were married! Oh, well"—she wandered over to one of the bookshelves and began scanning titles—"I thought I'd find a couple of good books to take home with me. What do you recommend?"

Jenny went to the new-fiction section. "How about a torrid historical romance?" She pulled out a thick volume.

"OK," agreed Doreen. "I could use a little romance in my life right now. What else do you have?"

Jenny crossed the room to another shelf. "Here's a new

biography of George Washington. You usually like biographies."

Doreen had returned to the desk. "Those will do."

Jenny removed the cards from the book pockets, and her mother signed them. Doreen stuffed the books into her shopping bag and smiled at Jenny. "If it were nearer twelve, I'd stay for lunch with you, but I'm too eager to get back home and start one of these books."

"Don't overtire yourself," Jenny disliked the idea of her mother climbing the hill alone on such a cold day. "Do you have the pills Dr. Weaver prescribed, in case you should need one?"

Doreen sniffed impatiently. "I always carry them in my purse, as Doc said. But I haven't needed one in weeks. Doc says sometimes that kind of thing simply goes away as mysteriously as it comes."

Atrial tachycardia, the doctor had called those attacks when Doreen's heart began to beat with a wild rapidity without warning and for no known reason, and she became light-headed and sometimes fainted. The medical term sounded awesome, but Doreen seemed convinced the condition was nothing to worry about. Jenny hoped her mother was right, but she was quite capable of denying the seriousness of her condition so as not to worry Gerald and Jenny.

"I'll be home by four-thirty," Jenny said as Doreen was leaving.

A few minutes before noon, Shirley Loomis, Jenny's best friend since high-school days, called to suggest that Jenny meet her for lunch at the coffee shop on Main Street. Jenny agreed eagerly, since she hadn't talked to Shirley in more than a week.

Shirley was holding a corner table in the crowded coffee shop when Jenny entered, her cold cheeks and nose smarting from the interior warmth.

"Over here, Jenny," Shirley called to her, waving broadly, her arm fully extended, several gold loop bracelets jangling.

Jenny made her way to the table, greeting several acquaintances en route. She threw her coat over the back of an extra chair and sat down facing the petite, dark-haired Shirley.

"Apparently," Jenny greeted her friend, "you've been keeping your nose to the grindstone—or should I say millstone? I haven't seen you around lately."

Shirley's brown eyes sparkled with their usual bright zest for living. "We've been working through the lunch hour for the past week, having sandwiches sent in." She wrinkled her pert nose. "It's not the same as getting away from the mill for a half hour, though." Shirley worked in the offices of the Highbridge Corporation, a job she had taken immediately upon graduation from high school. She was engaged to another high-school classmate of Jenny's, Kent Graham, a short, slender young man whose cheerful, optimistic outlook on the world was seemingly indomitable. Kent worked at the sawmill, and the couple planned to be married in the spring.

"Our office work always increases toward the end of the year," Shirley went on, "and now we are all a little anxious about our jobs; so everybody's putting his best foot forward."

The waitress passed by and left menus. While the two girls glanced over the list of sandwiches, which they already knew by heart, Jenny said, "Why the concern about your jobs? Business is good, isn't it?"

The waitress returned, and they ordered before Shirley replied in her usual breathless manner. "If business was any better, I'd have a big *S* branded on my forehead—for slave."

Jenny laughed. "So what's the problem?"

"Mr. Highbridge's stroke. Don't tell me you haven't heard about it."

"I've heard, but surely the mills and the plywood plant will continue to operate, regardless. They've been doing so for years."

"Oh, nobody thinks the place will close down, but we're a little skittish about having to answer to Luke Highbridge. Nobody knows how he'll run the business. He's young and inexperienced, and I hear he made some pretty radical changes during the short time he worked with his father before he went to San Francisco. The older employees, especially, are afraid of losing their jobs to a machine. I heard some of the sawmill workers talking out in the yard yesterday, and one of them described Luke as having a head full of foolish newfangled ideas."

"I knew Luke was coming home," said Jenny, surprised, "but I hadn't heard that he'd agreed to take over the business."

"Evidently he has. Somebody has to do it, and he's the obvious candidate. I doubt he had much choice in the matter. At least, all the employees assume he'll be the boss for a while, anyway." Shirley giggled and rested her small, dimpled chin in her cupped hand. "*I* say nobody as good-looking as Luke Highbridge can be all bad."

"An interesting theory," Jenny teased. "Completely illogical, of course. And you'd better not let Kent hear you talking like that."

"Oh, I can handle Kent," said Shirley complacently.

The waitress brought their turkey sandwiches and coffee then, and both girls were occupied with eating for several moments. Jenny felt famished, not having had her usual egg for breakfast. And Shirley had always been a hearty eater, one of those fortunate people who could eat everything and stay as slender as a reed.

After a while Shirley dabbed at her mouth with her napkin. "Enough shoptalk. Fill me in on your love life."

"Shirley," said Jenny, laughing again, "you know you'd be the first person I'd confide in *if* there was anything to confide."

Shirley frowned. "Don't tell me Tom hasn't proposed yet! What is *wrong* with that dolt?"

Jenny sighed helplessly. "You are an incurable matchmaker. No, Tom hasn't proposed, nor is he likely to. There's nothing serious between us. How many times do I have to tell you?"

Shirley brushed these objections aside with a wave of her small hand. "Maybe you're not serious, but Tom Irving is. I've seen the way he looks at you."

Jenny took a sip of coffee, set the cup down and shook her head emphatically. "Your imagination is working overtime. Take my word for it, Tom and I are friends, period."

Shirley tossed her dark hair back and studied her friend. "You're still seeing Tom, aren't you?"

"Yes. In fact he's taking me to the Copper Kettle for dinner this evening."

"I saw him early this morning," Shirley said after a moment. "He came into the mill office to talk to one of the men about something. He seemed kind of down."

Jenny was puzzled. "I can't imagine why. Maybe it's the weather."

"No," said Shirley seriously. "He asked me if I knew when Luke was due in. I got the impression that's what's bothering him."

Jenny wondered with amusement where Shirley got her outlandish notions. "I know Tom has never particularly liked Luke Highbridge, but what possible difference could it make to him whether Luke is here or in San Francisco?"

Shirley pursed her lips thoughtfully. "Maybe he feels uncomfortable having Luke around because of the gossip linking him with the murders. Tom wouldn't be the only person in town who'd sleep easier if Luke stayed in San Francisco. And, under the circumstances, Tom has more reason than most of us for disliking Luke."

Jenny stared at Shirley's pixie face. "Under the circumstances? Under *what* circumstances?"

Shirley's brown eyes grew wide. "You're forgetting that Mary Steed was Tom's cousin."

Jenny was truly astounded. "Cousin! Wherever did you get that idea?"

Shirley appeared to be confused by Jenny's reaction. "Why, one of the men at the mill told me only recently. But surely you already knew it."

"No, I didn't know it," said Jenny sharply, "and I don't believe it. I mean, why wouldn't Tom have mentioned it to me if it were true?"

"I don't know," said Shirley gravely. "Maybe he prefers not to dwell on it after what happened to the poor girl."

Jenny shook her head. "Since my aunt was murdered, too, it's only natural Tom would have mentioned a relationship to Mary, if there was one. No, I'm certain you're mistaken."

"There's one way to find out," said Shirley, studying her friend. "Ask Tom."

Jenny had no opportunity to respond to that suggestion, because Mazie Jones from the newspaper office interrupted their conversation just then.

"Mind if I join you two? I managed to slip out the back

door for a bite to eat." She plopped down in one of the vacant chairs at the table, her plump face red from the cold, and shrugged off her coat. "Lord," she groaned, "Wednesdays are hectic."

Actually, Jenny welcomed the interruption. She preferred to consider the news about Tom's possible relationship to Mary Steed at her leisure before discussing it with anyone, not that she thought there was any truth in the story. Still, if it were true, it would explain Tom's antipathy for Luke.

"The only thing that gets me through Wednesday," Mazie was saying as she deposited a well-chewed wad of gum in a paper napkin, "is thinking about Thursday, which is always the calm after the storm."

Shirley finished off the last of her chips and reached for her coat. "Listen, gals, it's not that I don't adore your scintillating company, but I have to get back to work. You should see my desk. Kent told me yesterday it bore a striking resemblance to a rat's nest. He suggested, not too subtly, that if I keep house the way I keep my desk, maybe we should consider hiring a cleaning woman once a week." She grinned as she put on her coat.

"Don't you desert me, too, Jen," Mazie implored. "I hate eating alone."

"I'll stay and have a second cup of coffee with you," Jenny told her.

"I'll probably see you at the Copper Kettle tonight," Shirley said to Jenny. "Kent and I are going out to eat."

"Good," Jenny said. "We'll get a table for four."

"Sounds great!" Shirley wound a brilliant scarlet wool scarf around her long dark hair, tossing the fringed ends over her shoulder with a flourish, and waved as she left. "See you both later."

Turning back to Mazie, Jenny said, "Business is not exactly booming at the library today. I feel a little guilty listening to you and Shirley talk about how busy your jobs keep you."

"Enjoy, enjoy," advised Mazie, rolling her round dark eyes, "and don't look a gift horse in the mouth."

The waitress arrived with a coffee pot to replenish Jenny's cup and take Mazie's order.

"You and Shirley have known each other a long time, haven't you?" Mazie asked when the waitress had gone.

"All our lives. We've been best friends since high school."

Mazie's brown curls bobbed. "Must be nice to have friends you've grown up with. I came here from Oregon after I was on my own, you know. It's harder for an adult to make close friends in a small town like this. People can be awfully clannish."

Not for the first time, Jenny wondered why Mazie stayed in Pine Valley. She was an attractive woman and far too young to be spending all her evenings alone in her apartment. "Do you see much of Marty Brubaker these days?" Jenny asked.

Mazie's mouth seemed to droop. "Only in passing."

"I thought you were seeing him a while back."

Mazie smiled briefly. "That was before your aunt entered the picture. Oh, heck, who am I trying to kid? Marty always had his eyes on Leah, even when he was dating me. It was infatuation at first sight. And"—she made a helpless gesture—"I saw the way he looked at her. I knew Marty was going to drop me if she ever gave him any encouragement, and he did."

"You can't have felt too friendly toward Leah after that," Jenny ventured. The thought was new to her.

"I blamed her at first," Mazie admitted, "but after I found out how much she'd hurt Marty, I stopped trying to place blame. Marty and I simply had the bad luck to fall for people who didn't return our feelings. It's nobody's fault when that happens. That's the way the old cooky crumbles, as they say." She smiled at Jenny. "And no use bawling over spilled milk, right? See, I've got an adage for every occasion."

"I'm not sure I understand why you mean about Leah hurting Marty," Jenny said. "It always seemed to me that they got along very well."

"Oh, I guess they got along OK," Mazie told her, "only Leah didn't love Marty, not the way he loved her."

Jenny felt a wistful pang. "It was awfully hard to tell what Leah was feeling. She often seemed to be distracted or preoccupied, as if she were in another world. I imagine Marty misunderstood her moods. In fact, she saw more of

Marty than any other man that I can remember. I really expected them to be married."

Mazie nodded emphatically. "Marty expected that, too, but Leah turned him down flat. Marty told me about it. He was feeling so low he had to talk to somebody, I guess, and I was handy. Oh, Lord, was I ever handy! I was still hanging around hoping for any crumbs that fell from Marty's plate in those days."

"When was this?" Jenny asked, amazed.

"A week or two before Leah was—before she died. You didn't know about it?"

"No. Leah never mentioned to any of the family that Marty had asked her to marry him. This is really a surprise to me."

"Yeah, I know what you mean," Mazie agreed. "Feeling the way I did about Marty, I couldn't imagine any woman turning him down. And, gosh, Leah couldn't have hoped to have many more offers, not at her age in a town this size." She darted a quick look at Jenny's face, flushing slightly. "I don't mean to speak disrespectfully of the dead."

"It's OK," Jenny assured her. "Frankly, I don't understand it myself. In her way, Leah seemed to care a great deal for Marty. I don't know, unless—maybe she couldn't bring herself to leave home. She'd lived with my parents since she was seventeen, you know. They treated her like another daughter."

"That's pretty weird for a woman in her thirties," Mazie said flatly.

"Oh"—Jenny smiled—"Leah wasn't your ordinary, run-of-the-mill lady."

The waitress brought Mazie's hamburger and malt and asked Jenny if she wanted more coffee. Jenny declined. "I must get back to the library," she told Mazie. "Some brave soul might venture out. It's a wonderful day for reading, after all."

"Amen," said Mazie. "Wish I were at home with a good book." She winked archly. "Don't tell your dad I said that. I wouldn't want to lose my job. Even though I complain a lot, Gerald's a terrific guy to work for. He tells me what he wants done, then lets me alone to do it. I used to work for a man who thought he had to look over my shoulder every half hour to make sure I wasn't goofing off."

"You must like your job," Jenny said. "I can't think of any other reason for your staying in Pine Valley."

Mazie seemed about to say something, then checked the impulse. Jenny caught a brief glimpse of pain in her dark eyes, and in that instant she realized that Mazie was still very much in love with Marty Brubaker, which probably had as much influence on her decision to stay as her liking for her job. She suddenly hoped that Marty would notice Mazie again. They seemed to be two lonely people whose lives could be much fuller together than they were apart.

Jenny put on her coat and said brightly, "I'm off." She left Mazie chewing reflectively on her hamburger.

Back at the library it took less than an hour to finish typing the reminders for overdue books. Then Jenny became engrossed in a newly arrived family saga, and the remainder of the afternoon passed quickly. It was almost quitting time when old Mr. Elledge appeared. James Elledge was in his seventies, but Jenny had never known him to miss his daily walk from his tiny two-room house a block off the business district along the length of Main Street and back, unless he was ill. Today he reminded Jenny of a rosy-cheeked, white-moustached Kewpie doll, his short body swathed in several layers of clothing, topped with a red-and-black-plaid lumberjack's coat, red rubber boots, and a red fur-lined cap with earflaps pulled down, the strap fastened under his round little chin.

Jenny assumed he'd come to berate her again about the book she had charged to him that he insisted he'd never checked out. Well, there was nothing to do but try to humor him.

"Good afternoon, Mr. Elledge."

The bright eyes, in deep pockets of flesh, were a startling blue, and they blinked at her now. "I been thinking on that book you say I took out, Jenny."

Today Jenny was ready for him. She reached for the card file and pulled out the card on which the last signature was J. Elledge, plain as day. "Here's the card, Mr. Elledge. *Basic Biology*." The old man was something of an amateur scientist, and most of the books he checked out had to do with various branches of the field. "Is this your signature?"

He blinked his eyes again and took the card from her hand, squinting at the name scrawled across the bottom. "Does look a bit like my handwriting," he conceded. "Could be a forgery, though."

Jenny fought back exasperation. "Why would anyone want to forge your name on a library card, sir?"

He glared at her. "Can't think, right offhand."

"The date's November 2, more than three weeks ago. I'm sure if you think about it, you'll remember getting that book."

"Nothing wrong with my memory, girl." He tossed the card back onto her desk. "I was in the hospital for a week the first of the month. Little flare-up with my kidneys. I did take several books with me to the hospital."

"Maybe," Jenny suggested, "this was one of those books."

"Except, when I got back home, that book was not among the ones the nurse had packed into my suitcase for me. So after I talked to you yesterday, I called the hospital and asked if they'd found it there after I left. They couldn't remember. Those nurses are mighty busy up there at the hospital, you know. They finally told me if they *had* found it, one of them would have returned it to the library. They always do that with books left there by patients." He turned and pointed toward the door, where a wide, flapped slot was provided for the return of books after hours. "They probably put it right in that drop there."

"If they had, I would have found it," Jenny said patiently. "That book is not on the shelf. I've checked several times." She indicated two stacks of books on her desk. "These are the books that have been returned during the last few days. I'm going to put them back on the shelf before I go home. I haven't had a chance to look through them yet, but I can do it now." She lifted each of the books in the two stacks, reading off the titles as she restacked them. Then she looked up at the old man. "No *Basic Biology*, I'm afraid. Look, Mr. Elledge, that book's several years old. It's not the kind of thing most people want to read, so it's hardly ever checked out. Why don't we just forget about it. I'll put the card here in my desk drawer, and maybe it'll turn up later."

The bright blue eyes snapped. "If I signed that card —and I'm not admitting that I did, mind you—I'll make it good. I'm a man of principle, Jenny Curtiss. Now, you figure out how much that book's worth, and I'll think on it some more and see if I can remember checking it out. I'll be back in a day or two, and we'll settle this once and for all."

"Any way you want to handle it, Mr. Elledge," Jenny said, "I'm sure will be fair."

"You're durn tootin'," James Elledge grumbled as he turned and stomped out.

Jenny smiled and shook her head. Touchy old gentleman, she thought, and as independent as they came. But he was right about one thing. There was undoubtedly nothing wrong with his memory, or any other part of his mind. James Elledge was as sharply intelligent as most men half his age. Jenny had always thought that if he'd had the opportunity to get a formal education, he might have been a great scientist. Even at seventy-two, he retained an avid appetite for knowledge, particularly scientific knowledge, and he read voraciously. But he wouldn't give an inch when he thought he was right, which he always did. Still, she couldn't help liking the old man.

By the time she had shelved the two stacks of books on her desk, it was time to close the library. She wrapped up warmly and started home, stopping at the post office to mail the overdue notices. She didn't stop at the newspaper office, because her father always worked late on Wednesdays.

Fir Street, which led to the Curtiss house, wound steeply. Several times she slipped and almost lost her footing, and her nose was soon numb from the cold. But the snow had stopped at last, and the street crew had started clearing the busiest thoroughfares. Halfway up the hill she paused to look back down at the village below. In the gathering dusk it looked like a Christmas-card scene with all the roofs and tree branches white with glistening snow and an occasional spot of bright color that was someone's coat or cap or scarf. There were even some children sledding down the hill west of Main

Street with a couple of small dogs running after them, barking.

Jenny stood there for some time, looking. Suddenly she flung her arms out as though to embrace the valley. What a lovely place in which to live, she thought joyously. But the mood did not last, for on the heels of this thought came a sharp memory of Leah standing in the backyard, looking up at the mountains and saying almost those exact words. Probably Mary Steed had felt the same way. And then came a wistful sorrow for the two women who had been young with much of their lives still before them.

She turned her back on the Currier and Ives scene and trudged up the hill toward home.

Five

She did not hurry for the remainder of her journey up the hill. For one thing, haste would certainly endanger her precarious footing in the deep snow. For another, she wanted time to think about the things she had learned during the past two days.

The first disturbing point was that something was definitely troubling her father. Standing outside alone in the middle of a frigid night, his uncharacteristic drinking, and avoiding Jenny's company as he had done that morning —all pointed to a disturbed mind. Doreen was aware of it, too, which was plainly why she had walked to town earlier. She had wanted to check up on Gerald, to see for herself that he was all right. But still Jenny didn't know what could be causing her father's obvious anxiety. Was it in some way connected to Harold Highbridge's stroke? Or Luke's return?

Underlying her puzzlement about her father was the notion that Shirley, and evidently others, believed to be true—that Tom Irving was related to Mary Steed. A fact that, if it *were* a fact, wasn't in itself surprising, since many of the families in the area had lived there for generations and were interrelated. The perplexing thing was that Tom had never mentioned it to Jenny. She tried to remember if they had ever actually talked about Mary Steed and couldn't recall that they had, except for a few passing remarks about the killings. In all fairness Jenny had to admit that she hadn't until recently been eager to discuss the murders with Tom or anyone else outside the family. The pain of remembering had been too fresh. Well, this was one question to which she would have an answer tonight.

But another puzzle remained. If Mazie Jones knew the truth of the matter, it seemed that Marty had proposed to Leah a few days before her death, and Leah had turned him down. Yet Jenny had been so certain that Leah loved Marty. Leah had been a loner most of her life. She had not been inclined to waste time on any man she didn't care for, and Leah had spent a great deal of time with Marty Brubaker. So it seemed that another factor had entered the picture. In spite of her love for Marty, Leah had had some reason for refusing his marriage proposal. At this point Jenny came up against a blank wall, for she could not think of any possible reason for Leah's behavior. It was true that Leah had been deeply hurt by Gideon Garfield, but that was years ago, and her aunt had probably not thought of the young actor for years before her death.

By the time Jenny reached the house, darkness was already beginning to creep into the valley. Doreen was curled up in front of the fireplace in the den with the George Washington biography.

"Is the book good?" Jenny asked, removing her gloves and coat.

Doreen laid the open book face down on the hearth. "It's all right, only I don't seem to be in a reading mood after all. I can't keep my mind on it."

"You're worried about Dad, aren't you?"

"I called him several times during the afternoon, but he was out of the office."

"You know he's always in and out a lot. You can't run a newspaper sitting behind a desk all day, not when you have to be publisher, editor, and star reporter all rolled into one."

"Oh, I know." Doreen rubbed at her eyes with both hands. "I've been kind of antsy today, and I've got a headache."

Jenny felt a trace of worry. "Are you sure that's all it is?"

Doreen looked up, the hazel eyes red from being rubbed but otherwise clear and direct. "Positive."

"Have you had any luck finding someone to help with the heavy cleaning, as Dad suggested?"

Doreen waved an impatient hand. "I don't need any help with the housework. I never did need that Steed girl, but your father overreacted to those little heart spells of mine. He's the one who found her and installed her upstairs. I nearly went mad having that child under my feet all day. It was an enormous relief when she decided to move to the Highbridges."

"Dad was only trying to help."

"I know, but I don't need that kind of help. I've little enough to occupy my time as it is." Doreen got to her feet. "How would you like something to tide you over until dinner?"

Jenny shook her head. "I'll wait. I think I'll go up and take a bath and wash my hair before Tom comes."

The hot bath was relaxing, and afterward she washed and arranged her hair in its usual casual pageboy. Since it was too cold for a dress, she put on heavy wool slacks knotted a tangerine-and-brown silk scarf around her neck. She was ready when Tom arrived and was admitted by Doreen, who called upstairs to Jenny.

Grabbing her gloves and purse, Jenny left her room. Tom watched her descend the stairs. He wore a brown tweed overcoat and leather gloves, and his ruddy complexion was deepened by the cold outside.

"Tom was just telling me," Doreen said, "that he almost didn't make it up the hill in his car."

"I should have had the snow tires put on, but I was running late," Tom explained.

"Well, if you were able to get away from the newspaper," Doreen said, "Gerald ought to be along any minute."

"He was still working in his office when I left," Tom told her. To Jenny he said, "You'd better wrap up. We may have to walk part of the way." Taking her coat, he helped Jenny into it.

"I'll be warm as toast," she said as she pulled on her gloves and turned to Doreen. "We shouldn't be out too late, Mother."

"Drive carefully," Doreen said, looking at Tom.

Outside, Tom took a firm grip on Jenny's arm and guided her to his car, a three-year-old maroon Pontiac. He handed Jenny inside, then waded through the snow to the driver's side and got in. When he started the motor and tried to pull away from the curb, however, the wheels spun and the car wouldn't budge.

Tom groaned. "What do we do now?"

"Simple," Jenny said cheerfully. "We walk."

Tom peered at her, his light-brown eyes dark in the shadowy car. "Are you sure you want to brave the elements?"

Jenny opened her door and stepped out, and Tom hastened to follow her.

"I don't intend to let a little snow keep me from having that steak you promised me," Jenny said. "Come along."

Tom laughed, taking her arm, and they started downhill, walking in the street near the curb. "Once we get to the bottom of the hill, it'll be easier," he told her. "The street crew got Main Street cleared." After several moments of silent walking, he said, "You're awfully quiet tonight. I haven't seen you for a few days. How is everything?"

"All right," she said, without much enthusiasm. "In fact, I've had a few surprises in the last couple of days, aside from Harold Highbridge's stroke, that is. One of them had to do with you."

"With me?" Tom echoed. "What are you talking about?"

"Mary Steed," Jenny said. "According to Shirley Loomis, she was your cousin."

In the light from the streetlamps, Tom looked disconcerted, but instead of denying what she'd said, he only remarked, "That's hardly a deep, dark secret."

Jenny looked up into his face. He was frowning, looking down at his feet, and she wondered if he was deliberately avoiding her gaze. "It was to me," she said, "which is my point."

Tom stared at her. "What point? I don't get it."

"Why didn't you ever mention it to me?"

He continued to stare at her. "Why would I? I haven't mentioned any of my other relatives. Mary was my second cousin, but I have dozens of them. If I started telling you about all of them, we'd be here until next spring."

"None of the others were murdered along with my aunt," Jenny said carefully.

"So?"

Jenny had the feeling he was being intentionally obtuse. "So I think it's strange you never mentioned the fact that you were related to Mary."

Tom stopped walking, pulling her to a stop beside him,

and looked down at her with a puzzled expression on his face. He startled her by grasping her arm and squeezing through her coat sleeve. "Are you trying to pick a fight with me?"

She looked at his hand where it had closed over her arm and pulled away. "I guess the best defense is a good offense," she retorted and walked away from him.

He caught up with her in two-long strides and took her arm again, but lightly this time. "Jenny, you and I weren't even dating when Mary was killed."

When she didn't respond, he went on. "Okay, you want me to tell you about Mary? She was raised on the farm next to my father's. She was one of six kids, four of them girls. Since she was six—no seven—years younger than I, I didn't pay much attention to her as she was growing up. She was just another little farm girl who happened to be related to me. Her mother is my first cousin. Her parents—her whole family—were shocked by what happened to her. The fact that she was pregnant hurt them almost as much as the way she died. They're a very religious family." He looked down at her. "Anything else you want to know?"

"Who do her parents think killed her?"

He shrugged. "They don't talk about it. It's as if they never had a daughter named Mary. She brought shame on the family, and they're the kind of people who don't easily forgive that sort of thing. It wouldn't surprise me if they interpreted her death as just retribution for her waywardness."

They had reached Main Street, and Jenny stopped, staring at him in amazement. "Shame! Just retribution! She was *murdered!*"

"Yes," Tom said, not ungently, "but she was pregnant and unmarried at the time." He studied her upturned face. "Maybe indignation is their way of dulling the grief. People have all kinds of ways of dealing with pain. They never wanted her to move to town. They were afraid she'd get into trouble. What happened convinced them they were right. None of the other girls managed to get away from home after that. The older girl is married now, and I imagine the others will marry, too, at the first opportunity, to get out of that rigid environment."

"How sad," Jenny commented, frowning.

"The ironic thing is," Tom went on, "if they hadn't been so strict, Mary might never have left home in the first place, and she wouldn't have fallen under the spell of the first fast-talking man that came along, and she wouldn't be dead now."

"So in a way her parents are to blame, though I don't suppose they would believe that."

Tom laughed mirthlessly. "They couldn't afford to. If they did, they'd have to question their values, their whole way of life. I don't think they're courageous enough for that." He led her to the sidewalk, and they walked east on Mill Street, toward the Copper Kettle. "Maybe I even feel a little guilty about what happened to Mary."

"Why should you?"

"I had moved to town by that time. I knew she'd been sheltered. I should have looked after her. When I talked to her, a few days before she died, I sensed something was was troubling her, but I was in a hurry to get back to work. I should have pressed her to tell me what was wrong. Thinking back on it now, I get the feeling she was scared."

"Being seventeen, pregnant, and unmarried would scare most girls. And, from what you've said, she couldn't count on help from her parents, and I doubt that abortion ever crossed her mind."

"You're probably right—but she might have been frightened of someone here, someone who had threatened her, maybe."

"The person who killed her?"

He shrugged. "It could be. Only I didn't take the time to find out, so I'll never know. Meanwhile the killer is free."

"I'm sorry," Jenny said truthfully. She liked Tom, and yet she had been ready to distrust his motives for not telling her about his relationship to Mary. He was not looking at her now but was staring ahead as they walked along the side street, his expression remote. What he had just told her about his own guilty feeings had been an admission he perhaps hadn't meant to make, and he probably regretted having done so.

"Here we are," he said curtly and opened the door of the restaurant for her.

Inside, Jenny said, "I promised Shirley we'd get a table for four. She and Kent are supposed to meet us here. I'm sorry I didn't think to mention it before."

He gave her a sharp look but made no other response as the waiter led them to a table. He seemed irritated, but whether about sharing their table with Shirley and Kent without being consulted or her curiosity about Mary Steed, she didn't know.

"Shall we have a glass of wine and wait until your friends arrive to order?" Tom asked her as they were seated.

She nodded, aware that his labeling Shirley and Kent "her" friends probably meant he wasn't too happy about sharing their table. She really should have talked to him about it before making the plans so glibly. Tom was in a bleak mood tonight, and she undoubtedly had herself to thank for that.

The waiter brought their drinks, and she sipped hers, glancing about the restaurant, which was the favorite haunt of the town's younger set. The Copper Kettle was decorated with used brick, dark paneling, and a beamed ceiling. Polished copper pans along with several Charles Russell prints hung on the walls. The small tables were spread with red-and-white-checked cloths, and in the center of each table a tall red glass held a lighted pine-scented candle. The dining room was beginning to fill up, and Jenny waved to several acquaintances as they came in.

Kent and Shirley arrived, breathless and rosy-cheeked from the cold. "Sorry we're late," Shirley greeted them as Kent held her chair, "but we had to walk the last three blocks."

"Consider yourself fortunate," Jenny told her. "We walked all the way from my house."

"How romantic!" Shirley said brightly, glancing at Tom from the corner of her eye. Tom, however, was gazing glumly into his wineglass and did not seem to notice.

Kent, a slight, brown-haired young man, took the fourth chair. As usual, a broad smile wreathed his pleasantly plain face. "The weather forecaster says we're in for more snow."

"Isn't it exciting?" Shirley said. "I simply love the snow. It means we'll have good skiing for the Winter Festival."

The Winter Festival was an annual event, usually held on the last Saturday of November, which heralded the beginning of winter. On that Saturday all the farmers and loggers came to town. The Christmas decorations would be strung along Main Street, and there would be special sales in all the stores, a parade, and a visit from Santa Claus. The young people would go skiing, sledding, and ice skating, if the lake was solidly frozen, and in the evening at the ski lodge there would be a huge fire for roasting wieners and, afterward, singing around the fire. For those who stayed in town, the day would end with a dance is the old armory building.

They ordered steaks and over dinner reminisced about past Winter Festivals. As a child, Jenny had looked forward to them with almost unbearable anticipation. This year she had not even thought about the coming event until Shirley had mentioned it. She supposed that was one of the drawbacks to growing up: few things were as much fun as they used to be.

By the time they had finished eating and were lingering over coffee, the restaurant was full. In the foyer, which Jenny could see from where she sat, several couples were waiting for tables. As she looked, a tall dark-haired man came out of the phone booth and made his way through the waiting couples toward the door. As he reached the archway leading into the dining room, he stopped, his glance raking the diners and coming to rest on Jenny's table.

She realized with a jolt of recognition that it was Luke Highbridge. He was taller, his shoulders broader, his eyes darker than she remembered. He wore an overcoat with a beaver collar, and his sharply angled face looked drawn and weary.

Suddenly he was coming toward their table, a smile lifting the tired corners of his wide mouth.

"Tom! Tom Irving! It's been a long time. How are you?"

Tom looked up at the man who was now standing beside him. There was no liking in his eyes. Since Luke Highbridge's hand had been thrust into his face, he shook it briefly. "Hello, Luke. I heard you were coming home."

"Just got off the bus. I called Mom, and I'm on my way to the hospital now."

"Sorry to hear about your father," Tom said, but his tone was cool. Then he shifted uncomfortably, his glance falling away from the dark eyes that seemed genuinely glad to see him and puzzled by the frosty undercurrents at the table. "I'm sure you remember Shirley Loomis and Kent Graham. They work for the Highbridge Corporation. And this is Jenny Curtiss."

The dark eyes came to rest on Jenny's face as a gleam of recognition sparked in them. "Jenny? Of course. You're Gerald and Doreen's daughter, the little girl who used to ride her bike up and down the street in front of the Tamaracks. I think you were away at college when I left Pine Valley. You've certainly grown up since I last saw you."

"Little girls have a way of doing that," Jenny said, feeling her cheeks grow warm. "What is the latest report on your father?"

"The doctor thinks the worst is past. Now it's a matter of time and whatever physical therapy can accomplish. That will depend largely on Dad's determination to get well."

"Mr. Highbridge is so—so energetic," Shirley put in. "I know he'll improve quickly."

Luke flashed her a grateful smile. "You're right about Dad—as he used to be. Only they aren't sure yet how much his mind has been affected by the stroke."

"I expect you'll be around for a while, then," said Tom reluctantly.

The slight smile vanished, and Luke's eyes darkened to a brooding black as worry closed in again. "Yes. Maybe we can get together for a drink soon, Tom." He glanced at Jenny, but his eyes had a faraway look as he said, "Since we're neighbors, Jenny, I'm sure we'll be running into each other." Fatigue had settled on his broad shoulders once more, and his face was remote. Jenny felt an unwanted stirring in her, a response to this tall, somehow inscrutable man that she did not wish to feel. She was saddened by his obvious concern for his father's health, but she could not let that blind her to the fact that he was possibly linked to Leah's death.

"Nice seeing all of you."

As Luke walked away from the table, Tom drank the last of his coffee and set the cup down on the checked cloth with a thud. "Let's get out of here."

Shirley shot Jenny a puzzled look. Kent scrambled to his feet and placed the money for the tip under the corner of the candleholder. As the two men were paying the checks, Shirley and Jenny went into the foyer to find their coats. As soon as they were out of earshot of the two men, Shirley whispered, "Tom's a regular barrel of laughs tonight, isn't he?"

Jenny answered offhandedly. "We had an upsetting conversation on the way here. Nothing major."

Shirley looked at her thoughtfully and decided against saying anything more. When the men joined them, Shirley and Kent bid a hasty farewell, Shirley saying with forced enthusiasm that they ought to get together more often.

Jenny and Tom set out for Jenny's house in silence. Several minutes later, as they turned onto Main Street, Tom burst out, "He's just as phony as he ever was!"

"I assume you mean Luke Highbridge," Jenny said. Indignation made Tom walk faster, and she had to run a few steps to catch up.

"Pretending to be happy to see me! Who does he think he's kidding?"

"He seemed genuinely glad," Jenny ventured.

Tom snorted, looking away from her. "Oh, he's still the big glad-hander. I'll give him that. The cocky son-of—" He glanced at Jenny. "Sorry."

Jenny took his arm, and he slowed down to keep pace with her shorter strides. "I don't know why you're so worked up," she said after a moment. "He's been away for a long time, and you're an old high school classmate. Didn't you play football together? It seems natural he'd be happy to see you."

He stared down at her. "Why are you defending him?"

"I'm not *defending* him. I simply think you're reading something into nothing."

"He had a nerve—to come back." Tom's tone was grim.

Frowning at his black expression, Jenny said, "You're being unreasonable, you know."

Suddenly he stopped and whirled her around to face him, gripping her shoulders. "He is responsible for Mary's death."

"You haven't any proof of that, Tom," she said flatly and realized with confusion that she *was* defending Luke, whom she had herself come close to accusing of murder, if only in her private thoughts.

Tom's face was rigid with anger, and she became aware suddenly that his fingers were pressing into her shoulders painfully. "You don't know Luke Highbridge as I do. He's arrogant and selfish and cares nothing for the rights of others. Rules that apply to ordinary people weren't meant for him. He took advantage of an ignorant little farm girl who knew nothing about men, least of all a man like the high and mighty Luke Highbridge. He seduced her and then didn't want to be bothered with her anymore. He may not have brought that rock down on Mary's head, but I know he was the cause of it. He probably hired someone to do the dirty work."

"Oh, Tom, that is a bit far-fetched."

"Is it? I don't think so. And because he has money and his family has influence, he walked away scot-free. Now he comes waltzing back to town, grinning and slapping backs as if none of it ever happened."

Jenny looked into Tom's tortured face, surprised at this rare burst of rage, and felt her heart tug. "I know how you feel, Tom. My aunt was killed, too."

His hands fell to his sides. "I'm sorry. I shouldn't be taking this out on you."

"I really do understand," she said. "You feel some responsibility for Mary's death. Do you think I haven't asked myself a hundred times if I could have done something to prevent Leah's murder? I knew she had something on her mind that day. She hadn't slept the night before. Yet I didn't do anything about it."

As she spoke, he put his arm around her shoulders. They started walking again. "To be honest, I'm probably a little jealous, too. I didn't like the way he was looking at you."

Again Jenny felt a strange, unexpected response, as if something stirred in her that she hadn't known was there, some taint of wild daring that must be subdued because it could be dangerous.

"You imagined it," she said, striving for lightness. "You were looking for something to be angry about."

He laughed shortly. "Maybe you're right." Then, after a moment, he asked, "Do you have plans for Saturday?"

"The Winter Festival? No."

"Would you like to spend the afternoon and evening with me? The skiing should be excellent."

"OK," she agreed. "Why don't you come by about two."

At her door he kissed her lightly. "See you Saturday." Then he trudged off down the hill again, since he would have to wait until the next day to have the snow tires put on his car.

Jenny went inside, spoke briefly with her parents, who were watching television in the den, and went up to her room, relieved that her father, though he looked tired, seemed to be himself again.

On her bed, Beast lazily washed his face. She took off her coat and hung it in the closet. Then she sat on the edge of the bed and watched the cat.

"If only you could talk, Beast," she said, a sudden urgency gripping her. "The way you slink around this neighborhood, you must know something about Leah's death."

The cat paused in his washing. The yellow eyes blinked at her. Then he rolled over on his back, paws straight up, waiting for her to scratch his stomach. She complied, laughing. "All you care about is your creature comforts!"

Beast yawned widely, rose and stretched. Then, looking back at her, he leaped from the bed and went to the door. She opened it for him, and he slipped into the hall without another glance in her direction.

Alone, she stretched out, fully clothed, on her bed, her arms behind her head, and stared at the ceiling. She did not feel as if she would sleep for hours. She thought about the meeting with Luke Highbridge and the warning bell that had gone off in her brain when their glances met. Yet, if she hoped to learn if he was involved in the murders, she would have to see him again. Until tonight he had thought of her as "little Jenny Curtiss," a neighbor child. Somehow she would have to get to know him as an adult. She would have to gain his confidence if she hoped to expose whatever dark secrets he was harboring. The whole idea filled her with such disquiet that she couldn't lie still. She got up and paced the room. She felt disturbed and torn. But more than anything else, she felt frightened.

Six

No more snow fell on Thursday, and by Friday morning Pine Valley's main thoroughfares had been cleared and sanded and the sidewalks on Main Street had been shoveled clean. People who had been shut in for the past two days came to town, and a number of them came into the library. Jenny was kept busy recommending, locating and checking out books most of the morning. It was almost noon when a man who worked as a trash hauler for the city approached her desk with a book in his hand. She'd never seen him in the library before, and in his dirty insulated coveralls and heavy scarred boots he certainly did not resemble the average library patron. Evidently he felt as out of place as he looked, for he shuffled his feet and cleared his throat self-consciously as he handed Jenny a worn, gray-bound book.

"We found this on the morning run."

Jenny took the book, glancing at the title. It was *Basic Biology*, the book James Elledge had checked out, which had subsequently been lost.

"Thank you," she said. "I've been looking for this. Where did you find it?"

"It was in the trash barrel behind the furniture store, ma'am. I always take home any books we pick up—for my kids. But I saw this one belonged to the library, so I brought it by."

"Mr. Elledge will be glad to hear about this. He checked it out and hasn't been able to find it. He thought he might have left it at the hospital when he was a patient there earlier in the month."

The man scratched his whiskery jaw. "The furniture store's a long ways from the hospital. It's a good piece from old man Elledge's house, too."

"Well, maybe somebody found the book, thought it had been discarded and tossed it into the nearest barrel."

"All they had to do was look inside the front cover to

76

see it belonged to the library. Some folks don't want to bothered, I reckon."

"I appreciate your taking the time to bring it back," Jenny told him. "Thanks again."

The man nodded and shuffled out of the library.

Jenny turned the book over. It didn't seem to be in much worse shape than when it had left the library almost a month earlier. The corners of the binding were worn, but, as she recalled, they'd been that way for some time. It was an old book. She began to flip through the pages, and the book fell open in her hand at page 213. She saw several ragged edges along the center line where the pages were bound together. The page on the right was numbered 213, the page on the left was 202. Someone had torn several pages from the book, and Jenny could almost swear it had been done during the past month. She checked every book as it was returned, before placing it back on the shelf. She must have examined this one the last time it was shelved, before James Elledge took it out. She had never known Mr. Elledge to damage a book. He had copied material from scientific textbooks on several occasions, but he had never torn pages from a library book before. If he had done it this time, it would explain why he hadn't wanted to return the book. But he had offered to pay for it, which wasn't very sensible, particularly since James Elledge was known to be extremely frugal and it would have been cheaper to copy the material. So either he had done it accidentally, which seemed unlikely, or the damage had been done after the book left Mr. Elledge's possession. James Elledge was coming into the library that afternoon. She would show him the book; it would be interesting to see his reaction.

She put the book aside on her desk and went to help another patron. By the time she'd had lunch and returned to the library, several people were waiting for her to unlock the door. She was very busy for the next hour or so and forgot about the book until late in the afternoon when James Elledge appeared.

She was helping the elder Sterling sister, Hattie, select an armload of mysteries. Hattie, a tiny birdlike woman in her late sixties, lived with her sister, Florence. They were retired elementary-school teachers; neither of them had

ever married. The two women read five or six suspense
novels every week. They belonged to two book clubs, but
even that did not keep them supplied; so they were regular
patrons of the library, as well, and often used the interlibrary loan system to borrow books from other state li-
braries. Keeping Hattie and Florence supplied with enough
mystery books was quite a challenge for Jenny.

After half an hour Jenny had found four novels that
Hattie couldn't recall having read. Then she said, "Oh, I
almost forgot. I'm starting a used-paperback exchange. I'm
going to clear out those shelves in the corner over there for
them. I've already collected a number of books in a box in
the back room. Let's go look through them."

Hattie followed her, twittering, "Jenny, you do have
such wonderful ideas. Some mysteries come only in paperback, you know."

"That's true with other kinds of books, too," Jenny said,
"which is why I wanted to start the exchange. The cost of
paperbacks has gone up so much in the last couple of
years that some people can't afford to buy all they'd like
to read. So why not trade theirs for somebody else's?"

Hattie's white head was bent over the box, her little
black eyes aglow. "Oh, marvelous, marvelous!" She shuffled through the books eagerly, reminding Jenny of a pi-
rate greedily raking through his pieces of eight.

"Oh, my goodness, look at this." Hattie grabbed a book
from the bottom of the box and held it out for Jenny's inspection. The lurid cover pictured a voluptuous redhead
in a skimpy black gown sprawled across a bed, a huge
dagger protruding from her breast and blood dripping onto
the floor.

"Looks interesting," said Jenny with a straight face.

"You never can tell about paperback covers," said Hattie seriously. "Sometimes they have absolutely nothing to
do with the story. But I haven't read this one, so I'll take
it." She hesitated. "Oh, goodness me, I forgot. I didn't
bring any books to exchange."

"Pick out what you want," Jenny suggested, "and I'll
make a note of it. You can bring me the same number of
paperbacks the next time you come in."

Hattie beamed. "That's awfully sweet of you, Jenny."

"Well, I wouldn't do it for everyone, so keep it under your hat."

Hattie nodded gravely. "My, yes. Mum's the word."

After more rummaging, Hattie found two other paperbacks she hadn't read, and they returned to Jenny's desk. James Elledge was waiting.

Hattie greeted him cheerily. "Hello there, James."

"Afternoon, Hattie." He indicated the biology book and said to Jenny, "I see that book's been turned in."

Jenny pulled the cards from the four hardcover books Hattie Sterling wanted to check out and handed them to the older woman. To Elledge she said, "One of the trash haulers brought it in this morning. He found it at the furniture store."

"What in tarnation was it doing at the furniture store?" Elledge asked.

"It was in their trash barrel," Jenny explained.

Hattie, who was signing the cards on the corner of Jenny's desk, stopped writing and looked from Elledge to Jenny curiously.

"I been thinking on this situation," Elledge said, "and I seem to recall taking that book to the hospital with me. I was awful sick for a day or two, and I don't remember seeing the book after that. Sure looks like somebody swiped it." As he picked the book up, it fell open where the pages had been ripped out. "What's this?" He scowled and ran his stubby fingers along the ragged edges. "Somebody's torn some pages out."

"I know," Jenny said. "I noticed it when the book was returned this morning."

Elledge's blue eyes glinted at her. "I hope you don't think I did it. Why, I'd never desecrate a book that way!" He looked so indignant that Jenny had to repress a smile. She was sure now that Mr. Elledge hadn't torn those pages from the book.

"Why in tarnation," Elledge went on before she could reply, "would anybody want to ruin a good book like that?"

"Clearly," Jenny said, "they wanted whatever was on those missing pages."

The pockets of flesh around Elledge's blue eyes came

together, leaving two narrow slits. "Why didn't they just keep the book? Nobody could have traced it to them."

Hattie Sterling moved suddenly. Her small hand fluttered to her cheek, then patted the knot of white hair on top of her head. "Oh, my goodness," she chirped. "Isn't this exciting?" Her mouth formed a little *O* of delight.

Elledge frowned at her. "What is so exciting, Hattie, about somebody tearing up a good book?"

"Oh, that isn't the exciting part, James." Hattie's black eyes sparkled. "It's *why* they did it, the motive. That's the mystery!"

"Consarn it, Hattie," grumbled Elledge, "this ain't no confounded trashy mystery novel. This is real life. Somebody just ripped those pages out from pure meanness. Complete disregard for other people's property. Probably one of those rowdy boys that hang around the pool hall all the time, when they ought to be at home shoveling snow or carrying in wood."

Hattie was shaking her head emphatically. "No, no, James, that's too simple. Haven't you any imagination?"

Elledge snorted. "Imagination! I reckon you got enough for you and me and most everybody in town. I tell you, Hattie, if you don't quit reading those cheap detective stories, they're going to come and cart you away to the nuthouse one of these days."

"James, James," said Hattie sadly, "you disappoint me. We have an honest-to-goodness, real-life mystery right here in Pine Valley, and you're ready to ignore it, just accept the easiest explanation and turn your back and walk away."

"Maybe we should send the book over to the courthouse to the sheriff's office," said Elledge sarcastically, "tell him to dust it for fingerprints."

"No," said Hattie, ignoring his tone. "Too many people have handled that book. Besides, see how rough the cover is? Why, that wouldn't take a fingerprint worth two hoots."

"Aw, shucks," drawled Elledge, beginning to enjoy himself. "What other clues ought we to look for, then, Hattie?" He glanced at Jenny and grinned wickedly. She couldn't help returning his smile.

Hattie didn't seem to notice, however. She struck a

thoughtful pose. "Now, we know that book was put in the trash barrel in the last three days."

"How'd we know that?" Elledge asked, his eyebrows rising.

"Because," retorted Hattie smugly, "the trash is picked up on Tuesdays and Fridays." She ran a finger across her chin reflectively. "Where was it before that?"

"Beats me," said Elledge.

"We'll worry about that later," Hattie said. "Jenny suggested somebody wanted what was on those pages, but what if they just didn't want other people to know what was there? That would explain why they didn't destroy the book."

"But they did try to destroy it, Hattie," Elledge pointed out. "They threw it into a trash barrel."

Hattie tapped a finger against her forehead. "That's right. Well, first we need to know what those missing pages contained."

"Hattie," Elledge said, "you ask me what's on any other page in that book, all I gotta do is turn over there and read it; but when you ask what's on those missing pages, the greatest genius in the world couldn't tell you, 'cause they're *missing*. Now, Hattie, I know you can understand that."

Hattie drew herself up to her full five feet and glared at Elledge. "Why, I just read a story where the villain hid a tiny microdot containing a secret formula on the page of a book. Used it for dotting an *i*."

Elledge started to laugh.

"Now, you wait a minute," said Hattie furiously. "I'm not saying this book had a microdot in it. No, it's the information printed on those missing pages that might tell us something. And it just so happens, Mr. Smartypants, there are ways of finding out what's on those pages." She thrust her hand out. "Jenny, give me that book."

Intrigued, Jenny complied. Hattie looked at the place where the pages had been torn away, then turned to the table of contents. "Now, we know that pages 203 to 212 are missing." She ran her finger down the page. "Here we are. Chapter 5, pages 190 to 232. Physiology. The study of normal functions of living things." She looked up at Elledge, her face falling. "What's that mean, James?"

"Why ask me?" said Elledge innocently.

Hattie stamped one small foot. "Because you're the scientist, not me."

Elledge tugged off his fur-lined cap and scratched his head. "Lemme see, now. Physiology covers a lot of things, Hattie. There's embryology, pharmacology, endocrinology—"

"You stop that, James Elledge!" Hattie snapped. "You know I don't know what all those words mean." She turned to Jenny. "Never mind. Jenny, I want to borrow this book through interlibrary loan." She glanced at Elledge slyly. "We'll find out what was on those missing pages without your help, James. Thank you just the same."

Elledge looked disgusted. "What if you do? What's that going to prove?"

"It will tell us," said Hattie with strained patience, "what it was that somebody wanted to know—or what they didn't want somebody else to read—so badly they were willing to tear up a library book. That will lead us to the motive. If you'd read a few mystery books, James, you'd know that much, at least."

Jenny was filling out an interlibrary loan form. "I'll try to get the book, Miss Sterling. I'll call you if it comes in."

"Call me, too," Elledge said, grinning again. "This is getting good. I want to see what crazy notion Hattie will come up with next."

"Go ahead, laugh," said Hattie sniffing. "You don't know the first thing about detective work, James. This is how they do it. A clue here, a clue there—it all adds up."

Elledge put his cap back on and started for the door. "Sure it does, Hattie." He was shaking his head and laughing as he stepped onto the sidewalk.

"Don't pay any attention to him," Hattie said to Jenny. "Oh, isn't this wonderful? A real mystery!" She finished signing the cards for the books she was checking out. "Now, you call me just as soon as that book comes in, Jenny." As she left, Jenny noticed a decided spring in her walk.

After closing the library for the day, Jenny went to the newspaper office.

"I've been waiting for you," Gerald said as she thrust

her head into his office. "Harold can have visitors now. I thought we'd go by the hospital and look in on him before going home."

"Good," Jenny told him. "I'd like to."

In the car he said, "We can only stay a couple of minutes. Doc Weaver doesn't want Harold tiring himself trying to talk. He can speak, but only in a whisper. Doc thinks that's temporary."

Remembering Harold Highbridge's big, booming voice and the way he had loved to use it, Jenny was glad that he would eventually be his old self, in that regard at least.

Beyond the business district where the street crew had been at work, the streets were still covered with hard-packed snow and ice. Gerald's car was equipped with snow tires, however, and by driving slowly they reached the hospital without mishap.

Harold was in a private room at the end of one of the halls that spread away from a central nurse's station like the spokes of a half wheel. Sarah, looking washed out and tired in a beige dress and little makeup, was sitting in a chair beside the bed, and Beau Gleason stood beside her chair. Sarah looked up as Gerald and Jenny hesitated at the open doorway, then left her chair and came toward them.

"How is he today?" Gerald asked her.

"Better," Sarah said. "He rested quietly during the night, and he's begun to be aware of the people around him."

"Have you been here all day?" Gerald asked.

"Most of it," she admitted. "Luke just left. He went down to Harold's office to take care of some things there. He'll be back later to drive me home."

"Do you think we might see him for a minute?" Gerald asked.

She wearily brushed at a stray wisp of auburn hair. "I think that would be good for him, Gerry, if you'll go one at a time. When there are too many people in the room, he becomes overexcited." She glanced over her shoulder. "Beau, would you mind staying with him until the nurse comes back? I think I'll go down to the snack bar for a cup of coffee."

"You go along," Gleason said. "I'll be here when you get back."

"I'll go with you," Gerald said to Sarah, "while Jenny looks in on Harold." Before Jenny could protest, her father had taken Sarah's arm and was leading her away from Harold's room.

She stepped into the room. Harold lay on his back, his head elevated slightly, the white sheet folded neatly across his chest. His arms, in blue cotton pajamas, were folded across his body on top of the sheet. His eyes were closed, and his sharply angled face was almost as white as the sheet, which made a ghostly contrast with the thick dark brows and hair only lightly sprinkled with gray. Jenny hesitated beside the bed, glancing at Beau Gleason, who stood opposite her.

Gleason's mouth above the full white beard pressed grimly in at the corners. "He's resting, and he needs that more than anything right now. I told them he shouldn't be allowed to have visitors outside the family, but they wouldn't listen to me. So I'm here to make sure he's not disturbed." Probably without his realizing it, Gleason's voice had risen as he talked. Harold stirred, and his eyes fluttered open. Jenny was so close she could see the pupils contracting in the brown irises as he focused on her face.

"Jenny?" he whispered, and the long fingers of his left hand moved toward her in a weak sort of gesture.

She took his hand in hers and smiled. "Hello, Harold. They tell me you're feeling better today."

"Yes," he whispered. "I'll be home for Christmas." His cold fingers exerted a surprisingly strong pressure on hers. "I haven't seen you for a long time. You don't come to the Tamarack anymore. You used to come often with Leah." His head turned away from her as he peered about the room. He looked lost for a moment and then troubled. "Is Leah here?"

"No." Jenny glanced at Beau Gleason, who had moved closer to the other side of the bed, his expression grim. Jenny didn't want to be there alone with Gleason and Harold clung to her hand too tightly for her to remove it.

The sick man was looking into Jenny's face once more.

His dark eyes were sad. "Forgive me, I forgot for a minute. Leah is dead, isn't she?"

Jenny nodded. "It was a long time ago, Harold." She attempted to retrieve her hand, but he hung on, pulling it toward him so that she was forced to lean over him. His dark eyes had the feverishly bright glitter of the very ill.

"Listen," he whispered close to her ear. His breathing was shallow and rapid, and she could feel it hot on her cheek. He was straining toward her, his head lifted from the pillow. "Mary Steed brought death. She was a liar—a schemer. Bad—evil. But Leah—Leah shouldn't have died. She was good. . . ." He fell back against the pillow suddenly, releasing her hand. Jenny could see tiny blue veins in his papery eyelids as he closed them. He was breathing more rapidly, and there were beads of perspiration around his mouth. As she watched, a tremor ran through his body.

Beau Gleason leaned over the bed, his rough hand resting on Harold's pale forehead. "You rest now, Mr. Highbridge. No more talking." Harold nodded almost imperceptibly and sighed.

Gleason straightened and strode to the foot of the bed. His eyes had a glaze of anger in them. He reached for Jenny's arm, pulling her toward the door. Even through the coat she was wearing, his fingers hurt to the very bone.

"Why do you always come where you're not wanted?" he asked her scornfully. "If he has a setback over this, you'll answer to me. Now, get out of here."

She obeyed him numbly, fearing that if she didn't, he'd break her arm. He muttered violently to himself as he released her, giving her a final push into the hall. "I'm sorry," she said. "If I'd known how weak he was, I would not have come today. Mrs. Highbridge—I didn't think he'd get so upset."

Gleason shook his head in disgust. "You didn't think about anything but your morbid curiosity. Wanted to see the biggest man in town laid out, helpless. No consideration for anybody else as long as you and yours aren't hurt. Just like your aunt."

Jenny stiffened against the cold wall, staring at him.

"That's not true. I wanted him to know his friends care about him."

He ran a hand through white hair and cocked his massive head to look at her. "You Curtisses are no friends of the Highbridges."

She folded her arms and met his gaze without wavering. Here was her chance to talk to Beau Gleason. But how could she, in his present mood? Why was he being so hostile to her? She didn't understand, but somehow she had to learn what he knew about Leah's murder. And she must be wary. She was no match for his shrewdness, and she knew it. Still she had to try.

"You have no right to speak unkindly of Leah. You didn't know her at all if you think she had no consideration for other people."

Gleason's dark eyes narrowed as he looked at her, his heavy white brows bristling. "Leah didn't even know when she was hurting someone else. She lived in a dreamworld." His voice grated.

"She didn't hurt people, she helped them. As she tried to help Mary Steed."

The sound he made in his throat caused a flicker of uneasiness to pass through her, but she stood her ground as he took a step toward her.

"Don't touch me again," she warned him "You'll have to deal with my father if anything happens to me."

He halted directly in front of her, and she sensed a dark frustration raging through him. She wanted to force him to voice his churning emotions now, before he had time to think.

"I have sometimes thought that *you* might have killed those women."

He glared at her for a long moment, struggling to contain his fury. "It wasn't me that did it. It was one of their men—their lovers. Mary Steed was a cheap floozy who thought she could turn her stupid mistake to her own advantage and force Luke to marry her. The Highbridges all thought she was sweet and innocent—but they found out. They thought Leah was something, too—put her up on a pedestal. But I knew better. If she was so grand, how come she made a friend of someone like Mary Steed? Birds of a feather, I say."

"Maybe the Highbridges knew Leah better than you did."

He snorted and, turning his back on her, went into Harold's room and shut the door.

Jenny thrust her hands into her coat pockets and walked down the deserted hall toward the nurse's station. Her heart, which had been pounding in her ears throughout the confrontation with Gleason, was beginning to slow down, but she still heard the caretaker's angry words. *"Why do you always come where you're not wanted?"* As if he knew of another occasion. In his anger he'd given himself away. He *had* recognized her that night outside the Tamaracks. He hadn't shot at a stranger, a potential burglar. He'd shot at *her*, Jenny Curtiss. She felt suddenly weak with the knowledge. He seemed to blame her for something, but what? When the time was right, she would confront him with that, but not here, not now. At the right time. She shivered at the thought.

As she reached the nurse's station, she met Gerald and Sarah coming from the snack bar.

"Everything all right?" Sarah asked, as if she saw something in Jenny's face that worried her.

"I—I think Harold tried to talk too much. I left so he would rest. Dad, he shouldn't have any more visitors today."

"I'll see Sarah to the room and just stick my head in," Gerald said.

Jenny wanted to prevent his going to Harold's room, but she didn't know how without telling him what had transpired between her and Beau Gleason. "I'll wait for you out here."

She had started toward the lobby when she met Marty Brubaker.

"Visiting Mr. Highbridge?" he asked.

She nodded. "Dad's in there now."

"Come on back to the snack bar," Marty said, "and I'll buy you a Coke."

She followed him down another hall and through the last door on the right, where there were several small tables and food dispensing machines lining the walls. At the moment the room was deserted. Jenny sat down at one of the tables. Marty got Cokes from a machine and took the chair across from her.

"Your mother was here visiting Mr. Highbridge earlier today," he said.

"Oh? I didn't know she planned to come. Dad must have told her Harold could have visitors."

Marty tipped the Coke bottle and drank, his Adam's apple shifting as he swallowed. Then he said, "I ran into her as she was leaving. Tried to get her to donate a pint of blood, but no dice."

Jenny was surprised. "Mother's usually not squeamish about things like that. Come to think of it, though, I can't remember her ever giving blood before. You know, I think she has some kind of aversion to the whole idea."

"Yeah." Marty grinned. "She informed me that when you were younger, more than one doctor diagnosed you as anemic. She suggested I check out my equipment. She didn't see how your count could be in the high-normal range now."

Jenny made a face. "I was kind of sickly as a child. I remember having to take those big, horrible-tasting iron pills the doctor prescribed. I guess they worked. Anyway, I'm hardly ever sick anymore, and I don't tire easily."

Marty's brow wrinkled. "I got to thinking about what she said, and it worried me so much I went back to the lab and changed all my solutions."

"You mean you might have been wrong about my blood count after all?"

"I don't really think so," he said, "but I'd like to check you out again, just to be sure."

"When?"

"Right now if you have time. Only a tiny prick on the finger this time. It won't hurt a bit."

Jenny shrugged. "Whatever you say."

He finished his Coke. "Come back to the lab, then."

It took only a few seconds for Marty to prick her finger and deposit her blood on the slides. When he had finished, she said, "You'll tell me if there's anything I should know, won't you?"

He looked at her and laughtd. "Don't worry. Even if the count's not as high as in the first test, I'm sure it'll still be in the normal range."

"OK," she said. "I better go find Dad."

As she reached for her coat, the gold medallion swung against her breast. For an instant Marty stared at it; then, reaching out, he took it in his hand. "Where did you get this?"

Jenny said, "It was Leah's," although she felt sure he already knew that.

Thoughtfully, he rubbed a finger over the raised head of the goddess. "What does it represent, do you know?"

"It's the Greek goddess of growing things, Demeter. Leah once told me she and Demeter were a lot alike."

His hand dropped, and he said nothing more. She wondered if he resented her wearing something that had belonged to Leah. "Why do you stay in Pine Valley, Marty?" she asked suddenly.

He gave her that quick, probing gaze. "You think it's time the rolling stone moved on?"

"No. I was thinking about Leah. This place must be filled with unhappy memories for you."

He glanced away, shrugging. "Yeah. Only I seem to have lost my adventuring spirit." He studied her for a long moment. "And this is a good job. A man ought to stay put after he passes forty."

She smiled, sensing that he wasn't telling her the full reason. She said good-bye and left the lab.

She had been waiting in the lobby for only a few moments when her father joined her. He looked concerned. "It's a shock seeing Harold so weak and helpless."

"I know," she said, wondering if Beau Gleason had mentioned anything of what had happened in Harold's room earlier. "Did he try to talk to you?"

Gerald shook his head. "I didn't stay. He was sleeping."

"Do you think he'll recover, Dad?"

"Sarah thinks so. Or maybe she won't let herself think anything else. Anyway, they're starting physical therapy tomorrow."

Gerald helped her into her coat, and they went outside, where darkness was falling fast. At the Curtiss house, Gerald let her out at the curb, saying he was going back to the office for a while.

Doreen was sitting in front of a fire in the den, reading. Jenny went to stand in front of the fire, rubbing her cold hands together over the flames.

Doreen put her book aside. "Where's your father?"

"He said he had some more work to do at the office. We went to see Harold for a few minutes, and then he brought me home."

"I was there earlier," Doreen said. "Harold looks terrible, doesn't he? He was always so full of life, and to see him like that . . ."

"I know what you mean, but there's still something of the old spark left. He told me he'd be home for Christmas."

"Oh, I hope so," said Doreen fervently. "I just don't know what will happen if he—if he doesn't make it."

Jenny looked at her sharply. Doreen was gazing into the flames. "If Harold doesn't recover, Sarah will survive. People do, you know."

"I only hope your father will believe that?" Jenny heard the pain in her tone, overlaid by bitterness.

To change the subject, Jenny said, "Marty Brubaker checked my blood again."

Doreen looked up, startled. "Why?"

"After you told him about my childhood anemia, he started worrying that maybe there was something wrong with the earlier test. He changed all the test solutions and took another blood sample. He promised to let me know if the first test was in error."

"If he keeps on," said Doreen sarcastically, "you won't have any blood left."

Jenny laughed. "Don't exaggerate, Mother. I really do want to know if I'm still anemic. Maybe I should be taking iron or vitamins or something. And if so, I certainly shouldn't be giving blood."

"That's what I've been saying," Doreen said. Then her eyes found the medallion, which Jenny had neglected to hide beneath her clothes. "When did you start wearing that?"

"A few days ago. If it bothers you, I'll put it back with Leah's things."

"Why should it bother me? Wear it if you want." She picked up her book again.

"I'm going to my room until dinner," Jenny said. Doreen mumbled her assent as Jenny left the room and went into the entry hall. At the door, she turned to look back at her mother.

The book was once more lying facedown on the hearth. Doreen sat with her head in her hands, not stirring. There was despair in every line of her body. This was her mother, who could cope with anything. Doreen Curtiss, who had brought her sister back to normality by the sheer unbending force of her will, who, in the early years of her marriage, had worked long, hard hours alongside her husband to make the newspaper a going concern. Doreen had always been the rock in the family, the one everyone else could lean on. Jenny could hardly bear to see her like this, knowing that she felt Gerald was somehow slipping away from her, going to Sarah because she needed him now. Jenny wanted to go and kneel beside her mother and put her arms around her. She wanted to comfort and support.

But she made no move. What could she say that would make a difference? She turned and hurried up the stairs and into the safety of her room. Beast was curled on her bed. She went to the big cat and lay down beside him, drawing her knees up so that the furry body was in her lap. She stroked the softness of Beast's fur and felt his warmth. He stretched lazily and began to purr so loudly it sounded as though he must have a small motor in his chest. Jenny sighed, wishing that human beings could find contentment as easily.

Seven

Jenny slept late Saturday morning. When she awoke, she lay in her bed for some time, thinking about the events of the past few days. Her mother's unhappiness, which Jenny had only dimly sensed before, had suddenly come home to her yesterday when she caught Doreen unawares in her dejected pose by the fire. Doreen was desperately afraid that the crisis in the Highbridge family was drawing Gerald closer to Sarah. But Jenny didn't know why her father should be more drawn to Sarah—and away from Doreen—now than in the past. Sarah Highbridge had suffered through unhappy circumstances before this—when Luke had left for San Francisco, for example—and Gerald, who had remained a friend to the Highbridges through the years, had always been ready to offer comfort and support when it was needed. Doreen had taken each of these occasions in her stride, feeling perhaps that it would soon pass. Why should this time be any different? Possibly it was only that Doreen was growing older and had not been completely well for some time, although she always managed to put up a good front for the family. Also, she had been deeply grieved by her sister's death, and she must need Gerald more than ever to help fill the gap left in all their lives by the loss of Leah.

It also seemed that Doreen hadn't liked the idea of Marty Brubaker's taking more blood yesterday. But perhaps when the results of the last test showed Jenny to be strong and healthy, as Marty seemed certain they would, Doreen's mind could be put at ease on that score, at least.

Marty's odd behavior when he noticed Leah's medallion around Jenny's neck was puzzling, too. But when she remembered how attached Leah had been to the medallion—so much so that she had hardly ever removed it—Jenny realized that Marty might see it as too special to be worn by someone else. She wondered if she should try to talk to him about it when she went back to the hospital.

If she went back. She wasn't sure she should risk exciting Harold again. She felt a pang of guilt over his unexpected reaction to her presence the day before. Unwittingly, she had upset him. He seemed to have felt a desperate need to communicate something to her. At first she had attributed his excitement to the fact that he was disoriented, thinking that Leah had come to the hospital with Jenny. And when he remembered that Leah was dead, he had evidently wanted to express his sympathy to Jenny. He might, in his slightly confused state, have thought that Leah had died recently instead of sixteen months ago. What had startled Jenny was Harold's obviously strong conviction that Mary Steed was the cause of everything that had happened, that the poor girl had been some kind of evil influence. Of course, Harold could hardly be expected to feel kindly toward Mary, since she was the cause of Luke's leaving home and the family business. But surely Harold didn't blame Mary entirely for what had happened between her and his son.

Thinking of Luke brought a sense of disquiet. Wednesday evening at the Copper Kettle, Jenny had felt a strange attraction to him. She had found herself alarmingly open to the appeal of a man she had never even liked. Oddly, he, too, had seemed momentarily drawn to her, curious about her—perhaps because the last time he'd noticed her, she was a child, and suddenly, as it must have seemed to him, she was a woman.

Then for the first time she understood, with a flash of uncomfortable self-recognition, what had disturbed her so about Luke. The way he looked at her had made her feel every inch a woman. It was as if the last trailing strands of her girlhood had fallen away in that instant. His glance had ignited a spark that seemed to have been waiting for just such a moment.

But probably the most alarming realization that had come to her during the past few days was that, for some inexplicable reason, Beau Gleason hated her. He seemed to feel that he had to protect the Highbridges from her. She did not understand how she could be a threat to them or to Gleason, but the caretaker evidently felt that she was. Was it because she was related to Leah, whose close relationship with the Highbridges had probably aroused jealousy in Gleason? For whatever reason, she knew that Beau Gleason and Luke Highbridge were dangerous men, and she must be on guard against them.

By noon a light snow had started to fall. She had a late lunch with her parents, who had decided to stay inside by the fire rather than venture out, even on the Saturday of the Winter Festival. Then it was time to get into her ski clothes. She went to her room and dressed rapidly, first pulling on long johns, then heavy socks. Her ski pants and hooded parka were bright red, with a narrow blue stripe down each leg and sleeve. Under the parka she wore a heavy white crew-neck sweater. Until she got to the slopes, she would wear her brown leather walking boots. She stuffed her red ski mittens in the pockets of her parka and got her black ski boots and skis from her closet. Carrying skis and poles over her shoulder, she went downstairs to wait for Tom.

When he arrived, he was bareheaded in dark blue. He took Jenny's skis and poles and strapped them on top of his car alongside his own. Dropping her ski boots onto the floor behind the front seat, she got into the car.

Tom slid into the driver's seat, rubbed his palms together and gave her an eager grin. "I've been looking forward to this all week." He started the car and pulled into the street. "Do you feel ready for Treacherous Hill today?" Tom, a much more advanced skier than Jenny, loved the more difficult slopes.

"I think I'll stay on the easier slopes," she said, "but don't feel you have to keep me company. You take Treacherous Hill, and we'll meet later at the lodge."

He glanced at her. "You can handle Treacherous, Jenny. I'll be right behind you."

She shook her head.

"Sure you don't mind if I go alone, then?"

"Not at all," she said and saw his obvious relief.

"You should at least try some of the intermediate slopes. You told me you skied the beginner slopes last year whenever you were home from college. They're not enough challenge for you now."

"They're plenty of challenge," she put in hastily. "I'm very happy plugging along with the beginners."

He gave her a puzzled smile. "You really mean it,

don't you? You don't feel in the least compelled to compete with anybody."

"Not on skis I don't," she assured him.

On Mill Street they turned west, soon leaving Pine Valley behind. They followed the highway for about a mile, then turned off on the road that led to the mountain where the ski area was located. They drove through stands of fir, spruce, larch, and pine as the road began to curve and climb toward the lodge. The snow continued to come down in big lacy flakes that splattered against the windshield, one by one. Their car was one of a line of several climbing up the mountain, and occasionally they passed a car coming down. At one point they passed a sign that warned, *"If your vehicle is not equipped with snow tires or chains, do not proceed beyond this point."* After that the road became steeper.

The lodge was not large, but with its brightly painted exterior of orange and brown and its snow-covered roof, it looked charmingly quaint, very like a gingerbread house sitting there against the mountain. Its basic construction consisted of two A-frame sections entirely walled with glass; a large deck extended across the front and along one side of the building. Several small cabins, their roofs wearing a frosting of snow, were clustered near the lodge on one side, and on the other side was the ski-patrol headquarters.

The mountain rose to the east of the lodge, the ski trails plainly marked. Tom found a parking place, and, as they got out of the car, Jenny could see small, brightly clad figures gliding down the trails. They got into their ski boots and clumped toward the small shelter at the foot of the trails. The snow had almost stopped falling, and the sun was trying to break through the clouds. Tom stood in line outside the shelter to buy lift tickets. Jenny sat down on a log railing to put on her skis and was ready when Tom returned.

In the chair lift, the safety bar snapped firmly into place, Tom said, "You can get off at Easy Rider halfway up, and I'll go on to Treacherous."

The chair rocked gently as it left the station. Jenny held to the bar tightly with one hand, the other hand grasping her ski poles. The lift carried them up a narrow aisle cut through the trees, and as their chair rose above the ground, Jenny felt a sensation of release tinged with exultation, a feeling she had come to associate with skiing, even though she was far from being an expert.

Beyond the lift track, winding trails had been cut through the trees, going in all directions toward the base. As halfway point approached, Jenny lifted the tips of her skis and, at the right moment, slid out of the chair. She headed for the ramp, waving a jaunty good-bye to Tom, who called to her, "I'll see you later at the lodge."

Left alone, for there were no other skiers waiting to go down Easy Rider at the moment, Jenny positioned herself, took a deep breath and started down, christying back and forth easily. She was pleased to discover that during the long nonskiing months she had not lost what confidence she had gained the previous winter. In fact, she was doing well, which was probably why she preferred the easier slopes. She felt in control of herself and the situation, and a surge of elation filled her. She saw a floundering beginner ahead and called, "Watch your right," and sped past, the cold wind in her face, the snow glistening underfoot as the sun broke through the clouds.

At the base, she took her sunglasses from her pocket and put them on. Then she clumped back to the lift line to wait her turn. She managed Easy Rider several times during the afternoon. Once, as she was going up in the lift, she saw Beau Gleason, his white hair sticking out from under a green stocking cap, several chairs ahead of her. When their glances met, she looked away quickly. Seeing him reminded her that he was said to be an expert skier; surprisingly, his injured leg did not seem to hinder him on skis. Gleason went on up the mountain to the more difficult slopes, while Jenny got off at the halfway point.

After two more good descents of Easy Rider, Jenny was feeling so confident she decided to go a little higher and try another hill. She preferred being alone the first time she tried one of the difficult trails. She didn't want to make a fool of herself in front of Tom. Remembering that Tom had said she could handle Treacherous, she decided in a sudden burst of daring to try it.

Her courage all but deserted her once she had slid from the lift and was standing at the top of Treacherous Hill. Compared to the beginner trails, this trail was unbelievably steep and winding and narrow. In places the snow-banks were thin, and she could see rocks protruding. She wished she hadn't given in to the impulse that had brought her here, but now that she stood atop the mountain, there was only one way down.

She removed her sunglasses, which she no longer needed. Then, taking a deep breath, she pushed off. After a few moments of snowplowing, she caught her ski in a bank, barely managing to keep from falling. She started off again, realizing for the first time that the sun had gone behind the mountains and dusk was falling. The trees seemed taller than they had farther down the mountain, cutting off even more of the failing light. When she caught herself in a bank a second time, she lost her balance, her skis flew out from under her, and she bumped a few feet on the seat of her pants.

Sitting there in the snow, she feared for the first time that she couldn't make it down. She brought her mittened hands up to cup her mouth and called Tom's name, but there was no answer, and she scrambled to her feet and got back on the trail. As she stumbled along, trying to stay on her feet, she heard the swish of skis behind her. Another skier was coming fast. And then, above her, through a gap in the trees, she caught a brief glimpse of a green cap and white hair and knew that it was Beau Gleason and that he would be upon her any minute. He had heard her call for Tom, had recognized her voice, and now he was coming after her! Panic clawed at her chest as she pushed herself along—faster and faster—amazed that she was taking the turns somehow without falling. But finally her momentum was so great she knew she had to slow herself or crash into a tree.

Abruptly, she sat down, letting her skis go out from under her. Above her, she could hear Gleason coming. It was useless for her to try to outrun him now. She ripped off her mittens and released her skis, pulling them loose from the boots. Then, shouldering the skis and poles, she staggered off the trail and into the trees. She ran and dodged in and out between the tall trunks that grew so close together there was sometimes barely room for her to pass. But she kept going, fearing that Gleason would try to follow her. Minutes later, when she had to stop to catch her breath, she listened carefully for the sound of a pursuer in the trees behind her. She heard nothing and, realizing that Gleason was probably far down the mountain by now, she started to turn back toward the trail. But she didn't know which way to turn. She was lost, and the light was growing dimmer by the second.

She stood frozen, fearing to move in any direction, for whichever way she chose could lead her farther from the lodge. She knew that in panic lay disaster. She must stand still for a moment and try to think. She turned about slowly, trying to see her own tracks, but it was too dark to make them out now, and if she did not find her way out soon, she would not be able to see her hand—or a tree— in front of her face. Deciding arbitrarily upon a direction, she took a few steps and stumbled into a drift, falling to her knees. The cold was beginning to penetrate her clothing. She clambered to her feet and propped her skis and poles against a tree long enough to pull up her hood and tie it securely beneath her chin. Her face was beginning to feel numb, and she was tempted to sit down and cry, to give up and wait to be rescued. But that is what Beau Gleason would expect her to do.

As she picked up her skis again and walked a few steps, she realized that the way she had tried to walk before, when she had stumbled into the drift, had been more difficult because it was uphill. Now she could feel that she was going downhill, which meant down the mountain. If she kept going downhill long enough, she should come to the lodge or one of the trails or the road. She felt a rush of warm relief and stumbled on.

It had grown quite dark when she saw the lights. She cried out, and then she heard a voice calling her name. Whose voice? She stumbled desperately toward the lights, falling, getting to her feet and going on, until she could make out the lighted ski-patrol building and, beyond that, the bright triangle of glass that was the top of one of the lodge's A-frames.

Then she saw a man coming toward her, and she stopped, almost falling. Relief flooded over her as, once again, Tom called her name, alarm in his tone. He came to her quickly and caught her about the waist. He took her skis and poles in his free hand and said, "Hold on to me." She clung to him as they went toward the lodge. He didn't try to question her immediately but concentrated on getting her to level ground.

Finally, as they came around the corner of the ski-patrol building, he asked, "What happened? I've been looking for you for over an hour. I was about to call out the patrol."

"I—I was lost. I tried to go down Treacherous and went into the woods." It was on the tip of her tongue to tell him that Beau Gleason had been following her, but she realized in time that he would probably think she was hysterical. And how could she prove otherwise?

"How could you be so foolish, Jenny? You shouldn't have tried that on your own the first time. Why didn't you find me to go with you?"

"I wanted to try it, and I didn't know where you were."

They had reached the lodge deck, and Tom continued to support her as they circled it and headed for the parking area. At his car he said, "Are you all right?"

"Yes." She disengaged herself from his arm. "I'm just exhausted, and I don't mind admitting I was scared there for a while."

He shook his head, looking down at her. "We can go back to town right now if you want."

"No." She set her chin stubbornly. "I want to stay for the wiener roast and everything." She wouldn't give Gleason the satisfaction of knowing she'd been in trouble, and she'd make certain she wasn't alone with him again. "But, Tom"—she put a hand on his arm as he opened the car door—"don't tell anyone I was lost. Promise?"

He turned back to her and smiled. "OK. Your secret is safe with me."

Tom strapped their skis and poles in place, and they exchanged their ski boots for walking boots before going to the lodge.

The large central room was open all the way to the peaked roof, the interior of which was pine-paneled and crossed at intervals with thick beams. The room had a central fireplace, open on all sides, where a pile of logs blazed, offering warmth and cheer against the cold outside. In addition to the two glass walls, the other walls were paneled like the ceiling, and there was a bright-orange shag carpet on the floor. Chairs, couches, wooden benches and stacks of square, leather-upholstered cushions in orange and brown lined three walls. On the fourth wall was the bar, and behind that the manager's office.

The manager, a former competition skier who had never attained championship status, was employed by the Highbridge Corporation. Jenny saw him arranging wieners, buns, chips and dips, buffet-style, on one end of the long bar. Beau Gleason was acting as bartender, but if he felt any surprise at seeing Jenny there, his face did not show it.

Most of the couches and chairs were occupied, and there were several people sitting on the floor near the fireplace.

"I've already bought our tickets for the buffet," Tom told her as they made their way around the furniture and through a group of people sitting on the floor to stand near the fireplace. After they'd warmed themselves, Jenny saw Kent and Shirley in a corner of the room, and they joined them, sharing the day's experiences on the slopes until the buffet line began to form.

Just as they took their places in line, Shirley nudged Jenny and pointed toward the door. "Look who's here."

It was Luke Highbridge, handsome in a yellow turtleneck sweater and brown corduroy pants. The worry and weariness that had been in every line of his body the night he'd arrived in Pine Valley were gone. Now his dark, dynamic presence seemed to have brought an added spark of life to the room. As several people called greetings to him, Jenny saw that a tall, attractive black-haired girl was with him. She wore a long black velvet skirt and a clinging jersey blouse.

"Who's the girl?" Jenny asked Shirley.

Shirley made a face. "Susan Nelson. Don't you recognize her? Look at that outfit! She's managed to outshine every female in the place, as usual."

"She hasn't been home for ages, and she's wearing her hair in a different style," Jenny said. "I guess that's why I didn't recognize her." Susan Nelson was the daughter of the president of Pine Valley's largest bank. She'd been two years ahead of Jenny in school, having graduated last spring from Vassar. Jenny had heard that Susan was working for a publishing company in New York City.

"It's not hard to figure out why she suddenly showed up here now," Shirley said. "She learned Luke was home. I'll bet her mother called her the minute he hit town. Susan's had her tentacles out for Luke for years. She wants to be Mrs. Luke Highbridge. I hate to admit it, but they make a striking couple, don't they?"

Jenny had to agree. Luke and Susan, their black hair gleaming in the light from the overhead lamps, were surrounded by a group of old acquaintances. Susan was laughing, her head thrown back, her hand tucked possessively under Luke's arm.

Tom, who had been watching the couple ever since they came in, frowned. "I didn't see them on the slopes today."

"They weren't here," Shirley said. "They must have just arrived. Perfect timing. Susan made quite an entrance in her sexy black outfit."

"Your claws are showing, hon," Kent teased.

"Yeah," Shirley said calmly, "I guess they are. It's pretty difficult to remain unruffled when every man in the room is about to drop his eyeballs ogling her."

Kent gave her an affectionate kiss on the cheek. "Every man but one, love. I only have eyes for you."

"Make that every man but two," said Tom tersely. "Susan Nelson's too uppity for my taste. She and Luke deserve each other."

They had reached the head of the line, and further conversation about Luke and Susan was forestalled as they filled their plates and ordered drinks. As Beau Gleason waited on them, Jenny looked at his thick neck and big hands and felt a shiver of revulsion, remembering the afternoon on Treacherous Hill, when Gleason had raced down the slope after her. When he handed her a drink, she made herself meet his gaze. He looked at her oddly for a moment, his shaggy white brows drawn down in a scowl, then moved away to wait on someone else.

Kent and Tom found a spot at the fireplace to roast the wieners, while the girls claimed a place for the four of them on the floor against one wall. Jenny was still tired from her ordeal in the woods, and she was grateful to be sitting down, her head resting against the wall behind her. All around her talk buzzed about the various slopes, friendly arguments about which was the most challenging. Some skiers bragged unabashedly about their skill; others described good-naturedly the falls they'd taken that day.

A small brown-haired girl of about fourteen, carrying a hot dog in one hand and a Coke in the other, sat down next to Jenny.

Jenny smiled at her. "Aren't you Tammy Nelson?"

"Yep," she said, taking a big bite of her hot dog, which she chewed vigorously before swallowing. "Great skiing today, wasn't it?"

"Yes," said Jenny, "although I'm a plodder. I spent most of the day on Easy Rider."

Tammy cocked her head, her large gray eyes studying Jenny curiously. "Have you been skiing long?"

"Occasionally for several years."

"You shouldn't still be on Easy Rider, then. My ski instructor says I'm about ready for Treacherous."

"You must be very good," Jenny said.

"I am," Tammy admitted immodestly, "and I'm going to be a champion someday. I love to ski better than anything in the whole world. I tried to get my sister to come with me today, but she wouldn't. She doesn't like to ski. Can you believe it?"

"Maybe Susan has been away from it too long. I saw her come in with Luke Highbridge a while ago. When did she get back?"

"Thursday. It's the first time she's come home in over a year. It took Luke to get her back to town. I asked her if she's going to marry him."

"And is she?"

"She said it was none of my business." Tammy's smile was mischievous. "But I heard her telling Mom later that she could plan on a June wedding."

Jenny realized she was pumping this talkative child and quickly changed the subject. Soon Tom joined her with their roasted wieners, and Tammy moved off to find some of her friends. Tom and Jenny sat together on the floor, their backs against the wall, eating and talking in a desultory fashion. The rising wind outside made a rattling sound as it pushed against the great panes of glass. When they had finished eating, Tom gathered up their dishes and went off with Kent to dispose of them. "I saw a couple of old friends across the room," he told Jenny. "I think I'll say hello to them before they leave. Want me to bring you another drink when I come back?"

"I don't think so."

When the men were gone, Shirley said, "I'm going to find a mirror so I can brush my hair and freshen my makeup. I feel like someone who's been on a three-day camp-out. Want to come?"

Jenny shook her head. "I'm too tired to stand in line for a chance at the mirror."

Jenny shifted her position against the wall and closed her eyes, listening with half an ear to the conversations around her. After a while the talk in the room began to die away, and the sound of a guitar being strummed randomly could be heard. Jenny opened her eyes and saw Susan Nelson perched on top of the bar, a guitar across her lap. Her skin looked fragile and white against the black of her blouse, her slender hands pale on the strings. She glanced about the room, her eyes appearing more violet than blue in the light from the fireplace. She smiled slowly and, as she bent over her guitar, her shining black hair fell forward, hiding her face from Jenny.

Susan began to sing, her voice low and richly beautiful. The song was "Bridge over Troubled Waters," and she sang it slowly, her tone sultry and sad. Some of the people in the room began to move their cushions and chairs closer to the bar, forming a half circle around the girl and her guitar, shutting her off from Jenny's view. Jenny stayed where she was, her eyes closed, listening to the song.

When Susan finished, there was a round of applause, and voices in the circle around her began to call out the names of songs. She sang "Rocky Mountain High" and "Country Roads," while others in the room joined in. Halfway through a fourth song, someone sat down on the floor beside Jenny. She opened her eyes and looked into Luke Highbridge's face.

"Hi," he said. "I saw you when I came in. I've been waiting for an opportunity to talk to you." In the firelight his brown eyes seemed black, and there was something in them Jenny could not read. He was sitting so close that their arms touched, sending a shock of electricity through Jenny. As casually as she could, she shifted away from him.

Oblivious to her discomfort, he smiled. "I understand you visited Dad at the hospital."

"Yes," she said guardedly, wondering who had told him—one of his parents or Beau Gleason. And how much did he know about her visit? "I hope I didn't tire him."

"He wants you to come back. He likes you, Jenny. You know, of course, that he was extremely fond of your aunt."

"Was he?"

His craggy brows drew together. "Of course. And he never understood why you stopped coming to the Tamaracks after Leah died."

Jenny laughed uncomfortably. "Is that really so hard to figure out?"

Luke looked puzzled. "What do you mean?"

Someone there killed Mary Steed and Leah. It is a melancholy house, a violent house, and even now it is harboring a murderer. She wanted to say these things to him, but the words stuck in her throat, and her couldn't answer him. There was a long silence between them during which Jenny was dimly aware of a log burning away and falling into the ashes in the fireplace, and singing. that seemed faraway.

The warmth in Luke's eyes was slowly replaced by remoteness. "You blame us, don't you, Jenny? You blame us for Leah's death."

"I—I don't know," she said. Then, after a moment, she added more steadily, "But Leah is dead and someone is to blame, someone who should pay for what he's done."

She saw the grim set of his firmly chiseled mouth, the slight flexing of a muscle along his jaw. "No one at the Tamaracks would have harmed Leah."

She hesitated momentarily before she found the courage to ask, "Or Mary Steed?"

A blaze of anger flashed in his eyes. "Or Mary Steed. Neither of them ever received anything but kindness there."

"I'm not so sure of that. And considering what happened, I don't see how you can be, either."

The sharp angles in his face seemed suddenly set and hard as cement. "Look," he said angrily, "why don't you stop these veiled insinuations and say what is on your mind."

She took a deep breath. "Your caretaker seems to feel that Leah and Mary were evil women, that they deserved what they got. Beau Gleason despised my aunt, and now he has transferred those feelings to me. In fact, I think he is a bit mad."

He stared at her. "I can't imagine where you got such an outlandish idea! Beau is one of the most faithful employees my father has ever had. He's like one of the family."

Jenny looked away from him, struggling to stifle the hot flash of indignation that rose in her. Why could this man make her so angry? And why did she feel so helpless in this confrontation with him? For several seconds she floundered in her confusion, and then she found her voice. "He shot at me. Beau Gleason saw me outside the Tamaracks the other night, and he shot at me. And at the hospital he was furious beause I had come to see your father. He pushed me out of the room and told me I wasn't welcome there."

Luke spoke sharply. "Beau would never do anything like that. Why should he care if you come to the Tamaracks or if you visit my father?"

She met his angry gaze steadily. "Yes, why?"

"Is that your answer to my question—another question?"

Hopelessness swept over her. She could not tell him why, because she was not sure herself. She had doubts, suspicions, but not one bit of tangible proof, nothing that would faze Luke Highbridge's arrogance. Still, she felt compelled to try. "He acts as if I'm a threat of some kind, as if I might know something, or might find out something, about who killed Leah and Mary."

"Are you suggesting that Beau killed those women?"

"I think it's possible."

"But what earthly reason could he have had?"

"Perhaps he was acting for someone else," she ventured, aware that she was stepping onto dangerous ground, "or trying to protect someone."

The dark eyes were wide. "You're making all of this up! But I can't fathom what you hope to gain by such wild accusations."

"Today on the slopes," she went on, determined to finish what she had started, but feeling an aching lump gathering in her throat, "he tried to run me down."

He laughed then, an amazed, but somehow humorless, laugh. "My God! you've built this up into a sinister campaign, haven't you?"

She bit her lip and blinked to keep back tears of frustration.

Suddenly his hand clamped over her wrist, and he scowled at her. "But don't let yourself get carried away, Jenny. Don't tell lies about a man because, for some unfathomable reason, you don't like him."

His words galvanized her. She shook his hand off and leaped up, glaring at him furiously as he scrambled to his feet. They stood facing each other for a long, heart-pounding moment. His face had a flushed look, and his eyes shot angry sparks.

"I don't lie!" she spat at him when she could speak. And then she whirled and stalked away, aware that several people near them were staring at her.

She met Tom halfway across the room. He was looking over her shoulder, his mouth twisted into a furious line. "What happened? What did Luke Highbridge say to you?"

Jenny pushed past him. "I want to leave, Tom." She made her way to the coatrack beside the door.

Behind her, Tom protested, "If he insulted you, I'll go over there and——"

She turned abruptly, tears springing to her eyes. "Leave it alone, Tom. It has nothing to do with you."

Outside, she stood still for a moment, letting the wind blast at her and clear away the conflicting emotions that churned in her brain. Tom followed her to the car, asking questions that she hardly heard. Neither of them spoke as they started down the mountain. The few tries they made at conversation were strained and soon trailed away.

After what seemed hours to Jenny, they pulled up in

front of the Curtiss house. As she started to open the door, Tom's hand on her arm stopped her. "Don't get involved with Luke Highbridge, Jenny. You'll get hurt."

She hesitated. "I don't know what you mean."

His hand fell away from her. "OK, pretend ignorance if that's the way you want to play it."

She opened the door and got out, pulling her ski boots from behind the seat. When she was standing beside the car, she said, "I am quite capable of taking care of myself."

"I hope so," he said gravely.

When he had lifted down her skis and poles, she took them from his hands. "I'm sorry I can't ask you to come in. I don't feel like talking anymore tonight. Thank you for the day." She hurried up the walk to the red brick house, where her parents had left the porch light on for her.

When she reached the front door and looked back, she saw that Tom was still leaning against the Pontiac, staring after her as though there were more things he wanted to say.

She called, "Good night, Tom," and went inside.

Eight

More snow fell on Sunday. At noon Jenny joined her parents in the den for a sumptuous brunch of scrambled eggs, sausage links, hashed brown potatoes, and Doreen's homemade buttermilk biscuits melting with butter and strawberry jam. Afterward, Gerald stretched out on the couch to watch a televised football game, and Doreen settled down in a chair near him, her competent hands moving rapidly as she crocheted bright multicolored "granny squares" for an afghan. Jenny went up to her room to read and nap most of the afternoon with Beast curled at her feet, while the thick snow slanted past her windows on the wind.

She rather expected Tom to call in a further effort to learn what had happened between her and Luke at the ski lodge and perhaps warn her again against getting involved with his old high-school classmate. When he didn't, she wondered if he had been hurt by her obvious eagerness to get away from him Saturday evening. She had never thought of her relationship with Tom as a romance, but Shirley had made a few observations lately that caused her to wonder if perhaps Tom had. She hoped not. She wouldn't like to hurt Tom, and she wanted to keep his friendship.

Monday the weather was clear. But the streets were freshly covered with several inches of snow, and the wind had piled drifts five or six feet high against buildings and fences. Jenny expected the library to be quiet, at least until the sidewalks along Main Street had been cleared again, and this turned out to be the case. She had only a handful of patrons during the morning and occupied herself with rearranging books, clearing the shelves where she planned to display the paperbacks available for exchange. She was preparing to leave for lunch when Marty Brubaker came in.

Surprised, Jenny exclaimed, "Marty! This is an unexpected pleasure. I assume this is your day off and you are so desperately bored you have resorted to checking out a library book."

Marty pulled off his leather gloves and stuffed them into his overcoat pockets. "Wrong," he said with a grin. "It's my lunch hour. The weather had landed a bunch of people in the hospital with upper respiratory infections, sprained ankles, and even a few broken bones, so I have been far too busy since dawn to be bored. I came downtown for lunch to get away from it for a few minutes."

"What can I do for you?"

"I'd like to talk, Jenny. Do you have a minute?"

"Several minutes. Evidently all those new patients up at the hospital are Pine Valley's book lovers. It's been like a tomb in here." She sobered, hesitating before she added, "Is it my blood test? Were the results of the second one different from the first?"

"Oh, no," said Marty hastily. "The two tests were practically identical. Your count's good. Everything's in tiptop shape." He looked around, then dragged a chair from one of the reference tables close to Jenny's desk. He unbuttoned his overcoat.

"I'm glad to hear that," Jenny said, expelling a small sigh of relief.

Marty studied her for a moment. "You were really worried, weren't you? I'm sorry. I guess I should have called you as soon as I ran the test. I just assumed you'd know that no news was good news."

"I wasn't worried exactly, but Mother will be glad to hear that everything checks out fine."

"Yes, I'm sure she will be. I got the definite impression she was concerned about you."

"Mother hasn't been completely well lately," Jenny said. "I think it's caused her to fuss—about everything—more than she used to." She tapped a pencil idly against the blotter on her desk. "If it's not my blood test, what is on your mind, Marty?"

He bent forward, his big hands braced against his knees. His eyes traveled to the medallion that lay against Jenny's brown cowl-necked velour shirt. "I want to talk about Leah."

"You still miss her, don't you?" Jenny asked sympathetically. "We all do. But, Marty, Leah wouldn't want us to grieve for her. She'd want us to go on with our lives." She thought of Mazie Jones. "She'd want you to find other interests, seek out other relationships."

He smiled briefly. "You sound very sure of what Leah would want."

"You know what I'm saying is true."

He shrugged. "Maybe. Only lately I'm beginning to wonder if I knew Leah as well as I thought I did. She was such a private person. And now, for some reason, I feel compelled to know everything about her before I can let go of her memory."

There was such remorse in his tone that Jenny had an urge to touch the lines furrowing his broad forehead— because they had both known Leah and loved her. "I'll tell you whatever I can."

Marty's thick fingers gripped his knees. "Do you know anything about that actor she was involved with? I know she ran away with him when she was barely seventeen and that they split up after a few months. And that's when she must have come back here to Doreen and Gerald. Did it take her a long time to get over him—that Garfield fellow?"

Jenny wondered what difference this could possibly make to Marty, especially now that Leah was dead. Did he have some inexplicable need to punish himself? "I wasn't even born when all of that happened. All I know is what I've heard Mother and Dad say about it. Leah never talked about him, and somehow I always knew that I shouldn't question her on the subject." She tapped the pencil against her cheek and smiled. "She wouldn't have told me anything in any case. You know how inscrutable she could be."

"Don't I!" Marty shifted in his chair and took his coat off, tossing it across the library cart, which was near the desk. Turning back to Jenny, he said, "I imagine your parents held a grudge against Garfield for some time."

Jenny nodded. "I'm sure my mother did. When Leah ran away, my grandmother was still living, but she never saw her younger daughter again. She died of a heart attack two or three months after Leah left. Mother always felt Leah's running away hastened Grandmother's death. And for that she blamed Gideon Garfield. Leah knew Garfield only a week before she left town with him. Did you know that?"

He shook his head, pain in his eyes. "Go on."

"Garfield was part of a touring troupe of actors—traveling summer stock, I guess you'd call them. Evidently they carried their props and everything with them. They'd set up in a town for a week and then move on. Mother told me that Leah had always been enthralled by actors and actresses. She went to the local movie house every time the film changed. Naturally, she was in the front row the first night Gideon Garfield performed here."

"Make-believe," Marty murmured thoughtfully. "Leah always seemed to prefer her dreamworld to reality. She must have been a pushover for Garfield."

"It was probably the first time in her life she had seen live theater," Jenny said, "the first time she had ever met any real actors, face-to-face, even if they were hardly more than amateurs. I'm sure the play, the actors, everything about it seemed glamorous and sophisticated to Leah. She went to every performance, and evidently she met Gideon Garfield after the show every night. Of course, neither her mother nor my parents knew anything about that until later. None of them went to see the show, but they weren't surprised at Leah's going every night, not the way she was. By the end of the week she had fallen head over heels in love with that young actor. I've always pictured him as tall and dark, dashing in a swashbuckling sort of way."

"Is that how your parents described him?"

"No. They never even saw him, and if Leah had any photographs of him she destroyed them when he deserted her."

"I can see why your mother hated him. Sounds like the bum deserved it."

"Oh, Mother had plenty of reasons. Besides Grandmother's death and the way Garfield treated Leah, Mother saw Leah at her lowest point. She went to New York and nursed her for several months before Leah was well enough to come home."

A muscle in Marty's jaw tightened. "Leah mentioned once that she'd been ill in New York, but she didn't elaborate."

"She had a complete nervous breakdown. From scraps of conversations that I've overheard through the years, I gather Leah was completely withdrawn for weeks and weeks. During that time she wouldn't or couldn't speak. Mother had to feed her every bite she ate. She had to dress her and bathe her and care for her like a young child. It couldn't have been easy for her. She'd recently lost her mother, and then having to leave Dad and the newspaper here and go east to care for Leah—all of this while she was carrying me. I was born in New York City, you know."

"Oh? I didn't know that, but, then, there's no reason why I should have." Marty ran a hand over his prominent chin, frowning thoughtfully. "It couldn't have been easy for Gerald, either, being separated from your mother all those months."

"He flew out to see her and Leah several times, but never for more than two or three days. He was just getting the newspaper started, and he didn't feel he could be away from it for long."

"I'm beginning to understand Leah's devotion to Doreen and Gerald. It sounds as if your mother practically forced Leah to get well."

"That's probably true. Leah had lost all desire to live, but Mother wouldn't let her stay in that safe little world she'd created inside her head. She made her come out and start living again."

Jenny was touched to see a film of tears in Marty's blue eyes. "She never told me any of this," he said after several moments during which he swallowed convulsively. "It hurts knowing she didn't trust me enough to confide in me."

"I doubt that it had anything to do with trust," Jenny commiserated. "As you said, Leah was a private person."

He shook his head in denial. "No. There's something you may not know. I think I can accept it now. Leah didn't love me."

"I know that she refused to marry you," Jenny said gently, and Marty gave her a startled look. Unwilling to reveal that it was Mazie Jones, and not Leah, who had told her this, Jenny rushed on. "But I can't help thinking that she would have changed her mind. Marty, if she'd lived. She cared very deeply for you. She wouldn't have spent so much time with you otherwise."

He took a deep breath. "Maybe. Leah may have loved

me, in her way, but the only explanation for her refusal to marry me is that she loved someone else more."

Jenny stared at him. "Oh, Marty, that's impossible! I mean, who else could she conceivably have loved? You were the only man in her life. Before she started dating you, she lived a solitary existence. Her days were occupied with her job here, and she spent her evenings at home. Leah had few friends. There were the Highbridges and—" The alertness in Marty's quick look caused her to hesitate. "Surely you don't think that someone at the Tamaracks—" She stopped, laughing in her amazement, "You don't think that Leah and Luke— Oh, no, Marty. Why, Leah was ten or eleven years older than Luke. And, besides, she never would have—" She stopped, stunned at this idea that had never occurred to her before. She laid her pencil aside. Then, elbows resting on her desk, she ran her hands down the velour sleeves of her shirt, feeling a slight chill.

"I did consider that possibility," Marty said after a moment, "the night Leah refused to marry me. I was a little frantic, I think, and I blurted out something about her and Luke. Know what she said?"

"What?"

"She said if I so much as mentioned anything like that again, not only would she not marry me, she would stop seeing me altogether. Said she had enough to worry about without having to deal with my jealous fantasies. Those were her exact words—my jealous fantasies. I think it was her total amazement at the idea that convinced me there was nothing between her and Luke."

Watching him, Jenny said, "But what did she mean? What could have been worrying her?"

"At the time, it went over my head. I was so furious at her crack about my fantasies. But I've wondered about it a lot since. I've even wondered if whatever it was could have had anything to do with her death. And I still think someone at the Tamaracks knows more than has been told about the murders. That lonely mountain path where Leah and the Steed girl were killed was closer to the Highbridge house than anyplace else. And it's odd the way Luke Highbridge cleared out when all that talk about him and Mary Steed was going around. If he was so darned innocent, why'd he run? Why didn't he stay here and stand up to the gossips? And—" he grimaced ruefully—"I've had even more bizarre thoughts in the middle of the night sometimes."

"Such as?"

"Such as Luke wasn't the only man living at the Tamaracks. It never entered my mind then to ask Leah about the others."

Astonished, Jenny stammered, "Are—are you suggesting that Leah might have been involved with Harold—or even Beau Gleason?"

"I'm not suggesting anything," Marty said quickly. "I'm just thinking aloud. Don't pay any attention to my wild middle-of-the-night ideas. The truth is probably that I can't stand the thought that Leah just plain didn't want to marry me. I keep looking for other explanations. The other day—" He stopped suddenly.

"What?"

"Oh, just a notion I had. Forget it."

Jenny nibbled her bottom lip. "If only we had some way of finding out what Leah meant by that remark—about something worrying her. It might lead to her killer."

Marty snorted. "I've wrestled that one around for the past sixteen months. I've kicked myself from here to Dallas and back for not pressing her for an explanation at the time. But I was too self-absorbed, too centered on how much I was hurting to think about Leah." He got up suddenly, as if he couldn't bear thinking any longer of what might have been. He picked up the chair in which he had been sitting and returned it to the reference corner. Then he gazed at Jenny intently, his hands in his pants pockets, as if he were reluctant to go. "Listen, as long as I'm here, do you happen to have anything on Greek mythology?"

Taken aback by this abrupt change of topic, Jenny laughed.

He looked puzzled. "Did I say something funny?"

She explained, "It's only that I didn't know you were into that sort of thing. Somehow the reading matter I associated with you is *Outdoor Life* or the sports page."

"Oh, I can see you have an inflated opinion of my intelligence," he said, shaking his head. "To tell the truth, I was always bored by that kind of stuff in school, but

I want to read up on Demeter. Maybe it'll help me understand Leah a little better."

"I didn't mean to sound flippant, Marty," Jenny said sobering. "Does my wearing Leah's medallion bother you?"

His thick blond brows came together quizzically. "Why should it?"

"I don't know, but you acted awfully odd when you noticed I was wearing it at the hospital the other day."

He stared at the medallion around Jenny's neck for a moment. "I can't think of anyone Leah would rather have wearing it." He straightened his shoulders as if to shake off a troublesome weight. "That day at the hospital it suddenly hit me that I'd gotten so used to Leah's wearing the medallion that I never even wondered what it represented." He shrugged. "Maybe she thought it was a pretty necklace and the engraving didn't mean anything special to her, but I'm curious about Demeter."

"We have Edith Hamilton's *Mythology*," Jenny told him, going to the proper shelf section. "It's become a classic in the field." She found the book and pulled it out.

When Marty had signed the card, he put his overcoat on, holding the slim volume between his hands for a moment. "I wonder how many times Leah handled this?" Then, abruptly, he slipped the book into his pocket. "Well, I'd better grab a sandwich somewhere and take it back to work with me. They'll be sending out a St. Bernard if I don't show up shortly." He went to the door. Turning back, he said seriously, "Thanks for talking to me about Leah, Jenny. I wish I'd known more about her illness while she was alive. I might have been a little more understanding if I had. At least I'd have known why she found it so hard to trust other people, why she always seemed to be holding something back."

It was several minutes before Jenny stirred from her dest after Marty had gone. Picking up her pencil, she doodled absentmindedly on a note pad while she thought about his visit. Why, after all these months of never even mentioning her name, had he suddenly wanted to talk about Leah? And why the questions about Gideon Garfield, who was so far in the past that he must have been only a dim memory to Leah in recent years? Marty's insistent words flashed into Jenny's mind: *"Leah may have loved me . . . she loved someone else more."* Was this merely the unfounded accusation of a rejected suitor? He had admitted that Leah accused him of jealousy. Was that the reason for the questions about Garfield? Did the thought still rankle that Leah had once loved another man enough to abandon family and home to run away with him? And what of Marty's suggestion that Leah might have been involved with Luke or another of the men at the Highbridge house? Was that only jealousy talking?

Abruptly, she saw Marty's strong hands, the way they had gripped his knees so tightly the knuckles showed white. Frantic and furious—those had been Marty's own words to describe his reaction to Leah's refusal to marry him. It seemed that the mild-mannered lab technician had a temper after all. Yes, she had always sensed something mysterious behind his usually calm facade. Had he been frantic enough to hurt Leah? Furious enough to seize a rock in a moment of blind rage and bring it down upon the head of the woman he loved?

He would have know where to find her. Leah was always going off into the woods alone. Everyone who knew her well knew that. The day of her death, she might have gone back to the spot where she had found Mary's body. It would have been like Leah to mourn her friend in that way. Had Marty waited for her on that lonely mountain path behind the Tamaracks?

Jenny stared at the note pad in front of her. Without being aware of it, she had written "the Tamaracks" several times. The explanation, of course, was simple. It seemed that all lines of investigation ventually led back there, like ski trails that although they twisted and turned in all directions as they wound down the mountain, always ended at the same base station.

She tore the top sheet from the pad, crumpled it and tossed it into the wastebasket. Then, trying to shake off her dark thoughts, she glanced at her watch and saw it was past the usual time for her lunch. But, as she locked the library door behind her and walked toward the coffee shop, the memory of the pain in Marty's eyes returned.

She thought about his statement that in the days before her death Leah had been troubled. *"I have enough to worry about,"* she had said. *Enough to worry about.* What had been worrying Leah? As Jenny made her way along the snow-covered sidewalk, she told herself that the answer to that question could be the first step to Leah's killer. But there was no way of discovering the answer, since no living person was privy to the knowledge. No one, that is, except possibly the murderer.

As she crossed the street, the blast of a car horn brought her back to alertness. She made a gesture of apology to the driver for dawdling after the light had changed and hurried to reach the opposite curb. At the coffee shop she took a seat at a table with several employees of Main Street shops and joined their conversation, more than willing to think about something besides the murders.

The afternoon brought more patrons into the library than had ventured out during the morning, and between customers Jenny finished clearing the shelves for the paperbacks. She wrote a short announcement concerning the new book exchange, to be run in next week's paper, planning to take it to the newspaper office when she met Gerald there after work.

A few minutes before four, Tom Irving came into the library, looking solemn and a little hesitant. "Your dad asked me to drive you home," he explained. "He's going to be working late."

"That isn't really necessary, Tom," she said, sensing that he was finding this situation a bit embarrassing, after their cool parting on Saturday. "I don't mind walking."

"I'd like to drive you," he insisted, brushing a strand of red hair out of his eyes in a rare gesture of self-consciousness. For a fleeting moment Jenny caught a glimpse of the backward farm boy Tom had been. "Are you still miffed at me?"

"I was never miffed," Jenny said. "I'm sorry if I gave that impression."

His smile was a mixture of relief and doubt. "I wouldn't blame you. I came on pretty strong Saturday night about something that didn't directly concern me."

Jenny dismissed this with a deprecating murmur and went to get her coat, tucking the announcement intended for the newspaper into her pocket. She would give it to her father later that night.

Then she rejoined Tom. As they were leaving the library, he said, "I had your best interests at heart, Jenny."

Jenny felt a flash of impatience, which she managed to hide. "Let's not talk about it anymore, OK?"

He nodded rather glumly, and they got into his car, which was parked at the curb. On the drive up the hill Jenny had the impression that he was on the verge, several times, of saying something more about Saturday. To forestall this, she kept up a spate of bright, inconsequential chatter, which Tom seemed hardly to be hearing.

As they pulled up in front of the Curtiss house, he turned to her with a look of perplexity. "You're different, Jenny. Something's happened to change you since Saturday. You feel uncomfortable with me, don't you?"

"Of course not," she protested, perhaps too vehemently, for it was true that a subtle sense of guardedness had crept into their relationship, muddying the waters of a friendship that had been as placid and undemanding as a mountain pool on a windless summer day. Perhaps Shirley's comments had done it. At any rate, Jenny now felt the necessity of being watchful with Tom lest he give voice to his true feelings for her, which she was beginning to suspect went deeper than friendship. She wanted to avoid any such declaration at all costs, for it could only prove embarrassing for both of them.

"Thanks for the ride," she told him, getting out of the car. Hurrying toward the house, she heard the Pontiac accelerating as he made a U-turn and started down the hill, but she didn't look back.

Inside, she called, "Mother, I'm home." But the only answer was a soft meow as Beast appeared in the entry hall and wrapped himself around her legs. Jenny stroked him absently, then took off her coat and hung it in the closet.

Disentangling the cat from her feet, she walked through the downstairs rooms, stopping to call up the stairs, but Doreen was not there. Peering out the kitchen window, she saw that the garage door was up and Doreen's car was gone. No fire burned in the fireplace, and dinner preparations had not been started, which indicated that her mother must have been out of the house for some time.

She poured a bowl of milk for Beast and looked into the refrigerator to see if she could determine what Doreen had planned for dinner. Three steaks were thawing on the shelf, so Jenny wrapped three potatoes in foil and put them in the oven to bake.

It was growing quite dark outside, and Jenny felt a twinge of concern. It was not like Doreen to be gone from home at this time of day without at least leaving a note to say when she'd be back. She went into the den and tried to read a magazine but soon abandoned the attempt. Finally, giving in to her growing uneasiness, she went to the telephone to dial the newspaper office, but as she picked up the receiver, she heard Doreen's car in the drive. She returned to the kitchen and opened the back door, which led through the utility room and into the garage. She heard the car door slam and the side door into the garage open and close; then Doreen appeared in the utility room, one hand gripping the door facing to steady herself, her face white.

Jenny ran to her side. "Mother! What's wrong?"

Doreen brushed aside Jenny's hand in a petulant gesture. "No, no, I'm all right. Just a little faint. Would you get the groceries from the car while I—lie down?"

Jenny, refusing to be dismissed so easily, took Doreen's arm. "You're shaking, Mother."

"It's cold," Doreen said as Jenny led her through the kitchen. In the den Doreen sank down on the couch. "Let me sit here for a few minutes. I'll be fine."

Jenny got an afghan and spread it across Doreen's legs. Kneeling, she took one of her mother's cold hands in hers and began chafing it, noticing that the fingers had a bluish tinge around the nails. "Where is your medicine?"

Doreen laid her head against the back of the couch. "In my purse—in the car." She closed her eyes for a moment. "And bring the groceries."

"I'll only be a minute," Jenny told her. Half running, she went through the kitchen and the utility room and into the garage, shivering as the cold air engulfed her. Doreen's purse lay on the front seat of the car, and two sacks of groceries at in the back seat. Gathering up both sacks and the purse, Jenny returned to the house. She set the groceries on the breakfast bar and turned to the sink for a glass of water. Then she rummaged in Doreen's purse until she found the bottle of pills Dr. Weaver had prescribed. She poured out one of the pills and carried it, along with a glass of water, to her mother.

Doreen had removed her coat. She was sitting bent over, rubbing her left arm with her right hand, but she stopped as Jenny entered the room. She swallowed the pill Jenny gave her without comment, and Jenny thought her color seemed slightly better.

"I'm going to call the doctor," Jenny said, ignoring Doreen's protests as she picked up the receiver. The line was dead. "Wouldn't you know it," she wailed. "I can't get a dial tone."

Doreen's head was resting on the back of the couch again, and her hand covered her eyes. "I forgot," she murmured. "The phone's been out all day. The wind must have blown down some of the lines. I'm sure they'll have it fixed soon, and, anyway, I don't need the doctor. I'm feeling better already."

Jenny returned to stand beside the couch. "Are you sure?"

Doreen lifted her head and looked up at Jenny. "Stop looking so scared. It's nothing. I went to town for groceries and then decided to drive on out to the hospital and look in on Harold. On the way back the car stalled on that lonely stretch of hillside between the hospital and town. I sat there for several minutes before I got it started again. I must have flooded it." Then, as if the effort of so many words had exhausted her, she let her head drop back against the couch and closed her eyes. After a moment she asked in a thin voice, "Where is Gerald?"

Jenny sat down beside her, wondering if she should go after the doctor in spite of Doreen's protestations. "Tom brought me home. He said Dad had to work late."

Doreen was silent for so long that Jenny thought she had fallen asleep. But then she said, "He wasn't at the newspaper office when I was there earlier."

"When was this?"

"An hour ago, no more. It was after I'd left the grocery store." Was this the reason for Doreen's impulsive decision to visit Harold? Had she expected to find Gerald there, perhaps with Sarah?

"Was Sarah at the hospital?" Jenny ventured.

"No." Doreen's face was void of expression.

"Mother," Jenny said after a moment, "I really think I should go after Dr. Weaver." She put her hand on her mother's forehead.

Doreen's eyes flew open. "No," she said. "If you must do something, find your father." She closed her eyes again and added wistfully, "I need him sometimes, too."

Frowning, Jenny peered more closely into her mother's face, finally assuring herself that Doreen's color was definitely more healthy-looking. She glanced at the hands resting in Doreen's lap. The skin under the fingernails was no longer blue. The pill was taking effect. Convinced that Doreen now needed the assurance of Gerald's presence more than medical aid, she said, "I'll go after Dad if you're sure you'll be all right here alone for a few minutes."

"I told you," said Doreen tiredly, "I'm fine."

"Promise me you won't get up until I come back."

Doreen lifted one hand, then let it fall against the couch cushion, effectively conveying her exasperation with Jenny. "I won't budge."

Quickly Jenny got her coat and took Doreen's car keys from her purse. She would drive her mother's car, since her own hadn't been driven for several days and it might take a few minutes to get it running smoothly.

Taking a final look at Doreen, who seemed to have fallen asleep and was breathing deeply and easily, she went to the garage for the car. She stopped for a moment in the street as she tried to decide whether she should go to the newspaper office first. Gerald hadn't been there an hour ago, and he hadn't been at the hospital. She turned the car north then and drove up the hill, following the road that led through the woods on the Highbridge property.

She had a sudden strong conviction that she would find her father at the Tamaracks.

Nine

Gerald's car sat on the paved drive that made a sweeping circle in front of the Tamaracks. Seeing it, Jenny felt such a burst of anger that she sat in the car for several moments fighting the impulse to rush inside and confront him. She longed to accuse him of neglecting a sick wife to spend time with a woman who had given up all rights to his time and sympathy years ago. Gradually, however, concern for Doreen's welfare won out, and her anger subsided. What good would it do her mother to create a scene in front of Sarah? The essential thing was to send Gerald home as soon as possible.

The pale light from the two yard lamps illuminated the clearing where the house sat. As she got out of the car, the wind running through the trees seemed to whisper dark warnings. And then, as if on cue, Beau Gleason appeared at the corner of the house. She had not heard his approach, and alarm coursed through her. He must have heard her drive up and waited silently until she got out of the car before stepping from behind the house.

He wore sheepskin jacket and the bright-green stocking cap that he had worn on Saturday at the ski slopes. Again she sensed that he was a man of tremendous strength and fearless courage. His weathered face showed his dislike for her, and she took a step toward him, then halted to hide the trembling in her legs. Yet she knew he would not harm her here within shouting distance of the house. On a sudden defiant impulse she blurted, "Why did you shoot at me the last time I came to the Tamaracks?"

Shaggy white brows came together in an angry scowl. "You'd better stay away from here, Jenny Curtiss. I know why you've started to come around again. Luke is back and you're scheming how you can bring about his downfall."

"I only want the person who killed Leah to pay for what he's done," she said.

"It was no one here, and I won't allow you, or anyone, to cause the Highbridegs any more trouble."

"How can you be so sure, when the Tamaracks is so close to where Leah died? Maybe you're afraid of what I might learn and you think keeping me away will protect the murderer." She wanted to say "will protect you," but she didn't dare.

He took a step toward her, and she saw cold hatred in his eyes.

"I don't know who killed Leah," she told him, "but I think you do."

He stood glaring at her, a reined-in violence in his stance. Involuntarily, she shrank back a step, frightened. She saw the dark, brooding presence of the Tamaracks behind him, and she told herself she could cry out and be heard if he attempted to come closer.

"Trying to run me down on the ski slopes won't stop the questions, either," she warned him. "I've already spoken to others about my suspicions."

His body, which had been coiled and dangerous, seemed slowly to unwind. The ungloved hands at his sides relaxed.

"It was talk like that—groundless gossip—that made Luke leave before. Now Mr. Highbridge needs him more than ever. You're acting like your aunt. But I know what you're up to, the same as I knew what she was trying to do."

"I don't know what you're talking about."

"Maybe I can't prove anything, but I can have my say, if it comes to that. Now, will you leave well enough alone?"

Feeling the question unworthy of reply, she persisted, "Why did you hate Leah? What did she ever do to harm you—or anyone?"

He answered in his rough voice. "She was nosy. She got what was coming to her, siding with that little floozy against Luke, knowing all the time he was innocent. Always telling people what they ought to do, horning into other people's business. They had it planned, the two of them, how Mary Steed could trap Luke into marriage."

Jenny did not believe a word of this, but she didn't

know why he was saying these things. "Why didn't you tell that to the police?"

He made a growling sound. "I can take care of things here. I don't need police to help me—not yet, anyway. And I don't have any burning need to see the murderer caught, since I think he did the world a service."

Appalled at his cruel words, Jenny felt suddenly light-headed and a little sick. She must have wavered slightly, for he was beside her, his vicelike hands gripping her arm.

"Look here, Jenny Curtiss," he said, "I got no personal grudge against you—if you'll just keep your nose out of the Highbridges' business. I won't stand for that. I owe them too much."

"How dare you!" she cried, jerking away from him. "How dare you threaten me! How do you think Luke would like it if he knew? He has invited me to come to the Tamaracks himself."

"Luke has always been foolhardy. Sometimes he doesn't know what's good for him."

"Anyway, it happens," she said, "that I did not come here to see Luke. I came to get my father."

"There's a handy little invention you may not have heard about," he said, his gravelly voice heavy with sarcasm. "It's called a telephone."

"Ours is dead," she said, moving around him, and she ran up the wide front steps to stand on the columned porch of the Tamaracks. She pressed the doorbell and turned to look down at Beau Gleason, but he had gone, as stealthily as he had come.

Luke let her in. Seeing the study door standing open to one side of the marble-floored foyer, she realized that he must have been working there when she rang.

"Hello, Luke. Is my father here?"

He stepped back from the doorway. "He's in the den with Mom," he said matter-of-factly. He was wearing a pale-blue sweater with no shirt, and dark, curling hair could be seen in the V neck. Although his tone was casual, she caught a sharp interest in his look. "Is something wrong?"

"He's needed at home," she said curtly, more disturbed by his nearness than she cared to admit.

"Let me take your coat, Jenny." She allowed him to help her out of it, wondering why he no longer seemed angry at her as he had Saturday at the ski lodge or if he were very good at hiding his feelings.

When he had hung the coat in the foyer closet, he turned and led the way down the long, carpeted hall to the den at the back of the house. She followed him, and when they reached the door leading into the den, Luke said, "Gerald, Jenny's here."

Sarah and Gerald were sitting on a dark-blue velvet sofa, which was placed at right angles to the massive stone fireplace. Two empty glasses sat on a low glass-topped table. Sarah and Gerald sat facing each other, their knees not quite touching. They looked up as Luke and Jenny entered, and suddenly Jenny felt as if she had to explain her presence to their satisfaction, as if she, not they, had been caught in a potentially incriminating position.

"I tried to call," she said to her father, "but out phone line's dead. I think you ought to go home, Dad. Mother's asking for you. She had a spell with her heart."

He got up abruptly and came toward Jenny. "Did you get hold of Doc Weaver?"

"Mother didn't want me to. I gave her a pill, and she seemed better when I left."

Gerald stood before her, his face gone pale, as if he had just received a blow to the stomach. There was a sadness about him, perhaps because he had been made aware that his presence here was a disloyalty to his wife.

"I'll go right home," he said, turning back to Sarah with a distracted air. "Thanks for the drink. Let me know if I can help."

"I'll get your coat, Gerald," Luke said, following him out of the den.

When Jenny started to leave, too, Sarah said quickly, "Won't you stay a minute, Jenny dear? Let me get you some coffee or hot buttered rum—something to warm you."

Jenny hesitated, wanting to go, yet knowing that Doreen would probably like a few minutes alone with Gerald. Also, she was recalling her vow to learn what she could about Leah's death, and since the Tamaracks was the place to start, she pushed aside her resentment of Sarah and walked back into the room. "Thank you. I'd like a cup of coffee."

Sarah, looking softly feminine in a rose-colored caftan, smiled at Jenny's acceptance. "I'll go ask Beth to bring your coffee. Sit down; I'll be right back."

Jenny sat on the sofa and glanced about the room, thinking that the furniture had been reupholstered since she was last here. Sarah was back in a moment, and so was Luke. "Jenny's having coffee," Sarah said to Luke. "Would you like some?"

He sat down in the leather armchair facing the sofa, stretching his long legs out to rest his feet on the matching footstool. "No, thanks, Mom. I had two cups in the study while I was going over some of the books."

"You needn't work day *and* night," Sarah admonished him. "Your father doesn't expect that of you."

"It's not a matter of what Dad expects," Luke said in a level tone that seemed to be conveying more than the words themselves, as if he were reminding his mother that he was his own man. "I want to be on top of everything. I can't run things efficiently otherwise."

"Oh, well," Sarah said, sitting down beside Jenny and throwing one hand out in a small gesture of capitulation, "if you feel that way. . . ."

The Highbridges' stout housekeeper, Beth Denton, came in then, carring a tray, which she set on the glass-topped table. Her broad face turned to Jenny as she straightened, and she smiled. "Hello there, Jenny. We haven't seen you around here in a while."

"No," Jenny said. "I've been busy."

"Well, if you want anything else, you just let me know."

"Thanks, Beth," Jenny said as the housekeeper left the den, and she lifted the coffee cup from the tray, cradling its warmth in her cold hands.

"I hope these attacks of Doreen's aren't serious," Sarah said solicitously.

"Mother says they aren't, but, then, she's the sort of person who doesn't give in without a fight—not to anything."

Jenny was aware that Luke was watching her closely,

and then he said, "An admirable quality." She could not tell whether this was meant as a snide remark or merely a casual observation, but she met his gaze steadily to show him that, either way, she was not affected by it.

"If I can be of any help—" Sarah ventured.

Jenny shook her head. "She doesn't have these attacks often, and when she does, she has pills that slow the rapid heartbeat in a matter of a minute or two. I think what she really needs is a little more of Dad's attention."

There was a long silence, and then Sarah grasped Jenny's meaning. She said gently, "Jenny, we certainly had no plan to keep your father away from his family. If Doreen thinks that, she's mistaken. Perhaps I should talk to her about it."

"No," Jenny said, thinking that this conversation was leading her no closer to learning anything about Leah's death.

"Gerald dropped by uexpectedly just a few minutes before you arrived," Luke said. "He wanted to ask how Dad's feeling. He would have been home shortly even if you hadn't come after him. He knew we'd be going back to the hospital soon."

Then why, Jenny wondered, did he tell Tom he had to work late? So he could come here to see Sarah without having to explain to Jenny where he was going? She sipped her coffee and stared out the large bow window. Against the dark background of the surrounding trees, something stirred at the periphery of the scant light coming from the den and kitchen. Was Beau Gleason watching the house, waiting for her to leave? She knew that if he was out there, he could see her sitting on the sofa beside Sarah. She wanted to tell them about Gleason's threatening behavior a few minutes earlier, to say that he was still out there watching her. But then Luke would go out to investigate, and if he found Gleason in his apartment, they would think Jenny was imagining things. Luke might even accuse her again of lying. She set the cup down and looked away from the window, glancing from Luke to Sarah.

"We've been friends of your parents since before you were born, Jenny," Sarah was saying, a slightly injured note still in her voice. "We want you to feel that you are always welcome here—all of you."

"I suppose the reason I haven't come recently," Jenny said, "is that the Tamaracks reminds me of Leah. I feel her presence here. Perhaps if her killer were behind bars, this house wouldn't have such a morbid effect on me." She smiled uncomfortably. "I imagine you think I'm being fanciful."

"Why should you feel Leah's presence here more than at your own house?" A puzzled frown wrinkled Sarah's smooth brow. "Unless you think— Oh, surely you don't think *we* know anything about Leah's death."

Luke's dark eyes seemed to bore into her, but he didn't speak. "She was here so much," Jenny faltered under Sarah's perplexed gaze. "I thought perhaps she might have told you something, Sarah."

"We talked frequently," Sarah admitted, "but if you're suggesting Leah might have given me a clue to the murderer—"

"Marty Brubaker," Jenny went on hastily, "said Leah was worried about something before her death. Leah didn't tell him what it was, but I thought she might have confided in you."

"She *was* worried," Luke put in sharply. "Don't you remember, Mom? That afternoon—it must have been two or three days before her death—she came by to talk to you. I'd come home for some papers Dad left behind, and I was just leaving to return to the office." He lowered his feet to the floor and sat forward in his chair. "She looked worked up about something. It was a little after four. She must have come here straight from the library. I remember that I thought she might be having problems with the library board, something like that. I let her in and called to you that she was here before I left."

"Yes—yes, I remember now," Sarah said reflectively. "We sat right here on this sofa and drank iced tea. I remember that her hair was all awry and she was perspiring, as if she'd been running—and it was so terribly hot that day. She barely tasted her tea, though, before she got up and started to walk about the room. She stood at the bow window a long time, just looking out at the trees. She was jumpy, like a wild creature peering through the bars of his cage, longing for freedom. I even remember thinking that her eyes had a brilliant look, too brilliant somehow."

Yes, Jenny thought. Yes, that was Leah, flitting about a room only half-aware of what was going on around her, as if she were waiting for the right moment to escape the confines of walls.

"What did she say?" Jenny prodded.

Sarah laced her slender fingers together and bent forward slightly to cup her knees. "As I recall, nothing significant. Oh, she rambled briefly about whether one person had a right to make a decision that affected the lives of other people, whether one could decide what is best for another, something like that, as if she might have been reading one of those depressing German philosophers at the library that afternoon. You know how she got caught up in her books." Sarah was silent for so long that Jenny thought she might not go on. She sat still, wanting to probe, to ask questions, but she waited silently. Sarah's tone softened when she finally continued, as if she felt deep regret over the loss of a beloved friend.

"Leah never seemed able to find contentment. It only made her unhappy, all that reading and pondering life's unanswerable questions. When I asked her that day what was troubling her, she went off on another tangent, something about dreams coming true too late to do anybody any good. Then she said she thought she'd go up and chat with Mary for a bit. I remember thinking as she was leaving that she had come here to tell me something but, for some reason, had decided against it."

"Why didn't you tell all of this to the sheriff after the murders?" Jenny asked

. Her question seemed to fluster Sarah, who began nervously stroking the silk kaftan over her knees.

"I think I can answer that," said Luke, his tone suddenly cold. "After Leah was killed and Beth told the police what Mary has said about me, you thought Mary must have told Leah, too, and that's what Leah had come here to tell you. Isn't that right, Mom?"

"I—I don't know. Oh, Luke, I knew it was a lie, anyway, although I can't fathom what that child hoped to gain by it. I didn't see any point in telling the sheriff what I *thought* Leah might have had on her mind."

"Aren't the lives of two people more important than —than anyone's reputation?" Jenny asked.

"It wouldn't have brought them back," Sarah said. "Once Humpty Dumpty had fallen, there was no way to put him together again."

Agitated, Jenny got to her feet. "And I suppose you feel the same way about finding the killer. Catching him won't bring Leah and Mary back—so why bother? I think you're heartless!" Jenny's voice broke on the words.

Sarah left the sofa and went to stand in front of the blazing fire, her back to the room. "I've told you," she said, and her voice had turned brittle, "that Mary Steed lied about Luke, but she might have convinced Leah that her ridiculous accusations were true. In fact, I think now that she did. The last time I saw Leah, she said there was something that had to be settled about Mary and that she was counting on our help. But Leah was so gullible." She turned to look at Jenny, her tall figure held regally erect. "Telling the sheriff about Leah's manner that day would have accomplished nothing."

"And what," said Jenny, hurt, "did you accomplish by keeping quiet?"

"I was trying to protect my son against the slander of a scheming woman. You will learn one day, Jenny, that a mother's first loyalty is to her children."

Jenny clasped her hands behind her to hide their trembling. She shot Luke a defiant look. "I hope not when they are in the wrong," she said. "If you will excuse me, please, Sarah, I must go and check on Mother."

Sarah inclined her head, but she didn't speak. Luke followed Jenny into the foyer. He got her coat and helped her into it, his lips pressed together in a grim line. Then, his fingers still clasped around her shoulder, he looked into her face and said, "I have to talk to you."

"But we have been talking," she said stiffly.

"Alone, when we aren't likely to be interrupted."

As she looked into his dark eyes, something twisted

in her that she wanted to ignore. "So that you can call me a liar again?"

He glared at her, anger vying with some other emotion that Jenny could not identify. "I've regretted that," he said finally. "I apologize."

She stepped back out of his grasp. "I accept your apology. Now what else could we possibly have to talk about?" As always when she was near him, she sensed danger. To her life or to her heart? She didn't know, but she was aware once more of the need to protect herself against this man who aroused such strongly conflicting emotions in her. She moved toward the door.

Ignoring the barriers she was throwing up, he said, "What about Saturday? We could go skiing—and we could talk."

She hesitated, her hand on the doorknob. Why was he being so insistent? What did he hope to gain by talking? Would he try to charm her into believing in his innocence because her suspicions were a threat to him? Or would he try to frighten her?"

She knew suddenly that her impulsive vow to unmask Leah's killer was getting her into something that was far too deep for her. Yet she also knew that she could not refuse his request. How could she hope to learn what he knew if she didn't spend time with him? She drew a deep breath and opened the door. Turning to look over her shoulder, she said, "Saturday will be fine."

His dark eyes seemed to be trying to read what she was thinking. "Is three o'clock all right?"

"Yes." She remembered Beau Gleason then. "Would—would you mind," she faltered, "watching at the door until I've driven away?"

If he thought this a strange request, he didn't show it. "Of course," was all he said.

Back at the Curtiss house, Jenny found her father sitting alone in the den, staring into the flames in the fireplace. "How's Mother?" she asked.

"She's all right, I think." Gerald got out of the chair, moved a few steps away from the fireplace and stood with his back to the flames. "I gave her a sedative and put her to bed. I sat with her until she fell asleep."

"There are baked potatoes in the oven," Jenny said,

"and steaks thawed in the refrigerator. I need to put the groceries away first, but that will take only a few minutes, and then I'll fix your dinner. Did Mother eat anything?"

"A bowl of soup. It was all she wanted."

Jenny hurried to the kitchen and laid two steaks in the broiler before putting away the groceries that Doreen had bought earlier. She sat at the breakfast bar, waiting for the steaks to be done, and thought about what had transpired at the Tamaracks. It was not a comfortable feeling, knowing people there did not wish her well. Beau Gleason hated her, and Sarah had seemed to be on the defensive when questioned about Leah. As for Luke, Jenny had not been able to read his reactions. But she felt that he did not trust her completely, and the feeling was certainly mutual. Of all the people at the Tamaracks, only Beth Denton seemed to be open with her, treating her as she always had, with affection. She wondered fleetingly what Luke's real reason was for taking her skiing Saturday. And how would he explain it to Susan Nelson, whom, according to Susan's younger sister, he planned to marry in June? Well, Jenny thought bitterly, Luke Highbridge was probably very good at getting around women. No doubt he would come up with a reasonable explanation for Susan.

When the steaks were done, she arranged plates on two TV trays and carried them, one by one, into the den. Gerald was sitting in the armchair, and when she placed his tray in front of him, he thanked her absentmindedly and began to eat in silence. She sat on the sofa and tried to eat, but she didn't feel hungry. After several minutes had passed and neither of them had made any attempt at conversation, Jenny looked up to find Gerald studying her gravely.

"You're angry with me, aren't you," he said, "for being with Sarah when your mother had her attack?"

Jenny did not know how to answer that. She had been angry, but now she only felt disappointed. Finally she said, "Mother needed you. I wish you could have seen and heard her. You'd understand why I was upset."

"Did it ever occur to you," he said heavily, "that Doreen is capable of using her illness to get her way?"

She stared at him. "If you had been here, you wouldn't

say a thing like that." She felt her anger stirring again. "Why are you treating Mother like this? Is Sarah still so important to you?"

He pushed his half-eaten dinner aside and restlessly paced across the room and back. "Jenny, you're old enough, surely, to realize that parents are human like everybody else."

"Is that supposed to excuse disloyalty?"

He stopped, looking down at her for a long moment. She wondered what thoughts passed through his mind in the silence. Then he said, "I have never been intentionally disloyal to your mother. Oh, I'm not claiming to have been a perfect husband all these years. I haven't always been as attentive or as considerate as I might have been. And sometimes our good intentions fail us in a moment of weakness. But whatever"—he hesitated, as if searching for the proper word—"whatever problems your mother has are of her own making. One person cannot own another. Nor can one be responsible for another's happiness. No, we all make our own happiness—or misery."

What did he mean, Doreen's problems were of her own making? Was he insinuating that the attack was staged? Jenny did not know how to respond. This was a Gerald she had never seen before. This unfeeling man who accused her mother of using her illness to manipulate him was not the father she had always known.

As if he were reading her thoughts, he said, "I don't expect you to understand." Wearily, he rubbed both hands across his face, then let them fall to his sides. "I'm tired, Jenny. I think I'll go to bed now. Good night." He turned away from her, walking from the room with that peculiar shambling gait of exhaustion.

"Good night, Dad," she murmured.

After a moment she cleared away the dishes. Beast, having caught the scent of the steaks, came streaking into the kitchen as she was arranging the dishes in the dishwasher. She gave him what was left of the meat and ran fresh water into his drinking bowl. Then, leaving him to his feast, she climbed the stairs to her bedroom.

After a long bath, she got into bed. Beast had not come

upstairs again, and there was no sound from her parents' bedroom below. The silence was intense. She found herself straining to listen. For what, she didn't know. She stared into the darkness a long time before she finally fell asleep.

Ten

The experience at the Tamaracks on Monday evening colored the rest of Jenny's week. Gradually, however, her first fear and shock over Beau Gleason's threats faded and she bolstered her courage by deciding to tell Luke everything that Gleason had said and done. And this time she would make him believe her. As additional protection, she even thought about writing a description of the caretaker's suspicious behavior and putting it away in a safe place, in case she should meet with an accident; but that seemed so melodramatic that she had to laugh at herself. No, she would simply ask Luke to see that Gleason stayed away from her, and if that didn't work, she would speak to Sarah about it.

As the days passed, she thought increasingly of the obligation to Leah that she had placed upon herself. More than ever she wanted to be able to say to her aunt's memory, *Your murderer will be punished.* And the conviction began to grow in her that the only way to solve the mystery was to see Luke whenever she could, to gain his confidence while somehow hiding her own distrust of him. She knew that it could be a dangerous game, but she was determined to play it.

When she had time on her hands at the library, she went over in her mind, again and again, Leah's enigmatic comments to Sarah Highbridge a few days before she was murdered. Unlike Sarah, Jenny did not believe Leah's mood had been created by reading philosophical works. Rather, from what Sarah had said, Leah had been trying to make a difficult decision, one that affected the lives of other people, but there was no inkling as to what the decision might have been. As far as Jenny knew, Leah's life had been going along as usual until she was killed—except, of course, for the testimony of several people that Leah was worried about something—probably the decision she was trying to make. She could not have been agonizing over whether to expose Mary Steed's murderer,

135

since both Marty and Luke had said that Leah seemed troubled two or three days before her death, and Mary was killed only twenty-four hours before Leah. Could she have known something incriminating about the killer before the murders took place, something she had almost confided to Sarah Highbridge? She had left Sarah to go upstairs to Mary's room. Had she decided to confide in Mary rather than Sarah? Was that confidence the cause of both Mary's and Leah's death?

And what had Leah meant when she talked about dreams coming true too late to do anybody any good? What had Leah dreamed of? Once, when she ran away with Gideon Garfield, she must have had a head full of dreams; but afterward, during the years when Jenny was growing up, Leah had seemed content enough to live her rather pedestrian existence—as content as Leah was capable of being, at any rate. It was true, as Doreen had said, that Leah often daydreamed, but no one had ever taken that seriously.

On Thursday evening she had dinner with Tom at the Copper Kettle. Although she tried very hard to get their relationship back on its former easygoing plane, a barrier stood between them. When Tom suggested that he take her skiing on Saturday and help her conquer Treacherous Hill, she had to admit that she was seeing Luke. This put an even heavier damper on things, and Tom had been uncommonly morose the rest of the evening, finally leaving her at her front door with a barely audible "Good night."

It was with some misgivings that she left the house with Luke on Saturday afternoon. The fact that Doreen obviously did not want her to go didn't help prop up her already flagging courage, either. "You would be better off," Doreen had said, "staying as far away from the Highbridges as possible."

Nor did Doreen make any effort to be hospitable to Luke when he arrived. Wearing forest-green ski pants and a matching parka open over a tan turtleneck sweater, Luke took Jenny's skis and ski boots from her hands and inquired politely about Doreen's health. To this Doreen replied curtly, "I'm fine, thank you."

Luke was driving a Bronco equipped with four-wheel drive for climbing snowy mountain roads. When he had tossed Jenny's boots, skis, and poles into the back, he climbed into the driver's seat beside her and said, "I don't think your mother was too thrilled to see me."

When Jenny didn't comment, he glanced at her questioningly, but then seemed content to let the matter drop. "I need to go by the office for a few minutes, if you don't mind."

"Fine," Jenny said.

They followed the steep lane downhill to the edge of the business district, then turned east on Mill Street.

"How is your father?" Jenny asked.

"Progressing. In fact, he's beginning to amaze his doctor and his therapist. He's made good progress with his therapy already. He's much stronger and is determined to come home for Christmas."

"He told me that," Jenny said, "when I visited him."

Luke glanced at her soberly, perhaps wondering why she had not been to visit Harold again. She looked out the side window, not meeting his eyes, and a silence fell between them.

The various buildings of the Highbridge Corporation sprawled across two hundred acres northeast of town, at the end of Mill Street, next to the river. The original sawmill had been built in 1885 to supply ties for the Northern Pacific Railroad and had already changed hands several times when Harold Highbridge's grandfather bought it in 1910.

Behind the tall chain-link fence along the western edge of the property, a long pipe was belching out a continual stream of sawdust, creating a small mountain. As they turned into the front entrance, Jenny said, "I haven't been out here for three years, at least. We used to take a tour almost every year when I was in school."

Braking in front of the partially glass-enclosed cubicle where a guard sat, Luke honked the horn. The guard saw who it was, waved and pushed the button that raised the gate arm, enabling them to drive through into the yard.

"We've made some changes since you were here," Luke said. "The plant is now eighty-five percent energy efficient. Those piles of sawdust you saw out in the yard, along with other waste products, fuel the boiler system that produces steam to run the plant."

They were weaving in and out between huge buildings, heading for the modern buff brick structure that housed the offices of the corporation. "And the old green chain," Luke went on, his voice animated, "has been replaced by an automatic sorter."

"I remember hearing about that," Jenny remarked. "Didn't it cause some friction with the union?"

Luke nodded as he turned into the paved parking area next to the office building. "That was only a tempest in a teapot. Eventually, as openings occurred, we rehired all the men who lost their jobs to the machine. There has been opposition to other improvements, too—people seem naturally to resist change—but fortunately the employees haven't as yet been unhappy enough to strike. Most of them feel the changes have worked out for everybody's benefit. The sawmill is turning out three hundred and eighty thousand board feet of lumber a day now."

He stopped the car and sat gazing toward the riverbank, where huge mechanical arms picked up logs from the river and deposited them on a conveyor belt.

Jenny thought, *He is still tied to all of this emotionally. His father was right; lumbering is in Luke's blood.* "You're happy to be back and running things, aren't you?" she asked.

He laughed. "It shows, doesn't it? To tell you the truth, selling insurance never seemed like real work. It's all on paper, which struck me as being somehow artificial. There's nothing you can sink your teeth into. Here I can be a part of something tangible, something important. There's a sense of accomplishment about all this."

"Will you stay, then?"

Unexpectedly, he turned to study her intently. "I never wanted to leave, but my pride was hurt." In the background, the mechanical arms creaked, and he turned to look at them again. "I've learned that pride is a luxury I can't afford. I'm needed here, and this is where I want to be. I'm selling my interest in the San Francisco agency. I won't leave here again."

"No matter . . ." She floundered over the words.

"No matter what happens," he said softly. His expression was inscrutable, and she could not tell whether the words were a vow or a warning.

After a moment he said, "I only need to check on a couple of things. It shouldn't take more than a few minutes. Do you want to come inside with me?"

She shook her head. "I'll wait here."

"Your ski clothes will probably keep you warm enough, but run the heater if you start feeling chilled." He got out of the car, leaving the key in the ignition.

While he was gone, she followed the progress of the logs as they were lifted by machinery and carried by the constantly moving conveyor to be jostled into position under giant saw blades that sliced them into manageable lengths. Then the logs were carried on another conveyor into the sawmill, where, Jenny knew from the tours she had taken, they were sent first to the edger and cut to the desired width, then on to the trimmer, where they would be cut to selected lengths. From there, they would travel through the automatic sorter and be conveyed to the proper bins.

True to his word, Luke was back after only a few minutes. "We're having some trouble with a bark disease out at the nursery," he explained as he started the car. They left the parking area and retraced their route through the yard. The gatekeeper was watching for them this time and had the gate arm up before they reached it. Luke waved his thanks as they passed through and out the main entrance.

"About three hundred of our four-year-old seedlings have died," he went on as they turned into Mill Street again, "but I think we've diagnosed the disease now, and there is a cure. I've been talking to a man with the forest service. They had an outbreak of the disease on federal forest land a couple of years back. Fortunately, we caught our problem before too much damage was done."

"Are you sure you wouldn't like to change your mind about skiing?" Jenny asked, feeling that perhaps he would prefer going out to the nursery now.

"Not at all." He looked at her sharply. "And we're still going to have our talk."

"I wish you would explain that to me. I don't know yet what you want to talk to me about."

"I thought you might like to know that I confronted Beau with your accusations."

"I'm sure he denied everything," she commented wryly.

They were on the highway now, headed toward the snow-covered mountain and the ski lodge. "No," he said, "but he did seem surprised at the interpretation you had put on his actions."

"Surprised!" She stumbled over the word. "I'll bet! I suppose I imagined that rifle shot and that shove at the hospital was only a playful little pat!"

"He remembers shooting the rifle one night not long ago," Luke went on calmly. "He heard something and went outside to investigate. He saw someone at the front of the house and, thinking that whoever it was intended to take advantage of my parents' absence from the Tamaracks to break in, he fired into the air. He didn't recognize you, Jenny."

"So he says," retorted Jenny hotly.

"As for the incident at the hospital," Luke persisted, "Beau admitted that he might have gotten a little carried away. He saw that Dad was becoming agitated, and he was trying to shield him from further excitement. He says he might have given you a push, but he doesn't remember it. He was too worried about Dad. What did you say to upset him—Dad, I mean."

"Nothing. He seemed to be trying to tell *me* something." But she didn't intend to let Luke change the subject so easily. "What about Gleason's trying to run me down on the slopes last Saturday?"

They were climbing up the mountain toward the lodge, and his gaze left the road for a moment to rest on her thoughtfully. "He knows nothing about that. Beau says the only time he saw you on the slopes last Saturday was as you were getting off the chair lift at the top of Easy Rider. If you were on Treacherous at any time, he didn't see you."

She opened her mouth to deny this, but then she bit back the words. She was sure Luke would not believe her. Gleason's explanations sounded reasonable, and she realized that, to an objective observer, his version might seem the true one. Nevertheless, she couldn't keep from saying a little sarcastically, "I can see why you might prefer to accept what he says at face value."

"Beau has never given me any reason to doubt his word," he told her abruptly.

"Maybe not," she said. "But I don't suppose he told you, either, that he threatened me again Monday night at the Tamaracks."

Luke's vaguely tolerant expression vanished, and the deep brown of his eyes darkened as he looked at her. "I watched you leave, Jenny, and Beau didn't come near you."

"It was when I arrived, before I rang the bell."

Understanding seemed to dawn on his face. "So that's why you asked me to watch until you had driven away. Exactly what did he say that you interpreted as a threat?"

"He told me to stay away from the Tamaracks, and his tone was definitely threatening."

"You must have misunderstood him."

"No, Luke," she said firmly. "I understood him perfectly. Can't you see that Beau Gleason is a dangerous man?"

They had reached the lodge, and Luke maneuvered the Bronco into a vacant parking space, switched off the motor and turned to face her. "Beau does have a hot temper, and sometimes he acts without thinking. He's always been fiercely loyal to my father. After he was injured, Dad gave him a job, when no one else would. Evidently Beau thinks he is protecting us. I'll certainly speak to him about Monday night, though. That was a bit beyond the call of duty." His thick brows came together. "Why are you looking at me like that?"

"I was wondering," she said slowly, "why Beau Gleason thinks you need to be protected."

His dark eyes clouded, and she saw the ice in them. "This isn't the first time you have insinuated that everyone at the Tamaracks is hiding something, as if one of us knows who was responsible for the deaths of Leah and Mary Steed." His voice was level, but there was an edge of steel in it.

"I'm not alone in my belief."

Luke's ungloved hands gripped the steering wheel. "What is that supposed to mean?"

"Marty Brubaker feels the same way. And don't look at me as if you think I put the idea into his head. He mentioned it to me first."

He was frowning. "Brubaker? The man Leah was seeing? The technician at the hospital?" He didn't wait for an answer. "Maybe I should have a talk with him. He might be more disposed to listen to reason than you are."

Luke looked away from her, his hands releasing their grip on the wheel. "I don't remember your being so unfair in the past, Jenny. I don't understand you at all."

"Unfair!" She gasped out the word. "Cold-blooded murder has been committed, and you talk about being fair!"

He opened the car door with a jerk and, stepping out, began to drag their skis from the back of the Bronco. "It's impossible to talk to you about this subject, so perhaps we should drop it. For whatever it's worth, however, you are dead wrong about Beau."

Seeing how prejudiced he was in Gleason's favor, Jenny was no longer sure she could continue on the course she had set for herself. Certainly she had not played her part well so far. Instead of gaining Luke's trust, she had managed to antagonize him. And how could she keep up the charade when there were moments during which she suspected Luke himself of having knowledge of the killings? For a few moments she sat unmoving, while he leaned against the hood of the car and tugged on his ski boots. Finally he straightened and peered through the windshield at her.

"Well, did we come out here to ski or not?"

Brushing aside her misgivings, Jenny got out of the car and reached for her own ski boots.

Together they clomped toward the chair lift. "What slope do you want to try first?" he asked.

"We'd better separate," she told him. "You're an expert skier, and I don't want to hold you back. I'll keep to the easier slopes."

"Suit yourself," he said, shrugging. "I'll meet you at the lodge when it gets too dark to ski. Five-thirty or so."

Jenny got off the lift at Easy Rider and trudged toward the top of the slope. Today several other skiers were waiting their turn to push off. She stood in line and pulled up her parka hood, tying it beneath her chin. On either side of the trail, spruce trees rose like Gothic spires. She inhaled the fresh mountain air and felt her face tingling with the cold. Then it was her turn, and she pushed off, feeling a sudden exhilaration as her skis clattered over the hard-packed snow. The spruces slipped past on either side. The wind numbed her face as she drove into it, but the sun overhead reflected the snowbank at her like millions of diamond chips. The cares she had brought with her to the mountain seemed to fly away behind her with the wind. She felt wonderfully free.

The afternoon passed quickly, and very soon, it seemed, the sun slipped behind the mountain and dusk crept across Easy Rider. Jenny made her last descent to find Luke waiting for her at the foot of the trail.

He smiled, his earlier impatience gone. "You're good enough for more difficult slopes."

She smiled in return. "Maybe I'll be braver next time."

They went back to the car and exchanged their ski boots for walking boots, then went into the lodge together. A number of skiers had already gathered around the blazing fire in the center of the room. Luke cleared a path for her through the groups of people and, at the bar, ordered mulled wine for both of them. Jenny was relieved to see that Beau Gleason was not tending bar today. Carrying their drinks, they found two unoccupied chairs near one of the huge triangular panes of glass. Outside it had grown dark, and the lodge, with its warm lights, the blazing log fire, and the murmur of voices in the background, seemed to Jenny, if only fleetingly, to offer contentment and safety. Soft music from the stereo added to the pleasant atmosphere.

As she sat down, Leah's medallion swung free of the open neck of the cotton shirt. She idly fingered the smooth circle and sipped the hot, spicy wine.

Then she noticed that Luke was looking at the medallion curiously, "Isn't that Leah's?" He bent toward her and took the medallion in his hand, turning it over to examine it closely on both sides.

"Yes," she answered, wondering uneasily why he was so interested. "It's Demeter, the Greek goddess. Leah felt a particular empathy with her."

He let the medallion fall from his hand and sat back in his chair. "Yes, I can see why she would. Demeter was a melancholy goddess—moody, like Leah. Do you know the story?"

"Only vaguely," Jenny said, settling back in her chair. "Would you tell me?"

He nodded and began. "Demeter was grieved over the loss of her daughter, Persephone. In her unhappiness, she withheld her gifts from the earth—all growing things. That was the first winter, I suppose."

Bits of the story were coming back to Jenny now, as Leah had related it to her long ago. "Persephone was kidnapped, wasn't she?"

He sipped his wine and said expansively, "By Hades, the lord of the underworld. Persephone was enticed by the bloom of the narcissus and strayed too far from her friends. Before she knew what was happening, Hades burst through a chasm in the earth in his chariot and carried her down to the underworld. Persephone cried out and Demeter heard her, but, search as she might, she couldn't find her daughter. Finally the Sun told her what had happened to Persephone. Her grief made the land so barren that men began to die of starvation."

"I seem to remember that Zeus intervened," Jenny put in, watching the sharply cut lines of his face soften, as if enjoyed telling the story.

His eyes on her were warm. "Of course, Zeus saw that something must be done to save mankind. He sent a messenger to Hades, telling him to send his bride back to Demeter. Hades knew he had to obey the word of Zeus, but he had a trick or two up his sleeve. Before he would let Persephone go, he made her eat a pomegranate seed, knowing that if she did so, she would have to return to him. When Demeter leaned that Persephone had eaten the pomegranate seed, her brief joy turned to sorrow again. But Zeus decreed that Persephone would return to the underworld only four months out of every year, and Demeter would have her daughter during the remaining eight months. So when Persephone is with Hades, we have winter, and when she returns to her mother, spring comes."

"I like that," Jenny said when he was done. "Man's imagination can come up with such lovely stories when he isn't bound by facts. It seems a shame that modern man has put all his faith in cold science."

Luke's eyebrows quirked in amusement. "Surely you wouldn't want to go back to the age of superstition, before the Industrial Revolution provided all our modern conveniences."

Jenny laughed. "Oh, no—but I do think we lost a lot of beauty when we lost the mystery."

He sobered, gazing at her with eyes that reflected the glow of the wood fire. "You are a complex girl, Jenny Curtiss. How does it happen that we never got to know each other before this?"

She said lightly, "You were far too occupied to notice a scrawny neighbor kid with braces on her teeth."

"And skinned knees," he said, grinning, "from falling off her bicycle. You see, I noticed more than you thought." His smile faded. "And somehow, while I was gone, you became a woman. What kind of woman, Jenny? What do you want from life?"

She felt her cheeks growing warm and was grateful for the soft light in their corner of the room. "An ordinary woman, I'm sure. I want what most women want—a home, a family, a job I enjoy doing."

"And what of the man who is to provide the home and family?" he asked softly. "Will it be Tom Irving?"

She shook her head, wondering what right he had to ask her these questions when he had Susan Nelson waiting in the wings. "Tom is a good friend, nothing more."

Luke stood and reached for her glass. "I'll get us some more wine." His fingers closed over hers and lingered there for a moment while he looked down at her with a puzzled expression, as if he wanted their touching to continue and was, at the same time, perplexed by the desire. Then he lifted the glass from her hand, and there was a gentleness about him that she had never seen before.

As he walked away from her, she had to remind herself that Luke Highbridge might have an ulterior motive for trying to charm her. If he had some dark secret to hide, it would be to his advantage to win her trust. The thought sent a chill through her, and she determined not to allow herself to fall under the spell of this man who could turn gentle or harsh with such confusing speed.

"Hello again."

Jenny looked up to see Tammy Nelson standing before her. "Hi, Tammy. Did you ski well today?"

The girl raised her shoulders in an elaborate shrug. "So-so. What about you? Did you stay on the sissy slopes again?"

Jenny laughed. "I must confess I did."

Tammy looked solemn. "You shouldn't be afraid of falling, you know. Everyone falls."

"Even you?" Jenny asked teasingly.

"Oh, yes! You wouldn't believe the falls I've taken. But I always get up and try again. My ski instructor says it's a drive I have—all ski champions have it. You must not have it, or you wouldn't be happy until you conquered Treacherous."

"I expect you're right," Jenny agreed.

In an abrupt change of subject, Tammy asked, "Are you here with Luke?"

"Yes. You don't mind, do you?"

Tammy grinned. "Not me, but Susan will." With that she turned and walked away, calling to someone across the room.

When Luke returned with the wine, he asked, "What were you and Tammy talking about?"

"The difference between championship material and sissies like me."

Luke laughed. "That kid has a smart mouth."

"I don't think she means things to sound the way they do. She's irrepressibly self-confident, though, isn't she?" Then Jenny couldn't resist saying, "She told me that Susan wouldn't like my being here with you."

His face took on a guarded look. "Susan doesn't own me."

No, Jenny thought, no woman could ever do that, not even a wife. To be married to Luke Highbridge might be infuriating at times, but it would never be dull.

"I'm going to the hospital to see Dad when we get back

to town," Luke said suddenly. "Would you like to come along?"

"No," said Jenny, fumbling for the right words. "I think I'll wait until Harold is back at the Tamaracks, until he's stronger. I wouldn't want to upset him again."

He frowned at that but did not try to persuade her. A few minutes later, after finishing their wine, they left, driving slowly down the mountain through the darkness.

At her door, she said, "Give my regards to your faher."

He nodded. "Good night, Jenny." He turned away from her and bounded down the porch steps. Watching him drive away, Jenny wondered how she could keep on in her efforts to unmask Leah's killer. It would mean seeing more of Luke, and that prospect troubled her deeply. She did not understand his moods, nor her own unfamiliar reactions to him. And yet she had no choice. She would keep on for Leah's sake. As for her own foolishness, she would conquer that. She turned and went into the house.

Eleven

On Monday morning Jenny could hardly open the library door for the pile of books on the floor inside, books that had been returned over the weekend. Finally she managed to shove the door open wide enough to squeze through. As soon as she had hung her coat in the back room, she carried all the returned books to her desk, where she stacked them until she could get around to shelving them. Then she scooped up from the floor a stack of mail that included a parcel of books she had ordered through the interlibrary system.

She tore into the parcel first, for she would have to telephone the people whose books had arrived. There were five books in all. Four thick volumes had been ordered by one of the high-school history teachers. The fifth book was *Basic Biology,* ordered by Hattie Sterling.

Curious, Jenny got the damaged copy of the biology book from her desk drawer and checked the missing page numbers. Then she turned to those pages in the book sent by interlibrary loan. Beginning at Page 203, she scanned all the pages through 212. The entire section dealt with inheritable characteristics—eye color, sex-related traits such as baldness, hair color and type, blood type, skin pigmentation, and race-related traits such as sickle cell anemia.

Nonplussed, Jenny flipped through the section a second time. She wondered how Hattie Sterling would find a mystery in these pages, but if she knew the elder Sterling sister, Hattie would try.

She called the high school first and left a message for the history teacher. Then, smiling, she dialed Hattie's number. Upon hearing that the book had arrived, Hattie was delighted.

"My goodness gracious, Jenny, I'll be down as soon as I can get there. You haven't called James, have you?"

"No," Jenny said, "but don't you think I should? After

148

all, he was the last person to check out the book. He should have the opportunity to help clear his name."

"Well," Hattie agreed reluctantly, "I suppose you're right. Go ahead and call him."

James Elledge seemed amused at the news that the biology book had arrived. "I'll be down there in a minute," he told Jenny. "I wouldn't miss Hattie's detective work for anything."

Jenny busied herself replacing the cards in the pockets of the books that had been returned, until Hattie Sterling arrived with James Elledge at her heels.

Hattie approached Jenny's desk, one arm outstretched. "Let me see that book." Her black eyes were aglow, and as Jenny handed her the book, she felt a pang of regret that Hattie's little mystery was about to dissolve.

Hattie shrugged out of her coat, holding the book in first one hand and then the other, as if she were loath to put it down for even a moment. Then she squared her narrow shoulders in the worn blue wool dress and took a small note pad and ball-point pen from her purse.

James Elledge watched her, the skin all around his blue eyes crinkling with amusement.

Hattie pulled a chair up to Jenny's desk and sat down, opening the book to page 202. Elledge moved closer, peering over her shoulder. They were silent for several moments as Hattie turned the pages.

"Well, I must say," Hattie declared at last, looking up from the book, "this is a real puzzle." She chewed reflectively on the end of her pen. "Why would anyone want to tear those particular pages out of the book?" She was silent for several moments then, seemingly deep in thought. Elledge shuffled his rubber boots against the floor and winked at Jenny over Hattie's white head.

After a while Hattie returned her attention to the book. "This is all very interesting, I'm sure, but why did our suspect want to hide this information?"

Elledge gave a loud guffaw. "Why don't you give up, Hattie?" There's nothing in those pages that isn't common knowedge. Everybody knows about inherited characteristics."

Hattie frowned at him. "*I* didn't know all of this," she snapped.

"Well, everybody but you, then," Elledge said, straight-faced.

"You can be so disgustingly smug, James," Hattie retorted. "I'm sure there must be lots of people who are fuzzy about how we inherit certain traits. Reading dry old science books isn't everybody's idea of fun, you know." Then, evidently deciding to ignore Elledge's skepticism, she flipped open the note pad that she had taken from her purse. "Now, here's what we know already, Jenny." She touched the end of her pen to the page in front of her. "First, that book was checked out by James on November 2. At that time none of its pages were missing."

"You're durn tootin'," Elledge put in.

Hattie scowled at him briefly, then returned to her notes. "Second, we can assume the book left James's possession while he was in the hospital sometime between 2:06 on the afternoon of November 3 and 10:48 on the morning of November 9."

Elledge's bushy white eyebrows bristled. "How'd you find that out?"

"Elementary, my dear James," said Hattie, not bothering to look at him. "I very cleverly drew the facts I needed from a nurse's aide who works at the hospital. The poor dear didn't even realize she was giving away privileged information, I dare say."

"Who was it?" Elledge thundered. "I'll report her to the hospital administrator! She can't go around telling every nosy old biddy who asks what's on *my* chart."

Hattie eyed him coldly; that look undoubtedly had quelled many a troublesome young student in Hattie's teaching days. "Calm down, James. Your face is getting red. I have no intention of revealing the girl's identity." She set her chin stubbornly. "Wild horses couldn't drag it out of me."

"I'm sure the girl doesn't make a habit of talking about patients," said Jenny, trying to smooth the situation. "Hattie was probably just too shrewd for her."

Hattie beamed. "Exactly right. Now, if James will settle down, we will get on with my list of clues. It seems certain the book was taken by a hospital employee, another patient, or a visitor to the hospital."

"I suppose," grumbled Elledge, "you finagled a list of the patients from that nincompoop, too."

Hattie looked regretful. "No, I couldn't manage that. But then I remembered that the newspaper runs the names of those who are admitted or discharged from the hospital every week. I checked through my old newspapers and came up with a list of sixty-four names. Of course, the other patient in the room with you, James, had the best chance to take the book." She looked at him expectantly.

"Sorry to bust your bubble, Hattie," Elledge said, "but I had a private room."

Hattie sighed. "Add to the sixty-four the one hundred and three full- and part-time employees of the hospital and we have one hundred and sixty-seven suspects, not to mention the visitors, whose names we would have to guess at."

"Ha!" Elledge snorted. "Like looking for a needle in a haystack. Besides, Hattie, why would a hospital employee take that book? The hospital owns books covering the same subjects, and much more thoroughly. I've seen them in the lab."

"Oh, my goodness," Hattie said, "I hadn't thought of that." Then she brightened. "Well, that cuts our list of suspects down considerably."

"Seems to me, Hattie," said Elledge, clearing his throat, "you are barking up the wrong tree here. It so happens that I am a very light sleeper. Even when I was the sickest, I refused to take sleeping pills or any other kind of dope. Don't believe in it. Nobody could have come into my room, gotten into my closet and rummaged around in my suitcase without my hearing them. I think we can say without a doubt that book was not taken from my room while I was a patient. Here's what I think happened: The nurse who packed my suitcase for me when I was discharged shuffled the books around to make room and accidentally left one out. The book was returned to the library, and it was taken from here."

"I don't see how that could have happened," Jenny

put in. "I still had the card in my file, which means I had not yet shelved the book."

Elledge's glance swept over the stack of books on Jenny's desk. "Are these the books that were returned over the weekend?"

"Yes," Jenny said.

"When will you get around to putting them back on the shelves?"

"This afternoon possibly, maybe not until tomorrow."

"You see," said Elledge confidently, "return books might stay on Jenny's desk a day or two. Plenty of time for someone to swipe one if he'd a mind to."

"I see what you mean," Hattie mused distractedly. "It does muddle things, doesn't it? Well, we'll just skip that for now. The book was taken, either from the hospital or from the library, the pages torn out and probably destroyed, and the book was tossed into the trash barrel behind the furniture store sometime between Tuesday, November 26, and Friday, November 29." Suddenly Hattie's face lit up. "I know what I'll do. I'll question all the employees of the furniture store and find out if one of them saw someone slinking around in the alley on one of those days." She got up and put her coat on with quick, birdlike movements. Then she returned the note pad and pen to her purse and clasped the biology book in her arms. "I'd better question the people in the businesses on either side of the furniture store, too, just in case one of them saw anything. Let's see, now. That would be your father's newspaper, Jenny, and the hardware store."

James Elledge shook his head. "You keep this up, Hattie, and they're going to send out those men in white coats with a straitjacket for you."

Hattie merely sniffed and started for the door.

"Good luck, Miss Sterling," Jenny called after her.

When she was gone, Elledge looked at Jenny with a wry smile, "She offered to help the sheriff solve those two murders, but he told her if he heard of her nosing around, he'd charge her with obstructing justice." Elledge cackled. "Should have gotten married years ago, that one. Needs a man to settle her down, knock some of those silly notions out of her head."

"Well, she's enjoying herself," said Jenny philosophically. "Let her have her fun."

Elledge said, "Might as well. Once Hattie gets started down a track, it would take a locomotive to derail her." He looked pleased with his own joke, said good-bye to Jenny and left the library.

Still smiling to herself over the way James Elledge and Hattie Sterling seemed always to rub each other the wrong way, Jenny finished slipping the cards into the pockets of the books on her desk. She wondered briefly if James Elledge was right about the biology book being taken from her desk after it was returned. She knew it could have happened. People came and went, and she was not always at her desk.

She did not get around to opening the rest of the mail until after lunch. Near the bottom of the stack of mail, her hand fell on a white envelope addressed with a pencil in childish block letters to JENNY CURTISS, PINE VALLEY LIBRARY, PINE VALLEY, MONTANA. There was no return address.

Frowning, she tore into the envelope and took out a single sheet of white paper, folded once. Her hands shook as she unfolded the paper and, thinking about it later, she realized that she must have had a premonition as to its contents. The message was short, the words cut from printed matter, which appeared to be magazine paper since it was slick to the touch, and pasted to the white sheet. She heard her heart pounding in her ears as she read:

FOR YOUR OWN GOOD, YOU MUST GET OUT OF TOWN.

That was all. There was neither salutation nor signature. Slowly she returned the message to its envelope and, going into the back room, thrust it deep inside a pocket of her coat. Then she sagged against the small table, staring blindly at its scarred surface. She heard the library door open, then female voices, but she stayed where she was, trying to decide what to do.

If she told her parents, it would frighten them, and they were having enough troubles these days without her adding to the burden. Only the evening before, after their return from visiting Harold at the hospital, Doreen had gone immediately to bed, saying that she was tired, even though it was not yet nine o'clock. And that morning, during the drive to town, her father had been morosely silent. Jenny thought something must have happened at the hospital or on the way home last night that caused her parents to quarrel. Whatever it was, she couldn't lay this additional worry on them just now.

Should she take the envelope to the sheriff? Perhaps. Yet she hesitated. Was it possible the message was somebody's idea of a joke? At any other time she probably would have accepted that explanation as the most likely one. But she couldn't now, not when so many people seemed to resent her questions about the murders. Saturday she had angered Luke, and before that Sarah and Beau Gleason. Would one of them have done this? Somehow it seemed more Gleason's style than the others, but she wasn't sure enough of that to disregard Luke or Sarah entirely.

It occurred to her now that the wording of the message seemed odd. FOR YOUR OWN GOOD, YOU MUST LEAVE TOWN. If it was meant as a threat, why hadn't the message been more direct: "If you value your life . . ." or "You have a month to get out of town or suffer the consequences." "For your own good . . ." struck her as more of a plea than a threat. But no well-meaning person would have to resort to anonymous messages.

A feeling of hopelessness swept over her. She didn't know where to turn. Even Tom, who until recently had been a loyal friend, was not feeling very friendly toward her just now. And she wouldn't dare confide in Shirley, who was too inclined to let secrets slip out in conversation.

The sheriff seemed the only confidante at the moment that she could trust. Yet that was a drastic step, and she might be more able than he to find out who had sent the message. He would ask a few questions and then bury the letter beneath the pile of papers on his desk, all of which needed his attention.

She straightened and drew a long breath, telling herself that she was safe in the library with its glass front and people coming and going all the time, and on Main Street she was surrounded by witnesses. At home the presence of her parents would provide protection. And she certainly had no intention of walking along any lonely mountain paths. She would wait a day or two before deciding what to do about the message.

Feeling calmer, she left the back room to help the two women who had just arrived to do research for the local historical society.

During the next two days Jenny found herself looking at the people around her with fresh eyes. In the middle of a conversation the thought would intrude, "Could *he* have sent the message?" And she began to find sinister double meanings in the most casual comments. At lunch on Wednesday, Shirley asked if she was coming down with something, since she looked tired and seemed unusually irritable. When Jenny insisted that she felt fine, Shirley suggested that she come to her house that evening for a good long visit. "We'll make fudge," Shirley said, "and talk. We used to do that at least once a month in high school. I can't think why we ever stopped."

Although Jenny was certainly in no mood for a marathon gabfest such as she and Shirley often had had in the past, she was finding her evenings at home with her parents something of a strain, too. The veneer of forced cheerfulness that she had been wearing around the house for the past two days was beginning to show signs of cracking. Tuesday evening she had snapped at her mother when Doreen inquired as to why Tom hadn't called recently. Jenny had apologized, of course, but afterward she caught Doreen regarding her with obvious concern when she thought Jenny wouldn't notice. She decided that an evening with Shirley might take her mind off herself.

And this proved to be the case. She left the house in her car as soon as she and her mother had had dinner. As usual on Wednesdays, Gerald was working late at the newspaper. But Doreen insisted that Jenny go on to Shirley's as planned; she would read the new George Washington biography until Gerald came home.

Shirley lived with her parents and two younger brothers in a big, old-fashioned house near the hospital. When Shirley announced that she and Jenny were going to make fudge, her brothers began to clamor for taffy and divinity, too, with the result that the candymaking developed into a family project, with Shirley's mother and brothers making taffy and divinity, while Jenny and Shirley made fudge.

They dirtied every pan in the house before they were through and laughed until their sides ached at the boys' version of the latest goings-on at the high school.

It was past ten before Jenny could drag herself away from the ebullient Loomises.

"I don't know when I've had so much fun," she told Shirley sincerely as she got into her coat in the entry hall.

"I'm glad," Shirley said. "I've been worried about you lately."

"Worried about me?" Jenny said lightly. "Surely you can find something better to do with your time."

Shirley's pixie face was grave. "You've had something on your mind, Jenny. Tom told me yesterday that he's been concerned about you, too."

Jenny dismissed her friend's comment with a laugh. "I haven't even seen Tom for several days."

"I know. He told me. He seems to think you're getting involved with Luke Highbridge. In fact, he asked me to try to talk to you about it. He thinks you ought to steer clear of Luke for your own good."

Shirley's final words brought Jenny to sudden alertness. "What did you say?"

Shirley frowned. "About Tom, you mean? Oh, he's obviously hurt and jealous. But, Jenny, I really think he believes Luke is no good for you."

"No. You said I ought to avoid Luke for my own good. Did Tom say that?"

"That was the gist of it, yes."

"Shirley," Jenny said insistently, "try to remember. Did Tom use those exact words—*for my own good*?"

Shirley looked puzzled. "Why, yes, I believe so. Yes, I'm sure he used those words. Why?"

For a moment Jenny was tempted to take Shirley into her confidence about the note that she still carried in her coat pocket. But the impulse passed, and she said only, "It isn't important. I was just curious." She buttoned her coat while Shirley studied her quizzically.

"Shall we meet for lunch at the coffee shop tomorrow?" Jenny asked.

"I think I can make it," Shirley said.

Jenny stepped back into the living room to say good night to all the Loomises. She left the house then and hurried across the front yard to her car, which she had left at the curb. Inside, she locked both doors and started the motor. Tom Irving's remark kept repeating itself in her head. Surely it was only coincidence that he had used the very words that had been included in her pasted-up message. In fact, it wasn't the first time Tom had expressed the thought. Earlier he had advised her not to get involved with Luke, saying he had her own best interests at heart.

For your own good. It was a common expression, used by almost everybody at one time or another. She couldn't believe Tom had sent that message. Why would he want her to leave town? Surely he didn't believe her leaving was the only way to avoid being hurt by Luke Highbridge.

She must, she told herself, stop searching for hidden meanings in people's conversations. Shivering in the cold car, she pulled away from the curb, adjusting the car heater as she started slowly down the steep, snow-packed road that led to town.

About halfway down the hill, a tremor ran through the small car, and it began to wobble unevenly. She had a flat tire. She had been putting off buying a new set of tires for weeks, and now she had no one but herself to blame for having to climb out on this deserted stretch of road on one of the coldest nights of the year to change a flat.

This settles it, she told herself as she opened the car trunk, *I'm going to see about new tires tomorrow.* After tugging and rolling the spare out of the trunk, she set the jack in place under the rear bumper and began to work the jack handle up and down. When the flat tire had cleared the ground, she felt around in the dark trunk until she found the lug wrench. As she straightened and turned around with the wrench in her hands, the lights of an approaching car came into view over the top of the hill, and the car slowed and pulled off the road, coming to a stop behind Jenny's compact.

The driver got out, leaving his headlights on, and came toward her. "Looks like you could use some help, Jenny." It was Luke Highbridge.

"Your lights are certainly welcome," Jenny said. "I didn't realize how dark it was tonight until I started to change this tire."

He took the wrench from her hands. "Here, I'll do that." Squatting, he wedged the sharp end of the wrench under the rim of the hubcap, dislodging it with ease. Jenny rubbed her gloved hands together and moved to stand beside him.

"Were you visiting your father?"

He was loosening bolts swiftly. "Yes."

"How is he?"

"Better than anyone would have thought possible. He can get in and out of his wheelchair now without help."

"Oh, I'm so glad to hear that, Luke. Maybe he'll be able to go home for Christmas, after all."

Laying the wrench aside, he lifted the tire off the rim and propped it against the side of the car. "It's beginning to look like it." He glanced at her. "Before going to the hospital, I went to see Marty Brubaker."

"At his apartment?"

"Yes. I wanted to ask him a few questions."

"Questions? You mean about Leah?"

"Yes. I wanted to know why he seems to think someone at the Tamaracks was involved in the killings. I had to tell him I'd heard it from you, of course."

"What did he say?"

"He was evasive, but I expected that. He finally admitted that he doesn't *know* anything. But he was cordial enough. We had a beer, and he loosened up a little and talked about Leah. He was very much in love with her."

"I know," Jenny said.

Luke got to his feet and reached for the spare tire, which was lying on the hard-packed snow between the two cars. He rolled it into position. "Ever hear of an actor named Gideon Garfield?"

The question astonished Jenny. "I can't believe Marty talked to you about him."

Luke had bent to work the tire into place, but he stopped and turned a sudden penetrating look on her. "He didn't."

"Then, how—"

"There was a scrapbook on the floor next to the divan.

When he went out to the kitchen to get our drinks, I flipped through it. It was full of newspaper clippings, play reviews mostly. They were yellow with age. I only read a few of them before he came back into the room. They were all dated in the 1950s. Gideon Garfield's name was underlined in every one of them."

"Garfield was the man Leah ran away with when she was seventeen. You've probably heard that gossip."

He nodded. "Everyone in town has, but I don't recall having heard his name before."

"I—I can't understand this, Luke. How did Marty get those clippings? He never knew Garfield. He did question me about him once. He said it might help him to understand Leah better."

"He went to a lot of trouble to gather so many clippings about a man he never even met."

Jenny stared at him, trying to make some sense of what he was saying. Somewhere behind her, she heard another car approaching, but all of her attention was on Luke and the incomprehensible information that Marty owned a scrapbook filled with reviews of plays in which Gideon Garfield had acted. Marty *must* have known him. Why had he questioned her as if he knew nothing at all about Garfield? What did it mean? Intent upon trying to understand, she took a step toward Luke.

He moved so suddenly that she didn't know what was happening. "Watch out!" His arms came up, and he shoved her roughly away from him. Somehow she was sitting in the snowbank alongside the shoulder of the road, and Luke had scrambled and fallen beside her. As she watched, wide-eyed, her car shuddered and fell off the jack, hitting the packed snow with a thud. At the same moment, the car she had heard approaching came to a stop in the road, and the driver rolled down his window to call, "Need any help?"

"No, thanks," Luke replied before Jenny had a chance to swallow her shock and speak. "The jack slipped, but no harm done."

"OK." The car moved off down the hill.

Luke got to his feet. "You are OK, aren't you?"

She brushed at the snow on her coat. "I—I think so."

Luke reached out to pull her to her feet, but when his

hands closed around hers, he lost his footing on the ice. His feet slipped from under him, and he landed once more beside Jenny in the snowbank.

"Damn," he muttered as he sat up and shook the snow off his gloves. Then he looked at Jenny, and suddenly their situation seemed hysterically funny. They began to laugh.

"Oh"—Jenny gasped when she could stop laughing—"my seat's wet."

Luke reached for her hand. "Shall we try again?" He was on his knees in front of her, and when their glances met, his laughter died away. For a moment that seemed to spin on and on, they looked into each other's eyes as if they were frozen there beside the road. He moved first. His arms reached out for her, and his mouth came down on hers in a searching kiss. Jenny's own swift response so stunned her that it was several moments before she could think clearly enough to realize that her lips had gone soft and yielding under his and that her arms had somehow entwined themselves around her neck. And then, much to her alarm, she discovered she didn't want to move—she wanted to stay there in the wet snowbank, to feel Luke's mouth on hers, to feel the wonder of his strong arms about her. A strange new warmth had invaded her body, driving out the cold.

But the memory of how near she had come to being hurt, perhaps killed, by the falling car intruded, effectively blasting her dreamy, drifting state and plunging her into harsh awareness of the danger of her situation. Bringing both hands against his chest, she pushed him away.

He looked down at her, bemused. "Jenny—"

"No." She scrambled to her feet. "Don't say anything, Luke."

"What's wrong?" His sharp words and the half-angry look in his eyes caused her to look away from him. Her hands shook as she fumbled beneath the car for the jack.

Instantly he was beside her. "Get away and let me do it." She did as he said, huddling against the front fender of his car, wet and shaking. With quick, angry movements, he set the jack in place once more and raised the car. In silence, he lifted the spare onto the rim, tightened the bolts and replaced the hubcap. Then he tossed the flat tire and lug wrench into her trunk and slammed it shut.

He turned to her and said stiffly, "I'll follow you, just to make sure you don't have another flat. Most of the tread's worn off that spare."

"I know," she said through chattering teeth. "Thank you for your help." She moved past him quickly, got into her car and started the motor before she looked into the rearview mirror. He was still standing behind her car, his head to one side, as if he were deep in thought. As she watched, he seemed to shake himself and turn abruptly. He got into his car. When she pulled away from the shoulder, he was right behind her, and he followed closely until she had turned into her own driveway.

She pulled into the garage beside her mother's car, noticing with half her mind that Gerald's car was not there. She turned off the motor and the lights and sat in the dark for several minutes, thinking. Another tremor ran through her as she realized that she could have been badly hurt by her falling car. But Luke had pushed her out of the way. Instead of reassuring her, as this knowledge should have done, it caused her to feel confused and shaken. What if that other car hadn't come along just then? Would Luke have been so quick to save her if there hadn't been a witness? A violent trembling started in her stomach and moved along her limbs. Could Luke have done something to the jack to make it fall? Had he intended for her to be hurt but been thwarted in his plan by the sudden appearance of the other car?

Her whole body was shaking now. Somehow she got out of the car and found the house key. Inside, she stood in the darkened utility room and took a firm grip on her runaway thoughts.

"Jenny, is that you?" Doreen's voice reached her from the den, and then she heard her mother come into the kitchen and switch on the light.

She entered the kitchen from the utility room. Doreen stared at her. "What happened to you? You're all wet."

Jenny slipped off her coat and gloves and laid them across the breakfast bar. "I had a flat," she said. She went into the den to stand in front of the fire.

"Your slacks are soaked," Doreen said behind her.

"I slipped in the snow," Jenny murmured.

"You'd better get those wet things off right away."

"I will, as soon as I warm up a bit." Jenny turned to look at her mother with what she hoped was a reassuring smile.

Doreen studied her gravely. "I'm going to make you some hot chocolate. You get changed and into bed, and I'll bring it up to you." She started for the kitchen.

Grateful that her mother did not seem inclined to question her further about what had happened, Jenny lingered in front of the fire for a few moments before going upstairs to her room. Beast leaped from the window seat as she opened the door and came to sniff at her wet clothing. She stroked him absently and quickly got out of her clothes and into a warm flannel nightgown. Leaving only the tiny dressing-table lamp on, she crawled into bed.

She stared into the corners of the room, seeing strange shapes in the shadows. What had really happened on that lonely road tonight? Had Luke saved her, or had he tried to kill her? In spite of the tumultuous feelings he had aroused in her with his kiss, she found she had no answer to that question.

Very soon Doreen came in with the hot chocolate. Jenny sat up and took the cup. Doreen sat on the edge of the bed, her hazel eyes clouded with unspoken questions.

"Where's Dad?" Jenny asked.

"One of the presses broke down. He probably won't be home until after midnight." Some hint of strain in her mother's voice caused Jenny to study her more closely in the dim light. She saw for the first time the worry lines etched on either side of Doreen's mouth and between her eyes.

"Are you feeling all right, Mother?"

"Yes, of course," said Doreen with what seemed to Jenny a little too much decisiveness, as if she were trying to convince herself as well as Jenny. "Drink your chocolate," Doreen went on, "and get some rest."

Jenny wondered fleetingly if she should get up and keep her mother company until Gerald came home. But suddenly she was far too sleepy to carry through with the thought. Her eyelids were heavy as she finished the rich chocolate, and Doreen took the cup from her hands. Jenny snuggled down into the warm bed, aware, as if from a far distance, that Doreen was tucking the covers snugly around her shoulders. She was already drifting into sleep when she heard her bedroom door close softly.

The memory of Luke Highbridge's warm mouth on hers came back in a soft haze as she slid away from consciousness into deep slumber.

Twelve

The alarm going off at seven-thirty drew her slowly from a sound and dreamless sleep. She reached out to turn it off, then stretched and opened her eyes. Her head was so fuzzy with sleep that it took a moment for her to orient herself. Then through the window opposite her bed she saw that it was snowing again. She watched the giant flakes falling silently, wishing that it were possible to stay in her room all day. She knew this was actually a desire to escape, if only for a day, the things that were happening in her life—her conflicting feelings about Luke, the anonymous message, the strain between her parents. She knew she must face these things squarely, however, and no amount of procrastination would make them go away. And she would also face Marty Brubaker and ask him about the scrapbook in his apartment. Since Marty's possible past acquaintance with Gideon Garfield seemed the least formidable of the puzzles facing her, she decided to tackle it first. There would be time to visit Marty at his apartment before going to the library, unless he was working the early shift today. She decided to chance it and, if he wasn't at the apartment, leave a note for him to call her as soon as possible.

With this goal in mind, she dressed quickly for the day in a silk shirt, a wool skirt, and warm knee-high brown leather boots. When she went downstairs, she let Beast out the front door before going to the kitchen, where Gerald and Doreen were having breakfast. Gerald looked haggard, and Jenny guessed the press breakdown had kept him up most of the night.

Jenny poured herself a cup of coffee and went to sit at the bar facing them.

"I'll scramble your egg," Doreen said, getting up.

Jenny surveyed her father's drawn face. "When did *you* get to bed last night?"

Gerald stifled a yawn. "Sometime after midnight."

From the stove Doreen said, "It was nearly two."

Jenny sipped her coffee. "Did you get the press running?"

"With Tom's help." He smiled. "In the proud tradition of American journalism, the *Journal* will be on the streets today."

Doreen put Jenny's scrambled egg along with a piece of toast onto a plate and carried it to the bar. "The world wouldn't end if the *Journal* was a day late."

"Don't rub it in," Gerald said wryly.

"I still think you ought to sleep in this morning."

Gerald drained his coffee cup. "I'll catch a nap at the office."

"Ha!" said Doreen crossly. "I can picture that. Even Beast couldn't sleep in that madhouse."

Gerald's tired features arranged themselves into a grin. "Wanta bet?"

Jenny finished her egg. "I'm going to buy new tires today, Dad. I was hoping you could advise me."

"If you like," Gerald offered, "you can drive my car and I'll leave yours at the filling station. They could have the tires on and balanced by the time I'm ready to come home."

"Oh, Dad, I'd really appreciate that. You know better than I what kind of tires I ought to buy. If you're sure it's not too much trouble for you."

"Not a bit." In spite of too little sleep the night before, Gerald seemed in good spirits. Whatever quarrel he and Doreen had been having must have been forgotten, by Gerald, anyway.

They exchanged car keys, and Jenny said, "I'm going to town early this morning. There are a couple of errands I need to run before I go to work." Putting on her coat, she hurried back through the kitchen and into the garage. She opened the overhead door and got into her father's car.

Marty Brubaker lived in a garage apartment about three blocks south of the hospital. He rented the apartment and the garage below from an elderly widow, Opal Whitlock, who lived in the house on the front of the lot. The snow was still falling as Jenny pulled into the narrow drive, coming to a stop near the stairs that led up to the apartment. She could see Marty's car through a small window in the stairway side of the garage.

At the foot of the stairs, she hesitated, her gloved hand on the snow-frosted banister. It hadn't occurred to her until then that Marty might resent her questions. But she could not let that stop her. She had to know how Marty had come into possession of a scrapbook of clippings about Gideon Garfield, and why he had pretended to know nothing about the actor. Anything that touched, even indirectly, on Leah's life might be a clue to her killer.

Her wavering determination firmer, she climbed the snow-encrusted stairs carefully. At the top, she stood under the shelter of the small roof overhang and knocked, the sound muffled by her fur-lined glove. After a moment she removed her glove and rapped sharply several times. She waited and knocked again, calling Marty's name.

There was no answer. She didn't think he would walk to the hospital in this weather, and his car was below. Perhaps he had been called back to the hospital last night and was sleeping too soundly to hear her knocking. She decided to ask Mrs. Whitlock if she knew where Marty was. If he was sleeping, she would telephone him from Mrs. Whitlock's house. The ringing of the phone might awaken him.

She put her glove back on and descended slowly, gripping the banister for a surer footing on the snowy stairs. The approach to Opal Whitlock's back door, about two hundred yards away, led past the front of the garage. Jenny was surprised to see that the overhead garage door was up, and the snow was drifting across the back of Marty's green Ford. Marty must have been tired last night to have forgotten to close the garage door in such frigid weather.

She was past the garage, looking back at the rear end of the Ford, when she thought she saw something on the floor in the dim space between the driver's side of the car and the garage wall. She halted and turned around. It looked like a man's shoe. Gingerly, she picked her way through the snow until she was standing at the open garage door. She took a step inside, peering down at what was lying beside the car on the cement floor.

She stood rooted to the spot for a long silent moment, and then her breath escaped her lungs in a sudden gasp of recognition. Marty Brubaker was lying with his legs half under the car and the upper half of his torso propped at a grotesquely awkward angle against the garage wall. He had been shot in the forehead. Frozen blood concealed most of the right side of his face.

Jenny's heart lurched fearfully in her chest. She turned and stumbled toward the Whitlock house, her boots crunching loudly in the snow. At the back door of the house, she banged frantically with her gloved fist and called, "Mrs. Whitlock! Let me in, please!"

Opal Whitlock was hard-of-hearing, and it was several moments before she became aware of Jenny's repeated knocking and yelling, enough time for Jenny to have reached a state of near panic. Standing in the falling snow, banging on the storm door, she remembered that Luke had been here last night and had talked to Marty. They had had a beer, Luke said, and Marty had talked about Leah. But what really happened? Had they quarreled?

The inner door finally opened, and the gray-haired Mrs. Whitlock peered through the door. Jenny gasped, "It's Jenny Curtiss, Mrs. Whitlock. Please let me in. Something's happened to Marty."

Mrs. Whitlock's wrinkled features drew together as she tried to comprehend. Finally she recognized Jenny and unlatched the door for her. "Oh, it's you, Jenny. I didn't know you for a minute with that hood half covering your face."

Jenny stepped inside. "I have to use your phone, Mrs. Whitlock," she said loudly.

The gray head nodded, trying to take it in. "Something about Marty, you say?"

"He's dead," Jenny shouted frantically. "In the garage."

This, at least, penetrated. *"Dead!"* Mrs. Whitlock's gnarled hand flew to her breast, and Jenny thought for a second that she might faint. But then the woman seemed to pull herself together, and she led the way into her living room, where the telephone sat on a corner table.

Removing her gloves, Jenny found that her hands were shaking so badly it was difficult to find the number she wanted in the book. But after flipping past it several times, she found it and dialed the sheriff's office.

Sheriff Turpin listened to Jenny's breathless recital and instructed her and Mrs. Whitlock to stay where they were until he arrived. They were not to go near the body, he side, an unnecessary bit of instruction as far as Jenny was concerned. She had no desire to look again at the horrible, blood-covered thing that had been Marty Brubaker.

Within a few minutes the sheriff's car pulled into the drive, with a second car behind it. Pine Valley's chief of police and one of his deputies got out of the second car, conferred with the sheriff briefly, then went along the driveway toward the garage, while the sheriff came to the front door.

Jenny let him in.

"Hello, Jenny, Mrs. Whitlock." Sheriff Turpin was a short, stocky man in his late fifties. He was bald except for a narrow fringe of reddish-blond hair, and he had a big hawk nose that might have made him wretchedly ugly, but his face was redeemed by fine, thickly lashed, dark eyes. He sat on the edge of a worn armchair, and Jenny took a seat beside Mrs. Whitlock on the couch.

"Now, Jenny," said the sheriff, "how did you happen to find the body?"

"I came by to talk to Marty before going to work this morning. I went up to his apartment and knocked. When he didn't answer, I decided to come here and ask Mrs. Whitlock if she knew where he was. I thought it odd that he didn't answer, when his car was in the garage. As I passed the garage, I—I saw him."

The sheriff was watching her with calm interest. "The garage door was open?"

"Yes. I thought that was odd, too."

Mrs. Whitlock shifted nervously. She seemed to be straining to hear.

"What did you do when you saw the body, Jenny?" the sheriff asked. "Did you touch anything?"

Jenny shuddered. "No. His face was all bloody. I ran

to Mrs. Whitlock's back door. She let me in, and I called you."

The sheriff looked at the elderly woman and raised his voice. "Did you hear anything last night or this morning, Mrs. Whitlock?"

Opal Whitlock cocked her head. "What's that?"

"Did you hear a car, a gunshot—anything at all—last night or this morning?" the sheriff roared.

"No, no—nothing."

The sheriff sighed. "No, of course you didn't." He resumed his normal tone of voice. "Can't hear it thunder, I don't imagine." He looked at Jenny again. "Why did you come to see Marty?"

Jenny had had time while waiting for his arrival to realize that he would ask this question. She had decided to tell him everything. "I'd just learned that he had a scrapbook full of clippings about Gideon Garfield, the actor my aunt Leah ran away with years ago. But Marty had pretended to me that he never even met Garfield and knew nothing about him. I wanted to ask him about the scrapbook, to see if it would clear up—anything."

Sheriff Turpin studied her with his fine eyes. "Making a little investigation of your own, eh?"

She didn't answer, and he raised his voice to shout at Mrs. Whitlock. "I'll need a key to the garage apartment, ma'am."

The widow understood and went into her bedroom to fetch the key.

"May I go with you, Sheriff?" Jenny asked.

He looked at her in silence for a moment. "Still want a look at that scrapbook, eh? Ah, well, come along. But you can't touch anything." Walking beside her toward the garage, snowflakes splatting on his bald pate, he said, "Dratted snow has covered whatever footprints or tire tracks were here." He pulled a stocking cap out of his coat pocket and put it on. "From what you've said, Jenny, it wasn't Brubaker who told you about the scrapbook. Who was it?"

Jenny had an impulse to evade the question, but she knew it would not be difficult for Sheriff Turpin to learn of Luke's visit to Marty the previous evening. If Mrs. Whitlock hadn't seen him, another neighbor might have.

Someone could have recognized his car. She found that she wanted desperately to believe that Luke had told her the truth about his meeting with Marty.

"Luke Highbridge told me," she said, finally, and then she went on as briefly as she could to tell the sheriff about Luke's visit with Marty and, later, her meeting with Luke on the road to town.

When she finished, Turpin said thoughtfully, "What time did you have that flat tire?"

"A little after ten."

"And you say he had just come from the hospital?"

She nodded.

"That'll be easy enough to check." He left Jenny beside the stairs while he went inside the garage to talk to the two policemen. After a moment he came back and led the way up the stairs. "Looks like he's been dead for several hours. We'll know more when the coroner sees him."

The small apartment was neat and clean. The bed did not appear to have been slept in. The sheriff saw the scrapbook lying on the floor at one end of the couch. With his handkerchief covering his hand, he picked it up by one corner and laid it on the chrome kitchen table. Still using the handkerchief, he opend it and turned the pages slowly as he and Jenny scanned the newspaper clippings. As Luke had said, they were reviews of plays in which Gideon Garfield had had small parts. The actor's name was underlined with a heavy black pencil.

Midway through the scrapbook they found a review that included a photograph of the cast. Reading the names below the photograph, Jenny picked out Gideon Garfield. He was the second from the left on the first row. Not at all as she had pictured him, he was blond and, compared with the actors on either side of him, appeared to be of no more than medium height. Curious, she studied his face.

"Sheriff," she said slowly, "look at the second man from the left. That's Gideon Garfield." She bent to see the face more closely. Were her eyes playing tricks on her? "Does he remind you of anyone?"

The sheriff bent nearer the photograph. "That could be Marty Brubaker twenty years ago."

Jenny stared at him. "But that can't *be!*"

He shook his head. "Easy to check, but I'd say the likeness is too clear for much doubt. He's put on a lot of weight, of course. Garfield must have been a stage name."

Jenny's knees felt weak, and she sat down in one of the kitchen chairs. "But why didn't they tell anyone? Why did Leah keep his identity a secret?"

"Never even told your parents, eh?"

Jenny shook her head, dazed. "They—they never saw him, you see, so they wouldn't have recognized him. He must have come back here because of Leah. He—he asked her to marry him."

"The acting career fizzled out, I'll wager," the sheriff said speculatively.

"Years ago," Jenny said. "It had to be that way. Marty was a salesman and a forest ranger before he came to Pine Valley. Leah told me that. All those years, I suppose, he was looking for something to take the place of acting."

"Finally had to be content with being a lab technician. So he came back for Leah. Must have felt he could have her, even if he wasn't an actor anymore." He shook his stocking-capped head. "Trying to recapture lost youth. It never works."

Jenny was remembering Leah's enigmatic words to Sarah Highbridge—about dreams coming true too late to do anybody any good. She must have been talking about Marty and herself, the dream of their being together. But why had it been too late? Jenny fought against a painful pressure in her throat. "I'll have to tell my parents," she said after a moment, "before they hear it from someone else."

"You go along when you're ready," Turpin said. "I may have some more questions for you later, after we get the coroner's report."

She got to her feet.

"We've got you blocked in the drive. I'll jockey the cars. You feeling all right?"

Jenny nodded, but the air in the apartment seemed uncomfortably stuffy. She wanted to get outside, to drive away from this place. She would go back home and talk to Doreen first; then she would phone her father. It was time to open the library, but that would have to wait until she had told her parents. The sheriff saw her to her car, where she waited impatiently for him to move the two cars that were blocking the drive. Then she drove away, rehearsing how she would tell her mother that Marty Brubaker was Gideon Garfield and that he had been murdered.

Jenny had been away at college last year; now she was beginning to understand how the residents of Pine Valley must have felt that first winter after the murder of the two women. The tensing of her stomach muscles, the dull throbbing behind her eyes—unlike the taut alertness with its surge of adrenalin that is triggered by a sudden unexpected threat, this fear would go on until the murderer was caught. In time it would fade into the background, but it would be there ready to surface at odd, unexpected moments. The murder of Marty Brubaker would bring that fear to the surface once more. It was all happening again. Would they catch the murderer this time? Or would there be other deaths?

Suddenly the anonymous message she had received took on even more sinister meanings. *For your own good, you must leave town.* For her own good? Was this a warning that she was marked for murder? That her presence in Pine Valley was a threat to someone? It was time to turn the message over to the sheriff. Slipping off her gloves, Jenny felt in her right pocket, and then her left, for the envelope. With a sinking feeling, she pulled over to the shoulder and stopped the car so that she could have both hands free. Then she turned her coat pockets inside out. The envelope containing the anonymous message was gone.

It was after ten when Jenny opened the library. By that time, news of the third murder had spread through the town like a fever. There was a notable lack of movement along Main Street. Most people were staying at home, telephoning neighbors and friends to talk about this newest horror. Violence was abroad once more.

Hattie Sterling called Jenny about noon to say that she was returning the biology book since her questioning of the furniture-store employees had resulted in no new clues. She was mailing it, she informed Jenny, because she had no intention of leaving her house for the time being. Hattie was giving up the investigation, and Jenny sensed that Marty's murder had knocked Hattie's vision of herself as a shrewd, sharp-witted detective quite askew. Like everyone else, Hattie was preoccupied with self-preservation at the moment.

During her lunch hour Jenny walked over to the courthouse and told Sheriff Turpin about the anonymous message and its subsequent disappearance. She thought that she had probably lost it during her tumble into the snowbank on the night Luke had changed her flat tire. The sheriff promised to send someone to search along the road for the envelope, but with several inches of new snow he didn't hold out much hope of finding it. Jenny had memorized the message, of course, and could even describe the type of paper and the printing used, but without the physical evidence their chances of tracing it were slim.

She spent the afternoon filling out a lengthy book order and cleaning up the back room with a vengeance that, nevertheless, did not keep a variety of frightening questions from filling her thoughts. What had really happened between Marty and Luke last night? Had Marty accused Luke of murdering Leah and Mary Steed? Had Luke just come from killing Marty when he stopped to help her change the tire? Had he caused her car to fall off the jack because of something Marty had said, something that convinced Luke she was a threat to him? Yet he had shoved her to safety. But if that other car hadn't happened along, what then?

A little before four, Tom Irving came into the library, an anxious scowl on his thin, faintly freckled face. "I'm going to follow you home in my car," he announced, "and I want you to promise me you won't go anywhere alone until that killer is caught."

He was clearly set to counter her protests, but Jenny was not inclined to argue. She merely went into the back room and put on her coat. When she returned, she said, "Don't you mean *if* the killer is caught?"

Tom brushed absently at a wayward red forelock. "If they don't catch him this time, this town is going to come apart at the seams. People are talking about moving. Your dad's editorial in next week's paper is going to lambast the sheriff's office, the police department, and everyone else even remotely involved in the investigation. Man, the heat is on."

"I was hoping Dad could spend most of the day with Mother."

"He went straight home after he vented some of his indignation in writing that editorial. It was about one o'clock. He had talked to your mother on the phone a couple of times before that. I gathered he was pretty concerned about how she's taking all this."

"Finding out Marty was Gideon Garfield really threw her," Jenny said. "It brought back all the old resentment and pain caused by Leah's breakdown. She kept saying, 'To think I entertained him dozens of times in this house.' And then to learn that he was dead—well, she's convinced now that his reappearance in Leah's life had something to do with her murder."

"He certainly seems to have been the source of most of Leah's problems," Tom said. "Do you think he killed her?"

Jenny pressed two fingers against her forehead where the headache that had struck that morning in Marty's apartment still throbbed dully. "That doesn't hold together, Tom. Marty loved Leah. What reason could he have had to kill her? And if he *did* kill her, did he kill Mary, too? And if so, who killed him? She massaged the bridge of her nose and groaned. "Oh, it just doesn't make any sense."

Tom laid a gentle hand on her arm. "Let's go. You look tired."

The snow had stopped, but dusk was gloomy with clouds and a certain dark sense of waiting. Jenny was glad to have Tom's car behind her all the way up the hill. He even followed her into the drive, got out, closed the garage door for her and saw her to the utility-room door.

"Come in and warm up before you go," Jenny said.

Gerald heard them and came into the utility room. "We appreciate your seeing Jenny home." He clapped his hand on the younger man's shoulder. "Doreen is making chili. Why don't you stay and have some with us?"

Tom hesitated. "I don't want to intrude, Gerald."

"Oh, stop that," Gerald said.

Tom gave in without further argument. The pot of chili was simmering on the stove in the kitchen, but Doreen was not in sight. After hanging up the coats, Jenny looked into her parents' bedroom. Doreen was lying on the bed, an afghan across her legs.

"Don't get up, Mother. Tom's staying for dinner. I'll fix him and Dad a drink and call you when it's time to eat."

Doreen's eyes were swollen, evidence that she had been crying. She seemed relieved that Jenny was taking charge. Later, when the food was on the table, Doreen joined the others in the dining room. Jenny had never seen her mother look so forlorn.

Doreen said little until the meal was under way. Then she looked at Gerald suddenly and asked, "Did you talk to Jenny about . . . ?"

Gerald shot Jenny a clouded look. "I wasn't going to mention it until Tom left, but—"

"Mention what?" Jenny asked, looking from one parent to the other.

"We know about that threatening letter you received," Gerald said. "Sheriff Turpin called to tell me. He was afraid you wouldn't."

"He had no right to do that!" Jenny cried.

"Of course he did," Doreen said sharply. "Jenny, you don't seem to understand the seriousness of this."

"May I ask," Tom ventured, looking around the table, "what letter you are talking about?"

"It was just a silly pasted-together note advising me to leave town for my own good," Jenny said, striving for lightness. "Somebody's twisted idea of a joke."

"Jenny, you can't just ignore something like that!" Tom exclaimed. "Especially not after what happened to Brubaker."

"Perhaps you should leave, Jenny," Doreen said pleadingly, "only for the time being—until all this is cleared up."

Jenny saw tears in her mother's eyes. "Oh, Mother, I can't leave you now. I'll take precautions—I'll—"

"I agree with Jenny," Tom said to Doreen. "Surely she's safer here, surrounded by family and friends. She's been forewarned. She must be very careful, but I don't think she should go away to a strange town. If someone is really intent upon harming her, he wouldn't necessarily forget about it just because Jenny left Pine Valley."

"That makes sense, Doreen," Gerald said placatingly.

Doreen's expression crumpled suddenly. "Why haven't they arrested him?" she cried, her voice rising.

Gerald half rose from his chair. "Now, calm down, Doreen."

Doreen turned on him abruptly, her eyes blazing. "You are as bad as the police! Luke Highbridge has been back in town for only two weeks and there has been another murder! How much evidence do you need? My God, are the Highbridges above the law?"

"Nobody is suggesting—" Gerald began.

Doreen shoved her chair back and leaped to her feet. "Yes, you are! Does he have to kill your own daughter for you to believe that the Highbridges are human like the rest of us?" Doreen's face had gone white, and her words tumbled over each other in a furious assault.

Jenny glanced at Tom and saw his discomfort and embarrassment at being a witness to this family conflict. She stood and tried to take Doreen's arm. "Mother—"

But Doreen shook her off. Nothing could stop her now. "Tell me, Gerald if it comes to a choice between the life of Sarah's son and your own daughter's, which will you choose?"

Gerald had risen, too, and his face was flushed with tightly reined rage. "Shut up, Doreen! It's bad enough to have to listen to your hysterical accusations when we are alone. I won't stand for this in front of guests!"

Doreen laughed wildly. *"You* won't stand for it! What about all that *I've* stood for?"

In a stunned, frozen moment of time, Jenny saw her father's hand fly out and strike her mother's cheek. There was a shocked silence before Doreen broke into hysterical sobs and ran from the room.

"Excuse me," Tom murmured, looking everywhere but at Jenny, "I—I think I'd better go." He stood uncertainly.

Without a word, Gerald turned and walked toward the den.

"I—I'll get your coat, Tom." Feeling as if she were

sleepwalking, she preceded Tom into the entry hall, where she pulled his coat off the hanger and handed it to him.

He looked down at her with a pained expression. "I'm sorry, Jenny."

She hadn't known she was about to cry, but at his words tears filled her eyes. She covered her face with her hands. "This is a nightmare," she said shakily.

Tom touched her shoulder hesitantly. "Your parents are worried sick." When she didn't answer or look at him, he added, "It'll be all right, Jenny." With that, he put on his coat and let himself out the front door.

After he had gone, Jenny stood there for several moments, wondering how anything could ever be all right again.

Thirteen

Doreen appeared in the kitchen the next morning only long enough to insist that both Jenny and Gerald go to work and not worry about her. Jenny rode to work with her father. She knew, now that her parents had been informed of the anonymous note, Gerald would insist upon accompanying her to and from work every day. Jenny was more than willing to accept this. As for the scene in the dining room the evening before, there seemed to be a tacit agreement among the three of them not to mention it.

Friday proved uneventful in the library. A few patrons came in, all wanting to hear about Jenny's discovery of Marty's body; they left as soon as they discovered that Jenny would not oblige them. At home Doreen and Gerald gave each other a wide berth, talking, when they talked at all, about trivial matters. Jenny had the feeling that her parents were waiting for the other shoe to drop. She made an effort to appear cheerful in their presence, but it was no easy task.

The second shoe dropped on Saturday. Sheriff Turpin came to the house about ten. Gerald led him into the den, where Doreen and Jenny were having a second cup of coffee. Doreen was still in her robe, but Jenny had dressed in faded jeans and an old sweatshirt before coming downstairs.

Gerald took the sheriff's coat and stocking cap and folded them over a chair, while Turpin greeted Doreen and Jenny, apologizing profusely for interrupting their morning.

"Got something I want to show you folks," he said. He peered about, spotted his coat on the chair and searched through the pockets, coming back to stand in front of the fire with a book in his hands.

"This seems to belong to the library, Jenny."

Jenny took the book. It was Edith Hamilton's *Mythol-*

ogy. "Marty checked this out a few days ago," she said.

"Strikes me as uncommon reading for a man like Marty Brubaker," the sheriff remarked.

"It would have been—ordinarily," Jenny told him, "but Marty said he wanted to try to understand Leah better, and she read a lot of mythology. She even wore this medallion with Demeter engraved on it." Jenny drew the medallion from the neck of her sweatshirt and offered it for the sheriff's inspection.

He stepped toward her and bent to examine the medallion, his hawk nose only inches from Jenny's face. "Demeter, is it?" he mused. "One of the Greek gods?"

"Yes. Marty wanted to read Demeter's story."

The sheriff stepped back. "Page 49," he murmured half to himself.

Jenny glanced at her parents, who were watching the sheriff curiously. "I beg your pardon?" she said.

"Demeter's story is on page 49, isn't it?"

"I don't know." Jenny was perplexed. "Let's see." She turned to the page and found the sheriff was right.

"You see what is written there?" Turpin said quietly.

Jenny turned the book around so that she could read the words scrawled in the margin with such pressure that the pen had torn through the paper in spots.

"The man who wrote that was in a highly emotional state, wouldn't you say?" the sheriff asked.

Jenny nodded, her heart twisting.

"What does it say?" Doreen asked sharply.

Jenny read aloud, " 'Leah, my darling, I'm so sorry.' "

Gerald took the book from Jenny's hands and looked at the scrawled words, frowning.

"Were those words there when Marty checked out the book, Jenny?" Turpin asked.

She shook her head.

The sheriff sighed. "I thought not. That's Brubaker's handwriting. We checked it against some papers found in his apartment. Any idea what he meant—any of you?"

All three of the Curtisses shook their heads. *We are like the three monkeys who see no evil,* Jenny thought and had a wild, fleeting impulse to laugh.

After a moment Doreen ventured, "I wonder—could that be a confession, Sheriff?"

Turpin stood in front of the wood fire, his big hands clasped behind his back, his legs spread apart. He lifted himself onto the balls of his feet and swayed slightly. "You mean Brubaker could have been confessing to Leah's murder? Well, I thought of that. Problem is, if he killed Leah, we've got two murderers on our hands."

"Yes," said Doreen gravely, "that doesn't seem likely, does it?"

"Well," the sheriff went on reflectively, "somebody could have killed Brubaker because they learned *he* killed Leah." He shook his head slowly. "But most people wouldn't react that way. They'd turn Brubaker over to the police. Not many people have the audacity to take justice into their own hands."

"I don't think Marty killed Leah," Jenny said. "He may have deserted her years ago, but his actions since he returned to Pine Valley indicate that he had come to regret that very much. He wanted to marry Leah. Maybe he was thinking about the time he abandoned her in New York when he wrote that."

"Could be," Turpin said. "We'll have to keep the book for evidence, Jenny."

Thoughtfully, Gerald closed the book and handed it to the sheriff.

Turpin eyed the other man speculatively. "Word's out you're taking pot shots at me and the police chief in next week's editorial."

"I'm not grinding my personal axe, Sheriff," Gerald said, "but I do have an obligation to my readers."

The sheriff's sandy brows lifted. "Do you think you're being fair, Gerald?"

"I think," Gerald replied curtly, "that if the murderer isn't caught and punished soon, the heart will go out of this town."

"Something is being done," Turpin said. "You ought to at least report the good along with the bad."

"Tell me what you've accomplished, Sheriff, and I'll consider it."

"The coroner has set the time of death between nine and midnight Wednesday night."

Jenny went to stand at the window, thinking, with a sinking heart, that Luke was at the Brubaker apartment about nine. She wondered if the sheriff had questioned him yet. She closed her eyes for a moment. They felt hot and dry, and another headache was beginning.

"Brubaker was killed," the sheriff continued, "with a thirty-eight-caliber slug. That could be a break for us. The killer may have slipped this time. Guns can be traced. Once found, the murder weapon can be matched to the slug taken from Brubaker's head."

"Once found," said Gerald doubtfully. "You don't think he'd be stupid enough to keep the murder weapon around, do you?"

Turpin balanced himself on the balls of his feet. "Not unless he is very sure of his invulnerability. But we're trying to run down every thirty-eight registered to anyone in the area."

Doreen spoke suddenly from the couch. "What if the gun wasn't registered?"

"You can help us there, Gerald," Turpin said, "by running a request in your newspaper, asking anyone possessing, or knowing anyone who possesses, a thirty-eight-caliber hand gun to report it to the police. Stress that informants' names will be kept confidential."

"I'll be glad to do that," Gerald said promptly.

Turpin clasped the mythology book in both hands, pressing it against his broad chest. "Oh, and by the way, Gerald, your name's on the registration list for thirty-eight-caliber guns. I believe you bought one about four years ago?"

The sheriff's quietly spoken words were punctuated by a sudden crackling of the logs in the fireplace. It was a moment before their meaning penetrated Jenny's aching head. She turned to stare at her father.

"That's right." There was a tightening of the muscles around Gerald's mouth. Doreen, gazing at her husband from the couch, looked stunned.

"May I ask why you bought the gun?" Turpin asked.

"It was during that rash of break-ins we had along Main Street," said Gerald curtly. "Since I sometimes work alone late at the newspaper, I wanted it for protection."

"We arrested two teen-age boys for those break-ins," the sheriff said.

"I know, but before you did, I stayed late at the newspaper every night for three weeks, hoping for a break-in. When a man sweats blood to make a business prosper, he doesn't cotton to thieves helping themselves to what has taken years to accumulate."

Turpin studied him gravely. "Maybe it's just as well we caught them before you did."

Doreen said, "You didn't tell me you bought a gun."

Gerald glanced at her. "I saw no reason to worry you."

"The gun's not here, then?" Turpin cut in.

"It's in my desk at the office. I haven't taken it out in months."

"We'd like to have it," Turpin said, "as soon as it's convenient for you to bring it by the courthouse."

"I'll do it now," Gerald offered.

"Good. I'll expect you in my office before noon. If I'm not there, leave it with one of my deputies." Turpin put on his worn overcoat, stuffing the stocking cap into one pocket and the mythology book into the other. He nodded absently toward the couch. "Good day, ladies."

When he was gone, Doreen spoke abruptly. "Gerald, why didn't—"

He cut her off. "I don't want to talk about it now, Doreen." He walked out of the room and took his coat from the entry-hall closet. Stepping back into the den, he said, "Don't worry. Tests will show my gun hasn't been fired in months."

After her father left the house, Jenny moved to sit down in a chair by the fire.

Doreen's hand clutched at the lapel of her robe. "How could he leave a gun lying in a desk drawer? What in heaven's name was he thinking of?"

Jenny pressed her fingers against her temples. "Mother, the gun has been there for four years. Recriminations at this late date will only anger Dad."

Doreen frowned worriedly. "Why didn't Sheriff Turpin ask about the gun the minute he arrived? It was almost as if he delayed dropping his little bombshell on purpose. Do you think he was waiting for Gerald to volunteer the information?"

"I don't know," Jenny said dully, "but it would be a mistake to underestimate the sheriff."

Doreen shot her a penetrating glance. "Well, if he's so smart, how come he hasn't figured out who murdered Leah?"

Jenny massaged her left temple. "Maybe he has figured it out."

Doreen's hazel eyes widened. "Why do you think that? He didn't say anything to you the other morning at Marty's apartment, did he?"

Jenny shook her head. "Why would he tell *me* anything? No, he'll wait until he has enough evidence to support a murder charge, and then he'll make an arrest."

Doreen rested her head in her hands. "Oh, God, I wish this were over. How long do you think it takes to run ballistics tests—or whatever they call them—on a gun?"

"Please don't worry." Jenny watched Doreen with concern. "Dad certainly doesn't seem to be. Checking all the thirty-eight-caliber guns in town is routine procedure."

"I wonder how many there are?"

"The sheriff said he had a list of names. There must be several. Do you think the Highbridges have one?"

"They could—easily," Doreen mused. "They have an arsenal at the Tamaracks. Both Harold and Luke hunt—"

"But they don't hunt with hand guns, do they?"

"No—" Doreen stiffened. "The other night when Beau Gleason shot at you—did you see the gun?"

"It was a rifle."

Doreen's shoulders sagged. "Well, they probably have some hand guns, too. I don't understand why the sheriff hasn't investigated Luke."

"He probably has. I—I told him something that he'll have to investigate. I didn't mention it before—but Wednesday night when I had that flat tire coming home from Shirley's, Luke stopped to help me. He said he'd been to the hospital, but before that he'd been to Marty's apartment."

"He *told* you that?"

had said to me—about his suspicions that someone at the Tamaracks knew something about Leah's and Mary's murders. Luke wanted to know what evidence Marty had."

Doreen's eyes narrowed. "Then, Luke must have told you about Marty's scrapbook."

"Yes. He said he didn't have a chance to take a good look at it, but it bothered me so much I wanted to talk to Marty. If only I had known sooner. Maybe we could have untangled some of this. I have the feeling Marty knew more about Leah's murder than he was telling."

"Wednesday night!" Doreen said, suddenly alert. "That's the night Marty was killed—and Luke was there!"

Jenny sighed. "Yes, about nine, I think."

"And the coroner says Marty was killed between nine and twelve." Doreen looked relieved. "Oh, Jenny, that may be just the bit of information Sheriff Turpin needed to solve the case. This could all be over soon—and we could get back to living normally again."

Sensing her mother's sudden optimism, Jenny felt only despondency. She found it hard to believe that the Luke Highbridge she was coming to know could have killed three people. Oh, he was proud—and he could be imperious—but he could also be gentle. And she didn't want to believe that he was a murderer.

"I think I'll go take some aspirin," she said, getting up, "and then I'm going to bake cookies. I—I have to keep busy."

Doreen followed her into the kitchen, sat at the bar and drank more coffee while Jenny mixed the batter. They talked little. Beast joined them and stretched out full length on the floor near the warm stove. But he watched Jenny's every movement alertly, as if he were aware of the tension in the house.

Jenny was taking the last sheet of cookies from the oven when Gerald returned. He came through the den to stand at the kitchen doorway.

Something in his expression alerted Jenny. "Is—is everything all right, Dad?"

He looked at her silently for a moment, then shifted his gaze to Doreen and said tonelessly, "My gun is gone."

Doreen stirred on her stool at the bar. "You took it to the sheriff, you mean?"

"No," Gerald said, scowling. "It wasn't in my desk. It's gone."

Doreen slid off the stool and stood staring at him fixedly. "Maybe you forgot which drawer."

Gerald was shaking his head. "I turned out every drawer in my office and the front desk."

"Could you have put it in the safe and forgotten it?" Jenny asked.

"I looked. That gun is not down there."

"I don't think you could have put it away in the house," Doreen said. "I would have run across it, cleaning."

"I know where I left it," Gerald insisted. "Somebody took it out of my desk."

"Was it loaded?" Jenny asked.

Gerald nodded.

Doreen gasped. "Did you tell the sheriff it's been stolen?"

Gerald made a harsh, sardonic sound.

"Oh," Doreen cried, "I don't suppose he believed you."

"He didn't say. Just looked at me and said, 'Interesting.'" He tried to laugh.

"What are you going to do now?" Doreen asked fearfully.

"Do? What can I do—except scrap my self-righteous editorial. I'm hardly in a position now to cast aspersions." Gerald made an effort to sound more cheerful. "It'll all come out in the wash, I guess. Well—what about a sandwich and some of those cookies, Jenny?"

"I'll get it," said Doreen.

Jenny didn't feel hungry. She went up to her room with Beast at her heels, his furry tail twitching restlessly. Closing her door, she went to sit on the window seat, and Beast leaped onto the cushion to rub against her arm. While she stroked him slowly, he curled up and was soon asleep.

Jenny looked toward the thick growth of trees surrounding the Tamaracks and admitted the doubts that were clamoring to be heard. What if her father had not wanted to turn his gun over to the sheriff? What if he had hidden it and then said that it had been stolen? If that were true, it meant he had something to cover up.

She let her forehead rest against the cold windowpane, appalled at the direction of her thoughts. But her mind continued to lead her down dark and twisting avenues of doubt. Could her father be a murderer?

Why? What reason could her father have for killing Marty? No! Jenny sat up, and a sob caught in her throat. It couldn't have happened. Someone must have stolen the gun, perhaps the person who had used it to kill Marty. One of the newspaper employees? In addition to Tom and Mazie, two other women worked for her father. She didn't know if either of them had even known Marty. Mazie had dated him of course, but that was more than two years ago. Mazie might have been dreadfully hurt by Marty's rejection of her, but if she were going to kill him, she would have done it immediately, in the first rush of humiliation and pain. No, it couldn't be Mazie. And Tom? Well, that was out of the question. She supposed Tom knew Marty, but they certainly hadn't known each other well enough to have the kind of disagreement that could lead to murder.

But it didn't have to be an employee who had stolen the gun. People passed in and out of her father's office at all hours of the day—advertisers, people wanting to place classified ads, friends. Gerald was not at his desk much of the time. Any number of people could have taken the gun.

The ringing of the phone made her jump. She hurried to her bedside table to answer, not wanting her parents to be disturbed. Snatching up the receiver, she said, "Hello."

"Jenny? It's Luke Highbridge."

"Yes?"

"What did you tell the sheriff about my visit to Marty Brubaker's apartment Wednesday evening?" He sounded terse and businesslike. She could not tell if he was angry, but he certainly did not sound happy.

"Only that you had been there," she replied, "and that you'd seen a scrapbook with Gideon Garfield's clippings. I'm sure you've heard by now that Marty and Garfield were one and the same man."

"Yes." Luke paused, and she heard far-away static on the line. "Evidently no one but Leah knew it—and that's strange." After a moment he asked, "Is that all you told the sheriff?"

"It's all I knew," said Jenny. "I had to tell him, Luke. He would have learned about your visit from someone else, if not from me."

"I know that, but I do think you might have warned me. He called me down to his office yesterday and grilled me—I believe that is the expression."

The indignant tone of his voice irritated her. "Well, I'm sorry if you were inconvenienced, but there is a murder investigation going on, you know."

"Mom's been upset all day," he went on, ignoring her sarcasm.

"She isn't the only one."

His interest was sharp. "What do you mean by that?"

"Nothing—" She hesitated. "Luke, is there a thirty-eight-caliber gun at the Tamaracks?"

The silence crackled with static. "Oh, I see. They must have identified the bullet that killed Marty, right? You've really got it in for us, haven't you, Jenny?"

"That's not true!" she said sharply.

"Well, I hate to disappoint you, but we do not own a thirty-eight. In fact, we don't have a hand gun in the house."

"What about Beau Gleason?"

Luke drew a short, impatient breath. "Beau has several guns, but I've never seen a thirty-eight and I've been in his apartment many times."

"He might keep it out of sight—in a drawer or something. Could you look? When he's not there, I mean."

He laughed shortly. "Jenny, I have no intention of searching Beau's apartment without his knowledge. I will ask him if he owns one, though. Incidentally, I spoke to him about the way he treated you when you came to the Tamaracks looking for your father. He admitted that he probably got too rough with you. By the way, he seems to think you're hiding something." There was amusement in the last remark.

"Talk about the pot and the kettle!" she sputtered.

He chuckled. "Anyway, I don't think you need worry about it happening again."

You certainly have more confidence in your caretaker than I do, thought Jenny. "How is Harold?"

"Better every day. The doctor has practically promised to let him come home before Christmas. His determination is really amazing."

"That's good. I know you and your mother are relieved. Since he's recovering so quickly, will he be back to work in the near future?"

"By spring, perhaps, but I'll be watching him closely to make sure he doesn't overdo."

"You still intend to stay, then?"

"I told you that." Luke paused. "Jenny, what's wrong? You sound odd."

"It's nothing," she said hastily. "I have a terrible headache."

"Dad asked for you again. I'd appreciate it if you could visit him in the next day or two."

"I—I don't know," she said hesitantly.

"If you really care about his recovery, you'll go."

"I don't want to run into Beau."

"He's hardly ever there now that Dad's better."

"All right," she said finally. "I'll try to make it Monday."

"Thank you," he said tersely. "Good-bye, Jenny."

Fourteen

When Jenny went to meet Gerald at the newspaper office Monday afternoon, Mazie was not in her usual place at the front desk. Hearing voices in her father's office, she walked to the open door. Gerald was seated behind stacks of papers, with Tom slouched against one side of the littered desk and Mazie standing near the other.

"Why did he insist on questioning us separately?" Mazie was saying, her voice shrill.

"He didn't want us to be able to compare stories," Tom explained quietly.

"I never saw the sheriff like that," Mazie went on, twisting nervous fingers around a pencil. "I have the feeling he thinks one of us did it. I don't mind telling you, I'm worried!"

Gerald, his elbows propped on the only bare spot on the desk, said, "Don't you see, Mazie? He *wants* us to worry. Then we might tell him something we wouldn't otherwise mention." He looked toward the door and saw Jenny. "Oh, hi, honey. Quitting time already?"

She nodded, coming into the room. "I gather Sheriff Turpin was just here."

Mazie's dark curls bobbed as she turned to look at Jenny. "For the last two hours. He made us come into Gerald's office, one at a time, and explain our whereabouts on the night Marty was murdered."

"Did you pass muster?" Jenny asked lightly.

"Not really," Tom said. "Gerald and I were working on the press that night, but we weren't here together every minute. Gerald went down to the Copper Kettle for sandwiches once, and later he had to go find the hardware-store manager to open up for us—we needed some screws and oil—and I went out for coffee a couple of times."

"I was home alone all evening," Mazie said. Her face looked chalky against her dark hair. There was a tight expression about her mouth. *This is doubly hard on her,*

189

Jenny thought, *because she loved Marty.* "Of course, I can't prove it. And he knew that Marty and I had dated before Marty took up with Leah. He asked if I'd felt angry when Marty dropped me. And he didn't seem to believe me when I said I hadn't known Marty was Gideon Garfield." She turned stricken eyes on Gerald. "I swear I didn't know it! I never saw that scrapbook, and Marty never said anything to me that would have made me suspect such a thing." Jenny saw a sheen of tears in Mazie's eyes before the other woman bowed her head to look at the floor.

"I know you didn't, Mazie," Gerald told her, "and I think the sheriff does, too. Leah didn't even tell her own sister."

Tom swiped at a falling lock of red hair. "I don't understand that. Marty and Leah were adults. Why did they hide Marty's identity? Unless he had a criminal record or a wife somewhere or—"

"No," Gerald interrupted. "Turpin checked him out. Apparently Marty never even got a speeding ticket, and there's no record that he was ever married. Leah might have wanted to keep it from Doreen, knowing she would disapprove of Leah's seeing Marty if she knew his true identity."

Jenny said, "But Aunt Leah never seemed to care what other people thought about her."

"I think it was Leah's idea, all right," Mazie said, "but not because she was worried about Doreen's reaction."

Gerald looked at her quizzically. "Why do you say that?"

"I hadn't thought about it until now, but the night Marty came by my place to tell me that Leah had refused to marry him—you remember, Jenny, I told you about that—he said something about being sick and tired of playing his part in Leah's little charade. And then he said it hadn't done him any good, anyway, and that she was up to something and he wished he knew what it was. I didn't understand what he was talking about, but he was so upset at the time I thought he probably wasn't thinking clearly." Mazie's voice caught suddenly, and Jenny changed the subject.

"Any word about your gun, Dad?"

Gerald shook his head. "The sheriff's trying to pin down when it was taken, but that's going to be hard. Tom was the only one I took into my confidence when I bought it, but he never saw it again after the day I showed it to him."

"There's only my word for that," Tom said wryly.

"Turpin wants the names of everyone who passed through this office during the past month—as near as we can remember." Gerald looked at Mazie. "I'll list everyone I can think of, and then we'll see if you can add to the list, Mazie."

Mazie nodded glumly. "Could run to over a hundred."

"A lot of them can be eliminated as possible suspects, I imagine," Gerald said.

"I'm not sure Turpin is eliminating anybody." Mazie shuddered visibly. "That man has blood in his eye."

"Logically," Gerald said, "the murderer was somebody who knew or had some contact with all three of the victims."

Mazie frowned, chewing the end of her pencil. "Let's not talk about this anymore. Murderer, victims—it's giving me the creeps."

"Why don't you go home, Mazie," Gerald said. "You've had enough for one day."

She flashed him a grateful smile that faded quickly. "I forgot. I rode to town with a neighbor this morning, and she won't be off work for over an hour yet."

"I'll take you home," Tom offered.

"Would you?" Mazie asked. "Gosh, I'd appreciate that, Tom. I'll go get my coat."

"I'd like to go by the hospital to see Harold," Jenny told her father after Tom and Mazie had left.

"Good idea," Gerald said, getting up carefully so as not to disturb the piles of paper on his desk. "Just let me lock up here."

In the car Jenny said, "I want to ask you, Dad—how did Sheriff Turpin really react when you told him your gun had been stolen?"

"I haven't the faintest idea," Gerald said, "but I know one thing. I wouldn't want to play poker with that man. Nothing shows on his face!"

"It opens up all sorts of possibilities, doesn't it?" Jenny

went on. "Especially if your gun turns out to be the murder weapon."

He looked at her sharply. "The gun could have been taken months ago. Somebody could have needed cash and pawned it for a few dollars. Besides, I think Turpin is shrewd enough to realize that if I were going to shoot somebody, I wouldn't do it with my own gun."

Jenny glanced at him hopefully. "And if the gun *was* taken months ago for some less sinister reason than murder, it may never turn up at all."

"I would rather have it turn up," said Gerald a bit dryly, "and be shown not to be the murder weapon. But if it was used to kill Marty Brubaker, I have a feeling it will definitely be found."

"You mean the murderer would want it to be found," Jenny said, "because it would point suspicion away from him."

"That thought has crossed my mind, but that presupposes the murderer took the gun specifically to kill Marty —and to do that, he would have to have known I had the gun in my possession. To my knowledge, only two people in town knew that—Tom and myself. I know I didn't kill Marty, and I'd wager everything I have that Tom didn't, either. He didn't even know him very well."

"Obviously somebody else knew about the gun," Jenny said quickly.

"Or happened upon it accidentally," Gerald said, adding, "at a rather auspicious moment."

His words puzzled her. "What do you mean?"

"I have a theory," he said. "I worked it out during the night hours when I couldn't sleep. What if Marty knew who killed Mary and Leah? He couldn't have known long, maybe only a day or two, or he'd have gone to the police. And what if, on impulse, he went to the killer and told him what he knew, perhaps threatened to expose him to the police. Loving Leah as he did, Marty wouldn't have been above wanting a little vengeance, twisting the screw to see the murderer squirm. The murderer knew he had to stop Marty or be exposed. And while he was caught in the dilemma of what to do about Marty, he found my gun."

"But why would he have been looking in your desk?" Jenny asked.

Gerald shrugged. "That's the one thing I haven't worked out, but a dozen people, possibly more, have spent time alone in my office during the past couple of weeks—in addition to my employees. Most of them were waiting to talk to me about an ad or something. If one of them was the murderer, and if Marty had accused him— or even hinted that he knew something—the murderer was undoubtedly in a highly anxious state of mind. He would probably have been restless, and he might have looked in my desk drawers absentmindedly simply because he couldn't sit still."

They had reached the hospital, and Gerald pulled into a parking space and switched off the motor.

Jenny put a hand on his arm as he started to open the car door. "Dad, has anyone from the Tamaracks been in your office during the past two weeks?"

He stared at her blankly for a moment. "Luke came by, soon after he arrived in town, to thank me for the moral support I'd given his mother."

"Was he alone in the office?"

"For only a few moments, I think. I found him there one day when I came back from lunch."

She swallowed the lump that appeared suddenly in her throat. "Anyone else?"

He spoke softly, as if he wanted to deny the implication of his words, and there was a sadness of manner that she had seen in him several times of late. "Beau Gleason brought Sarah by one afternoon. She wanted me to run an ad for a used hospital bed—for Harold when he goes home. I was in the pressroom when Mazie came back and told me they were there. I had to wash up before I could talk to them, but, to my knowledge, neither of them was left alone near my desk."

He did not wait for a further response from Jenny. He opened the car door and, without looking back, moved quickly into the brisk wind and up the front steps of the hospital.

Both disturbed and surprised, Jenny got out of the car to follow him. If what he said was true, neither Sarah nor Beau Gleason could have taken that gun. Her father could be mistaken, of course, and Sarah might have gone out to talk to Mazie, for example, leaving Gleason alone for a few minutes. But there was no doubt at all about Luke. He had been alone in her father's office during the past two weeks. Taken by itself, this fact meant little, but added to other things she knew about Luke, the weight of evidence against him could no longer be denied. He was with Marty during the time span the coroner had set for Marty's death, and he was the only person as yet known to have seen Marty that evening. Marty himself had voiced certain suspicions about Luke and the others living at the Tamaracks. For sixteen months there had been no murder in Pine Valley, and within days of Luke's return Marty was killed. For most of her life Jenny had disliked Luke; yet, as she walked the last few steps toward the front door of the hospital, a feeling that something very dear was slipping away possessed her. It was as if she had been cast adrift in unfriendlly waters only moments after having found something to cling to.

Someting to cling to? What a strange thought to cross her mind. Surely Luke Highbridge could not be thought of as an anchor, a place of safety—not for her, anyway. This was nonsense.

When she reached Harold's room, Gerald was sitting beside the bed. No one else was there.

Harold turned his head toward the door and motioned with his right hand for her to come nearer. "'I'm glad you've come, Jenny." The husky whisper of his voice sounded stronger. He turned to Gerald and croaked, "See where that nurse went will you, Gerald?"

Gerald nodded and left the room.

Harold's dark eyes surveyed Jenny's face. "Luke says you're still blaming us for Leah's death."

Startled, she looked into his eyes, trying to see if he was becoming agitated again, wishing fervently that the nurse would return. "I—I haven't said that."

"Luke is innocent! He was fond of Leah, and he was not the father of that other girl's child," he whispered hoarsely. "Mary Steed lied. You ask Luke. He'll tell you."

"Don't upset yourself," Jenny said gently, reaching to touch his hand.

"Leah knew," he said, his fingers tightening around hers.

She forced a smile and said, "It's all right, Harold."

"Leah knew Luke wasn't the father of that girl's child," he persisted with great earnestness.

"Did she tell you that?"

He shook his head on the pillow. "No, no, but she would have. She was going to tell us something, and then —but she knew something, something Mary Steed told her." This was the same thing Sarah had talked about, only Sarah had seemed convinced Leah thought Luke *was* the father of Mary's child.

Harold's plump, starched nurse strode briskly into the room on her rubber soles. "Here we are, Mr. Highbridge." She placed a glass of orange juice on the table next to Gerald's bed, found a flexible straw and thrust it into the glass.

Gerald stepped into the room then, and Jenny gently extricated her hand from Harold's grip.

The nurse bent over Harold. "Have a sip, now, Mr. Highbridge."

"No," grumbled Harold, "not now. I want to talk to my visitors."

The nurse set the glass back on the bedside table and bustled about for a moment, smoothing the sheet and plumping the pillow. Then she retired to her chair in the corner, casting a stern look at Jenny and Gerald.

"I want you to come to our open house," Harold whispered, looking at Gerald, "on Christmas Eve."

Gerald moved to the side of the bed. "Sounds like Doc Weaver is sending you home for Christmas. Doreen and I wouldn't miss your first party at home for anything."

"Will you come, too, Jenny?"

"Yes," she said, "of course I'll come."

"It'll be like old times," Harold told her solemnly, "when you used to come to the Tamaracks with Leah. We're going to banish all the ghosts, aren't we Jenny?"

She nodded reluctantly. What had he meant by saying that Leah knew Luke was not the father of Mary's child? Was his mind still confused? Or was it simply wishful thinking on Harold's part?

"Mr. Highbridge needs to rest now," the nurse said sharply.

Harold smiled feebly. "She's too bossy, that one." His husky whisper could be heard all over the room.

The nurse smiled thinly and came to Harold's bedside again. "Let's have your orange juice now and rest awhile."

"You rest," Harold grumbled. "I'm not tired."

The nurse made a clicking sound with her tongue and raised her eyes to gaze at the ceiling, as if this were just one small example of what she had to put up with from her cantankerous patient.

"We'll go now," Gerald said quickly.

"I'll see you both on Christmas Eve," Harold croaked as they left.

They left the hospital and walked to the car in silence. The air smelled as if fresh snow would arrive soon. Gerald rubbed ink-stained fingers across his forehead, as if he fought a headache.

In the car Jenny said, "Harold told me that Luke was not the father of Mary Steed's child and that Leah knew it."

"Of course he'd lie to protect Luke," Gerald said tiredly. "Harold has been known to lie in the past to get something that he wanted very much."

She had never heard him say anything derogatory about Harold before, and she looked at him with an air of surprise. Had Harold lied to take Sarah from Gerald years ago?

"The trouble with lying," he went on, "is you have to keep telling new ones to cover up the old."

"But what if it's true?"

He glanced at her with a pained scrutiny, "Listen to me, Jenny. Harold has found out about Marty's murder, and he's grasping at straws. If he had any knowledge that would have helped Luke's case sixteen months ago, why didn't he reveal it? Why has he waited until now to mention something so vital to the case? Think about it. Did you ever hear of Mary Steed having a boyfriend? Did you ever once see her in the company of a man?"

"No," she admitted.

"And ask yourself this: Why did she leave so suddenly,

if not to be near Luke? And why did she tell Beth Denton that Luke was the father of her child, if he wasn't? She couldn't have hoped to brazen out a lie like that."

Jenny could see the futility of trying to defend Luke. Perhaps she, like Harold, was grasping at straws.

"Then," she asked quietly, "you think Luke did kill Mary?"

"I haven't wanted to," Gerald said and when he did not go on to elaborate, she did not press him. Perhaps she din't want to hear what he might say. But after a moment his inherent sense of fair play seemed to win out, for he added, "I'm saying there is scant chance that anyone but Luke could have fathered Mary's child—and that's all I'm saying."

Tuesday morning Sheriff Turpin called Jenny at the library and asked her to come by his office during her lunch hour. When she arrived, he was sitting with his legs propped on his ancient desk, the mythology book open in his hands to the page where Marty had scrawled the note in the margin.

Looking up, he swung his feet to the floor, sat forward in his chair and tapped the open book with a stubby forefinger. "My hunch tells me the answer to Brubaker's death is here somewhere, Jenny."

She took the battered wooden chair beside his desk and slipped off her coat. "Are your hunches usually right, Sheriff?"

He waved the book at her. "At least half the time. The question here is, what was Brubaker saying he was sorry *for?* Deserting Leah years ago—crushing her skull with a rock—or someting else? Until I have more evidence to the contrary, I'm inclined to eliminate Brubaker as Leah's murderer."

"So am I," Jenny said.

The sheriff went on as if she hadn't spoken. "You said the words in that anonymous note of yours were cut from slick paper, the kind of stuff found in the magazines on the newsstand." He closed the mythology book and, putting it aside, made a steeple with his fingers. "We didn't find a single magazine in Brubaker's apartment. And my deputies have checked every place in town that sells magazines. Nobody remembers Brubaker ever buying one." He looked at Jenny thoughfully. "Conclusion: Brubaker did not read magazines and would not have had any on hand."

"As far as I know," Jenny said, "he didn't read much of anything except what was necessary for his job. He was in the library only once since I've been there."

"It's possible he could have gone out and bought a magazine for the purpose of cutting out words for an anonymous message—but I don't th'nk our mystery man did that. He'd have been afraid someone might remember it later, especially if he wasn't in the habit of buying magazines. No, he'd have used whatever was handy for the note." He stared at his steepled fingers. "So—I think we can eliminate him as Leah's murderer. Consequently, this belated apology to Leah"—he indicated the mythology book—"is not a murder confession."

"You are assuming that the same person who killed all three people sent my note?"

"That's my most promising theory at present," Turpin said, eyeing her steadily. "But I'm wondering why."

Jenny didn't catch his meaning. "Why what?"

"Why did the murderer see fit to warn you, when, as far as we know, none of the three victims received a warning?"

"Isn't it possible," Jenny ventured, "that somebody other than the murderer sent my note? Maybe somebody who thinks he knows who the murderer is but hasn't any real proof?"

Turpin nodded slowly. "Anything is possible at this point. But whichever, it seems clear that you are somehow a threat to the murderer. He doesn't want to kill you, but he wants you out of the way." He paused, then went on, "This threat to the murderer whatever it is, must be of recent origin. Otherwise, you would have received that warning months ago. Something you've learned lately—something you've said or done. Any ideas what that might be?"

"One," Jenny admitted with some reluctance. She went on to tell the sheriff of Beau Gleason's shooting at her outside the Tamaracks and her subsequent confrontations with the man, culminating in the one during which she had accused him of knowing the identity of the killer.

Turpin penciled some notes on a pad in front of him, but when he looked at her again, his face was expressionless. "Anything else?"

Jenny shook her head.

Turpin drummed the nub of the pencil against the note pad. "OK. Now, Jenny, I want you to try to remember everything you and Brubaker talked about the day he came to the library to check out the mythology book."

"He wanted to talk about Leah. It's strange, now that we know who he really was, but he also asked what I knew about Gideon Garfield. Maybe he was thinking of revealing his true identity and wanted to know how my family felt about him. I made it pretty clear that Mother would never forgive Gideon Garfield for the way he had treated Leah."

"I see," mused the sheriff.

"And then he seemed to want to know about Leah's breakdown in New York. From his reaction, I truly don't think he knew how deeply his desertion had affected her. In fact, he said that Leah had never told him any of it. He was hurt that she hadn't confided in him. That's why I think he was saying, in his note in the mythology book, that he was sorry about the desertion."

She paused and Turpin urged, "Go on."

She tried to remember that day in the library, and she saw again Marty's thick fingers gripping his knees tightly, revealing the tumbled state of his emotions. "He did say one thing that I thought was odd. He said that Leah wouldn't marry him because she loved someone else more."

Although Turpin's expression remained unchanged, Jenny saw a sudden glint of interest in his eyes. "Mention any names?"

"No. He—he did say he once had thought it was somebody at the Tamaracks."

The sheriff pursed his lips and stared at the pad on which he had been jotting.

"And," Jenny went on, "he said something had been worrying Leah before she died, but he didn't know what it was. When I tried to pin him down, he said he was probably imagining things because he didn't want to believe Leah hadn't loved him. Then"—she hesitated as the memories of her conversation with Marty came back, more clearly now—"he started to say something. I think he was going to tell me something he'd learned recently. He said, 'The other day . . .' But when I tried to get him to go on, he only said, 'Just a notion I had. Forget it.'"

Turpin scowled. "He didn't say anything to indicate what he was thinking?"

"No, and right after that he asked about the mythology book and checked it out."

The sheriff's sigh was the only outward sign of the disappointment he must be feeling. "That is all—absolutely all—you talked about?"

Jenny thought about the question for a moment. "When he first came in, I asked about the results of my blood test. I'd gone to the hospital a few days prior to that to give blood, and later Marty asked if he could do another test just to make sure everything was OK."

Turpin frowned. *"Was* everything OK?"

"Yes. He said both tests showed my blood count was good and I would be able to give blood when it was needed."

"Isn't it a bit unusual, though, to take a second blood test?"

"I suppose, but he had to be certain my count was high enough because I have a rare blood type and he wanted to put my card in his walking-blood-bank file."

After a silent moment, the sheriff said, "Anything else you can think of that might help me, Jenny?" When she shook her head, he asked. "You aren't going out much these days, are you?"

"Only when there are people about," she admitted. "I feel safe at the library and on Main Street."

He pressed his lips together. "Well, if you think of anything later, give me a call."

She said that she would and left Turpin's office. Walking along the dim gray hall of the old courthouse, however, she did think of something else, the mysterious disappearance of the biology book and its reappearance with several pages missing. It occurred to her that the missing pages had dealt with, among other things, human blood types. Could Marty have taken the biology book? But why? To keep someone else from reading those pages? Reaching the courthouse door, she pulled her hood up and stepped out into the cold December day. She remembered what James Elledge had said—there were other similar books at the hospital. Would Marty have taken it from the library, then? She frowned, trying to remember the sequence of events. No, Marty had come to the library *after* the book had disappeared. She turned the corner and, with the wind in her face, hurried toward the Main Street coffee shop. She puzzled for another few seconds over the biology book but finally dismissed it as having no bearing on the investigation.

Fifteen

Upon returning home that evening, Jenny discovered that the sheriff had also questioned Doreen. He seemed to feel that if anyone knew what was on Leah's mind in the days before her death, it would be the sister who had always taken care of her. Unfortunately, Doreen had been no more able than others to fathom Leah's thoughts at any time. After telling Jenny about her session with the sheriff, Doreen said, "He's questioned all the Curtisses and the employees of the newspaper, and from here he was going to the Tamaracks and the sawmill. Sheriff Turpin is really scattering his shots—on the off chance, I suppose, that one of them will hit something."

Hopefully, Jenny thought, someone among all the people being questioned would say something that would aid in tracking down the killer. She had to believe this, for the thought of never knowing, of spending the rest of the winter—and perhaps months afterward—suspicious of every unexplained look or comment, fearful of being alone, especially at night, was too horrible to contemplate.

Over dinner Gerald finally got around to informing Doreen that they were invited to the Christmas Eve open house at the Tamaracks. At that point Doreen confessed to having had another spell with her heart that morning. Ordinarily she would not have mentioned the incident for fears of worrying Gerald and Jenny, so Jenny suspected she was laying the groundwork for a later refusal to attend the open house, using her poor health as an excuse. Knowing how uncomfortable Doreen felt in Sarah's presence, Jenny couldn't blame her. However, when Gerald said that Harold had made a special point of inviting all three of the Curtisses, Doreen seemed to reconsider. "It's little enough to ask, isn't it, after all he's been through?"

And Gerald gave her a grateful smile and said, "We needn't stay long, but I know Harold will be hurt if we don't put in an appearance." He very prudently did not mention Sarah at all.

Jenny herself had reservations about going. The thought of being near Luke, possibly even being alone with him at some time during the evening, disquieted her. But she had promised Harold, and she felt obligated to keep her word.

Jenny managed to fill the cold December days with whatever activity was at hand. The newspaper announcement had brought piles of paperbacks into the library, donated for use in the book exchange. Consequently, during working hours she was kept very busy assisting patrons and cataloging and arranging the donated books. News of the exchange circulated quickly, and within a week of the newspaper notice the number of people coming into the library had risen dramatically.

Evenings and weekends she shopped for gifts, wrapped packages and made a variety of candies and cookies for the holidays. Thus the time passed quickly, and she found. that sometimes hours would go by without a thought given to the continuing murder investigation. Nor did she give much thought to the coming open house, deciding it was not even important enough to merit a new dress.

On Christmas Eve she kept the library open until noon, although few people found the time to come in. At lunchtime she rode home with Gerald and, her many activities of the past few days having finally caught up with her, went to her room for a long nap. She had already decided to wear her floor-length plum-colored velveteen skirt and a soft pink crepe blouse with a froth of pink lace at the neck. She slept so long that, when she awoke, it was time to get ready for the evening.

The Highbridges' open house proved, from Jenny's viewpoint, to be a mixed success. To begin with, snow had fallen most of the afternoon and continued well into the evening. Sarah, acting the gracious hostess, looked beautiful but distracted, so that her presence did little to foster a holiday air.

It was clear to Jenny that Sarah would have preferred a quiet day alone with her husband and her son. And, of course, by the time the evening crowd arrived, Sarah had been smiling and moving from one person to another, attempting to be welcoming, all afternoon. When Sarah's eyes met Gerald's, there was a woebegone look in them that was close to anguish. Jenny, who had never found herself so intensely in sympathy with Sarah before, shrank inwardly and did her best to avoid the woman for fear the wrong word might bring on a rush of frustrated tears. For Sarah's sake, Jenny wished Harold had not insisted upon the open house. It was obvious that the entertaining on top of the sheriff's investigation, which undoubtedly had been aimed to some degree at the Tamaracks, was too much for Sarah.

A young girl from the town, hired for the evening, took their coats at the door and directed them into the dining room, where lace-covered tables were laden with trays of tiny finger sandwiches, fondue dips, cheeses, meats, candies and cakes. Beau Gleason, in an ill-fitting brown suit, stood at another table serving coffee, punch or champagne, as requested. Jenny took a finger sandwich and champagne and wandered into the den, where there were even more people than in the dining room. Harold was ensconced near the fireplace in his shiny new wheelchair. His face, above the blue silk lounging jacket, was flushed with excitement at being surrounded by so many well-wishers and his pleasure at being home.

Jenny skirted the room and, to her surprise, saw Tom Irving and Mazie Jones standing unobtrusively in one corner. She made her way to them. "I didn't know you two were coming tonight."

Tom, looking casual but polished in a gray suit, smiled sheepishly. And Mazie giggled and said, "I'm only here as the guest of an invited guest." She pointed to Tom with her empty champagne glass.

Tom grumbled, "I'm sure Luke didn't think I'd come. He invited me to be democratic. So I decided to take him up on it and bring Mazie along for moral support."

"*I'm* having the time of my life," Mazie confided. "I've never been inside the Tamaracks before." She smiled happily. "I'm impressed!"

Jenny laughed, thinking that she herself had rarely seen the lovely old house looking so festive. Strands of holly tied with huge red velvet bows were strung everywhere.

Clumps of bright poinsettia, cedar boughs frosted with artificial snow, and mobiles of sequined balls and animal figurines glistened on all sides.

The ceiling-high tree, a fat pine heavily flocked with white and trimmed with red balls, candy canes and bells, claimed one corner of the large den. Each of the guests had been directed to find his gift from the pile beneath the tree. The parcels weren't tagged, except for being tied with red ribbon for the women and green for the men.

"Have you opened your gifts yet?" Jenny asked.

"That was the first thing we did," Mazie said. She extended her wrist from which dangled a tiny silver angel charm on a linked silver chain. "Tom got a tie tack."

"I think I'll claim mine now," Jenny said, moving away from the couple. As she crossed the crowded room, she examined the surprise she had felt upon seeing Tom and Mazie together. She wasn't jealous—her feelings for Tom could never go deeper than they did now, and she wished both of them well—but she had been surprised, because they had worked together for years and had never shown any interest in each other outside the office. Remembering Tom's offer to take Mazie home the afternoon Sheriff Turpin had questioned the newspaper employees, Jenny smiled, wondering what had happened on the drive across town. Well, she thought, they made a good-looking couple.

She had lost sight of her parents, and she had not, as yet, seen Luke at all. She didn't know whether to be concerned or relieved about that. Halfway across the room, Harold, in his chair by the fire, caught her eye and motioned for her to come to him.

As she did so, the group of people surrounding the chair moved back to make way for her.

Harold took her hand. "You look lovely tonight, Jenny," he said in his hoarse whisper.

"Thank you, Harold." She smiled down at him. His hand, pressing hers, was warm and pulsing with life.

"Where are Doreen and Gerald?"

"They're here somewhere," Jenny told him. "I expect they'll find you before long." She started to pull her hand away, but he held on.

"It's almost the new year, Jenny." His dark eyes glowed

with an intensity Jenny did not quite understand. "A new year and a new leaf—for all of us."

She did not see how the new year could be a fresh start for her family or for those at the Tamaracks unless the murderer were caught. Her hesitation must have shown in her manner, for Harold said, close to her ear, "I believe there will be no more tragedies. People will forget soon enough. Things will be as they were before, only better because Luke is home to stay."

Could he really believe what he was saying? she wondered, looking into the dark, burning eyes. "I don't think Sheriff Turpin will abandon the case so easily. And you have no way of knowing there will not be another murder."

He squeezed her hand in his effort to convince her—or was it to convince himself? "The sheriff is on the wrong track. Brubaker was an outsider, concealing his true identity. No man does that unless he has something to hide. Isn't it likely his murder had something to do with the double life he had?"

Jenny pulled her hand free, standing erect. "I would hardly say Marty was leading a double life. Gideon Garfield was a stage name, and that part of his life was behind him."

For the first time, Jenny noticed that the right side of Harold's mouth still drooped slightly. The clenching of his jaw muscles on the left made the sagging muscles more pronounced by contrast. "People can't separate the past from the present so handily," he insisted. "I'm convinced Brubaker left something besides his stage name behind him in New York, something he wanted to conceal. Perhaps gambling debts or some connection to illegal activities. That is what the sheriff should be investigating."

"I know that he has already done some checking into Marty's past and found nothing suspicious," Jenny said.

"He must dig deeper, then!" The effort of speaking was making Harold's neck muscles stand out like thick ropes. Jenny glanced around and saw Sarah making her way through her guests to her husband's chair. Sarah's gown of black jersey had been an unhappy choice. It only pointed up more vividly her pale, strained face. She smiled briefly when she saw Jenny and put her hand on Harold's shoulder as she spoke.

"The nurse says it's time for you to go to bed, dear. She's waiting for you upstairs."

Harold gave his wife an impatient sidelong glance. "Let her wait. I'm not tired, and I want to stay here and talk for a while yet." He turned back to Jenny. "Jenny and I were having a conversation."

"I'll come to see you in a few days," Jenny said quickly. "We can talk more then." She walked away from him before he had time to protest.

There had been fear in Harold's face, she realized as she made her way slowly through the press of laughing, chattering guests. Perhaps the sheriff was concentrating his investigation on Luke and his movements the night of Marty's murder. This would account for Harold's rather desperate insistence that Turpin should turn his attention to Marty's connections in New York. The elder Highbridge must be seething inwardly at being confined to a wheelchair while all of this was going on. No wonder Sarah looked so worried.

In spite of the festive air that was beginning to touch the party, much of the talk she heard around her had to do with business. Pine Valley was a lumbering town, and many of the people present were employed by the sawmill, the paper mill, or the plywood plant. As Jenny approached the Christmas tree, she saw Luke for the first time, standing near the snow-laden boughs with a group of Highbridge Corporation executives.

One gray-haired man was speaking fervently. "I know we've shortened the time between planting and harvesting by twenty years, but it has taken us half a century."

"The newer strains are of better lumbering quality," another man said.

"But can you imagine," said the first, "what this newest strain could mean to the industry? From planting to harvesting in thirty years!"

As she bent over the pile of packages beneath the tree, Jenny heard Luke say, "It's still in the experimental stages, Frank, and, from what I've heard, extremely susceptible to insects and disease."

"Increased spraying will take care of that."

She heard irony in Luke's reply. "And have the environmentalists on our necks again. That last series of protests cost us nearly a million for the pollution-control system. Not that I'm complaining. It was long overdue." If Luke was worried about the sheriff's investigation, it wasn't evident in his manner. He appeared relaxed in a gray flannel suit worn with a white shirt, open at the neck, and a cable-stitched, V-neck sweater.

Jenny moved farther away from the men, intent upon picking out her gift. It seemed almost a shame to tear into any of the elaborately wrapped parcels. She chose one arbitrarily and was reaching for it when there was a movement beside her. "Take this one."

Luke produced a package that had been tucked out of sight beneath one of the huge pine boughs. He handed it to her and watched as she unwrapped it. Inside was a bracelet of yellow gold with a single charm—but not an angel or a reindeer as Jenny had seen the other women wearing. Examining the small circle, Jenny saw that the head of Demeter had been etched with painstaking intricacy into the smooth gold surface.

She turned the circle over and found words engraved on the back: FOR JENNY, MAIDEN ALL LOVELY.

"That's Homer's description of Demeter," Luke said.

Uncertain, she looked into his face. She had thought before that he was relaxed, untroubled, but upon closer inspection she saw that brooding shadows touched his dark eyes. "Luke, I—"

But before she could go on, Susan Nelson, stunning in a halter-topped gown of emerald green, hurried up to them and clasped Luke's arm. "Here you are, darling. I've been searching everywhere for you."

"Hello, Susan. You're looking ravishing this evening." A shade had been drawn over his eyes, and the face he turned to the beautiful black-haired girl was mildly amused.

Susan glanced at Jenny. "It's Jenny Curtiss, isn't it? I haven't seen you in ages. How are you?"

Jenny met the girl's sharply curious gaze with what she hoped was a friendly smile. "Fine, thank you."

Susan's glance took in the gold bracelet dangling from Jenny's fingers. "You've opened your gift, I see." The perfectly arched black brows rose questioningly. "Oh, yours is gold. All the others I've seen are silver. And what's this?" She took the golden charm between her fingers.

"One of the Greek gods," Jenny said.

Susan dropped the charm and looked up at Luke, her head tilted to one side. "A bit inappropriate for a Christian holiday, isn't it, darling? But, then, I don't suppose you had anything to do with choosing these things." She laughed. "Sarah must have sent Beau or Beth to do the shopping. I wonder what other bloopers they've made?"

"Actually, I'm very pleased with my gift," Jenny said, looking at Luke, whose face betrayed nothing of what he was feeling. "If you two will excuse me," she went on, "I'll dispose of these wrappings." In her hurry to get away, she bumped into an elderly gentleman. "Oh, I'm sorry," she murmured and kept moving toward the door that led into the hall. Her thoughts were troubled with the memory of the unhappiness she had glimpsed in Luke's eyes, unhappiness which had been quickly concealed for Susan's benefit. She didn't know what she would have said if Susan had not interrupted them. The words engraved on her charm tumbled in her brain, confusingly enigmatic. FOR JENNY, MAIDEN ALL LOVELY. Luke had been quick to inform her that the description referred to Demeter, as if to make certain she didn't draw a wrong conclusion. Yet, in spite of what Susan had said, she knew he must have chosen the bracelet, since he was the only one of the Highbridges who had seen her wearing Leah's medallion.

She followed the long hall to the kitchen, where Beth Denton was supervising two girls in green-and-white uniforms as they arranged hors d'oeuvres on silver trays.

A long-suffering smile crossed the stout housekeeper's face as she saw Jenny in the kitchen doorway.

"I'm looking for a trash basket," Jenny said, coming into the kitchen.

"Over there in the corner," Beth said. "No, Elsie, not like that! Here, put the ones with the avocado spread next to the pimiento and cream cheese. There. You see how much prettier that is?"

Looking slightly harried, Elsie nodded and, followed

by her uniformed companion, carried the freshly filled trays toward the dining room.

Beth shook her head. "These town girls don't have the first idea how to serve at a doings like this." She hunched her broad shoulders and gave a resigned moan. "Ah, well, I have to make do with what I have. If Mr. Luke stays on, we may have to hire another girl full-time. Having folks in the house again means more entertaining. Might be kinda nice, at that. We haven't had much gaiety around here for a while. Not since—" She shot Jenny a quick, embarrassed look.

Glancing away, Jenny tossed the wrappings into the waste basket and turned back to face the housekeeper. "Not since Leah and Mary were murdered. That's what you started to say, isn't it?"

Beth nodded glumly and stooped to open the automatic dishwasher. "Better unload this batch so I can wash some more glasses."

Thoughtfully, Jenny fastened the bracelet around her right wrist, then said, "Do you mind if I stay and visit a few minutes?"

Beth was putting the clean dishes into the overhead cabinets. "I'd enjoy that, Jenny. Sit down at the table, and I'll get you something to drink. What would you like?"

Seeing the large percolator at one end of the cabinet, Jenny said, "Coffee. I'll get it. Where's a cup?"

Beth handed her one and, after filling it, Jenny went to sit at the kitchen table.

Beth leaned against the stove and looked at Jenny. "I didn't mean to bring up Leah's death, but with that lab technician getting shot the other night, I'm a bit on edge. Reckon the whole town is."

"Sarah looks strung out," Jenny said.

Beth began to stack dirty glasses in the dishwasher. "Sheriff's been here three or four times, asking all kinds of questions. And what with bringing Mr. Highbridge home and finding a nurse to care for him, it's all been awful hard on her."

Jenny sipped the strong coffee. "Has the sheriff questioned you again since Marty's death?"

"Oh, yes," Beth said heavily. "He's questioned all of

us, but Mr. Luke more than the rest. That boy seems to have nothing but bad luck, being at that Marty Brubaker's apartment the night he died and all." She sprinkled detergent into the dishwasher, flipped the door shut and turned on the machine. Then she came to sit across from Jenny, her big-boned face flushed with the kitchen heat. "Now, I ask you, Jenny, how could the sheriff suspect Mr. Luke of killing that man? Why, that's the craziest thing I ever heard of!"

"His questioning Luke," Jenny said haltingly, "doesn't necessarily mean he suspects him of shooting Marty."

Beth grimaced. "But coming after that Steed girl's murder and all the talk that went around then, it sure doesn't look good for Mr. Luke." She paused, pursing her lips. "Sometimes I wish I'd kept my big mouth shut when Mary died."

"But you had to tell what you knew," Jenny said, "that Luke was the father of Mary's baby."

Beth gazed at her reflectively. "I swear I'd think that child lied about Mr. Luke if I hadn't had to drag it out of her. She sure didn't intend to tell me or anybody, that's for sure."

Curious, Jenny asked, "How did you get her to talk?"

"She'd been drooping around here for days, and I knew something was wrong. Then I found her urping up her toenails one morning, and all of a sudden I knew what it was. 'So, you've got yourself in the family way,' I says to her while I held a cold cloth against her head. And she looked up at me with the scariest eyes I ever saw. The poor child was terrified. So I tried to calm her down, and I says, 'You'd best be telling the father and getting yourself married. It won't be the first baby to come too soon.'" Beth glanced down at the hands that rested in the lap of her white apron.

"What did she say to that?" Jenny asked.

Beth looked up with a little frown. "Said she could never tell the baby's father anything. Said she was in an awful fix and didn't know what she was going to do about it. But I says nonsense, she had to tell the father. The man's always at least half to blame. And then her eyes got big and she began to shake her head and said, No, she couldn't ever tell the father, that he couldn't marry her anyway, and then she started sobbing like her heart would break." Beth drew a long, unhappy breath. "Well, it didn't take much thinking to add it up. She'd been mooning after Mr. Luke ever since she came to work here, and I don't suppose you can expect a man to turn down what's offered so freely."

"Did Mary know what you were thinking?" Jenny asked.

"Oh, I just blurted it out, I was so stunned. I says, 'It's Mr. Luke, ain't it, Mary?' Well, of course, then I knew why they couldn't marry. Can you picture any more mismatched pair than that? Besides, Mr. Luke didn't care no more for Mary than he did his hunting dogs—not as much, probably."

"Mary's cousin told me that her parents would have washed their hands of her if they'd known. She really was in deep trouble, Beth. But surely the Highbridges would have taken care of her and the baby until she could get on her feet."

Beth looked at her hands again. "That's what I tried to tell Mary, but she grabbed hold of my arm and begged me not to breathe a word to anybody. Said she'd think of what to do, but she didn't want the Highbridges to know. Made me swear on the Bible not to speak a word about her condition." She shook her head. "What could I do? I promised to keep her secret. And I did, until the sheriff came around, after she was killed, asking questions. Asked me point-blank if Mary had ever said anything to me about being pregnant. Well, I couldn't lie. So I told him about that conversation Mary and I had. It was the only time she ever mentioned the subject to me, and she died a few days later."

Jenny swirled the remaining drops of coffee in the bottom of her cup. "Beth, do you think Mary told Luke after all?"

Beth stared at her. "No. I'd bet my life on it. He didn't know she was pregnant, so he didn't have any reason to kill her, Jenny. I don't care what the sheriff thinks." She bent forward and said with great earnestness, "Mr. Luke didn't do any of this. I watched that boy grow up. He was always high-spirited but never mean. Why, he wouldn't have harmed a hair on Leah's head. She used to tramp through the woods with him and tell him stories. He loved her, like we all did."

Their glances caught, and Jenny tried to push back the shadow of fear that hovered in the room. "Then, who could it have been, Beth?"

The housekeeper's glance slid to the window over the sink, where the black night pressed against the glass, and she shivered. "I don't know, Jenny. I don't know, but I sure do wish they'd catch him."

They sat in silence for a moment, each occupied with her own thoughts. Then they heard the voices of the two serving maids in the hallway.

"I'd better go back to the party." Jenny got up.

"Come and see me again," Beth said, "when I'm not so busy."

"I will," Jenny told her.

The girls entered the kitchen then, one of them carrying a stack of empty trays. "I swear I don't know where all that food is going," Jenny heard one of them say as she walked down the dimly lighted hall toward the front of the house.

Passing the den on her way to the powder room, she almost ran into Tom. "Oh, I'm sorry. I didn't see you standing there."

"I came out here to look for Mazie. I lost sight of her in the crowd. Have you seen her?"

"No, but if I do, I'll tell her you're looking for her."

He peered down at her for a moment. "I saw you talking to Luke beside the tree a while ago, and I realized why you're different lately."

"I don't understand," she said, beginning to feel uncomfortable there in the dark hallway with Tom.

"I think you do, Jenny. You've fallen in love for the first time in your life. Ever since we started dating, I've wanted to see that look in your eyes—only I hoped it would be there for me."

"Tom, I—"

He cut in. "Don't bother denying it. Your face is an open book. You never learned to dissemble, did you? You're in love with Luke Highbridge, and I hope to God he doesn't hurt you too badly." He seemed to be holding himself stiffly erect, as if he had to restrain himself. "He always takes what he wants, and he's never had to pay. Only he will pay for Mary, I swear it." Then, before she could reply, he turned and walked away. She stared after him. Why should he say those things to her? Because he was wrong, she told herself. She had not fallen in love with Luke; she couldn't have. She shook off her disquiet and continued down the hallway. The thick carpeting silenced her footsteps, so that the couple standing close together in the dark corner ahead did not hear her approach. When she became aware of them, she hesitated, wondering whether to make her presence known or to turn and go back to the kitchen. Before she could decide what to do, however, the man spoke, and she realized with a start that it was her father.

"You must get hold of yourself."

"Sheriff Turpin thinks it's Luke, Gerry. He keeps coming back to ask more questions." Sarah Highbridge's voice, though low, was taut with a nervousness that verged on hysteria.

"He can't arrest him without evidence, Sarah, and we must believe he won't find it."

The soft noise Sarah made was half laugh, half sob. "Even you aren't sure of his innocence. Oh, dear God . . ." Her voice trailed away as if she were momentarily overcome with the hopelessness of the situation, but after a moment she went on, "Besides, there *is* evidence, even if it is all circumstantial, and innocent men have been convicted of crimes before this."

"It would be hard even to bring the case to trial without the murder weapon, and Turpin knows it. Try to hold on to that. You are getting yourself so worked up you're making yourself ill."

The two moved closer together in the shadows, and Jenny sensed that her father had drawn Sarah against him to comfort her. She heard Sarah's soft, muffled sobs now. Riveted to the spot, she didn't dare move for fear of being noticed. If she had been going to make her presence known, she should have done it earlier.

Sarah was saying, "Harold is beside himself. Everybody keeps saying how wonderful he looks, how happy, but it isn't happiness, Gerry. The unnatural flush that's been on him tonight is caused by anxiety and anger because he can't get out of that chair and help Luke. He —he could have another stroke—"

There was a long pause during which Gerald murmured something Jenny could not understand. And then Sarah said, "He refuses to go upstairs to rest, but the nurse says he must."

"Would you like me to have a try at convincing him?" Gerald asked.

Sarah stepped back as if she felt a sudden necessity to put distance between herself and the man who had been holding her in his arms. "Oh, would you, Gerry? He might listen to you."

The two walked down the hall then, away from Jenny. Jenny did not move for several moments, wanting to give Gerald and Sarah time to cross the foyer and head back through the dining room to the den. A knot had formed in her stomach as she had watched Sarah being held close in her father's arms, even though everything her father had said could be construed as the giving of comfort to an old friend. Still, the sight of them together like that had sent a feeling of loss stabbing through her.

She walked slowly toward the foyer then, still pondering what she'd seen and heard.

Jenny was startled by the sound of the study door being opened and dismayed when Doreen stepped into the foyer. Had her mother overheard the conversation between Gerald and Sarah in the hallway? Had she come in search of Gerald and, upon seeing him with Sarah, stepped into the study to avoid a confrontation? Doreen's face appeared pale, but that could have been a trick of the soft lighting.

Seeing her daughter, Doreen said with what seemed to Jenny artificial brightness, "Oh, there you are, Jenny. Shirley was asking for you. Have you seen her?"

"No." Jenny studied her mother's face with concern. "I was in the kitchen with Beth Denton."

In the silence that followed, Doreen glanced behind her at the study door. "I was looking for my coat. They ran out of closet space and put some of the wraps in the study."

"Are you leaving already?"

"No, not just yet. I wanted the lipstick I left in my

coat pocket. I thought I could use a bit of color." From the look of Doreen's white lips, she had not found the lipstick.

"Would you like me to help you find it?"

"No," Doreen said quickly, "it's not that important. I want to speak to Harold before he retires." She blinked suddenly several times, as if she fought to hold back tears.

Jenny took a step toward her. "Mother—"

Doreen's lips curved in the caricature of a smile. "If I don't go, I'll miss Harold." With that she hurried toward the living room, moving quickly out of Jenny's line of vision.

Jenny bit her bottom lip, struggling against the desire to follow her mother and offer comfort, but she knew that would only embarrass Doreen. It would be best to pretend she hadn't seen Gerald and Sarah together in the hall. This, at least, would spare Doreen the humiliation of knowing others saw the secret meeting. Gerald had only been trying to calm Sarah, Jenny told herself, and to put any other connotation on what she had seen would be unfair to everyone concerned. But the knot, though slowly uncurling, still lay in the pit of her stomach, and she wanted to be alone for a few more minutes before going in search of Shirley. She stepped into the study and closed the door behind her.

In the book-lined room, sounds of the festivities were muffled and seemed far away. Sighing, Jenny walked slowly across the tan carpet toward the massive desk, where a single lamp had been turned on, leaving the corners of the dark-paneled study in shadow. Coats, the overflow from the foyer guest closet, were heaped on top of the desk.

Skirting the desk, she stood at the window behind it and looked out into deep darkness relieved only slightly by the peripheral glow of the yard lights around the corner in front of the house. Squinting into the pale glint of light, Jenny could not detect falling white flakes. It would appear the snow had stopped. Christmas day would be quiet with the hush of so much snow on the ground, except perhaps for the laughter of children trying out new sleds.

Absentmindedly nibbling her bottom lip, she wished she felt more in a holiday mood, but with a murderer who killed three times loose on the town and with people she knew under investigation, the coming day promised little gaiety for her or her family.

Sarah was convinced the sheriff thought Luke was the murderer, and it was true the circumstantial evidence against him was strong. He had been in Marty's apartment the night the lab technician was killed, and he had been the father of Mary Steed's unborn child. Jenny thought back over her conversation with Beth Denton, realizing for the first time that it had been Beth, not Mary, who named Luke as the baby's father. But Mary had not denied it. It came to Jenny that she was hoping for some scrap of evidence to support Luke's innocence, but there didn't seem to be any. Although the study was warm, she shivered, blinking to clear the moist film from her eyes.

She heard the study door behind her open and close and, feeling regret at the interruption, turned to see Luke standing there. She did not know if the sudden racing of her heart was fear or something else.

"Hiding from someone?" His dark eyes swept over her with a curious intensity.

"No." She pressed her lips together on the word.

He smiled fleetingly. "You look as if you might have been crying. Are you hurt because Tom Irving brought another woman tonight?"

She manged to laugh. "Don't be ridiculous. I told you Tom and I are only friends."

"Then, why have you shut yourself away here, with a party going on out there?"

When she didn't answer, he cocked his head to one side and gazed at her speculatively. His glance followed the line of her throat and breast in a bold sort of way that made her cheeks grow warm.

Flustered, she said haltingly, "I—I want to thank you for the bracelet. You must have gone to a lot of trouble to find it."

He shrugged carelessly. "No trouble at all. I had it made."

She stared at him. Such a special order must have cost a great deal. "Why?"

He was silent for a moment, holding her eyes with the luminous depths of his own. "For a lot of reasons, which I won't go into at the moment. Let's just say I thought it would please you."

Nervously, she fingered the lace at her throat, and her glance fled to a shadowy corner of the room.

"Does it bother you that I wanted to please you?" he asked quietly. He took several steps toward her, which caused her to stiffen defensively.

"What bothers me," she said, "is that I think there is more to it than that. I'm not so naive as to believe I'm the first girl you've ever given a special present. There must have been many others. I'm sure you have lost count by now."

"I won't deny that," he said, an edge of amused irony in his voice. He was standing beside the desk, close enough for her to see the almost imperceptible shifting of his dark brows downward.

Somehow she managed to whip up a semblance of indignation as protection against the strange weakness in her legs. "But to give it to me under Susan's nose!"

He frowned darkly. "If you will recall, we were alone beside the tree when I gave it to you. I had no way of knowing Susan would appear at that moment."

"And that is supposed to make it all right?"

He grimaced in irritation. "I fail to see what you are driving at."

His casual dismissal of the girl he was supposed to marry in June sent a flash of anger through her. "No honorable man would give such a—a special gift to one woman when he is engaged to another!"

To her amazement, he threw back his head and laughed. "Why are you so shocked? Haven't you heard? I'm not an honorable man. Almost anyone in Pine Valley will tell you that."

Jenny tossed her hair furiously. "Oh, I feel sorry for Susan!" She tried to sweep past him, but he grabbed her arm and whirled her around to face him.

"You seem to be laboring under the false impression that Susan is my fiancée." The words had a sharp, biting edge. "Nothing could be further from the truth, I assure you."

His fingers gripped her arms through the thin crepe of her blouse, making it impossible for her to move. "Do you take me for a fool! Tammy Nelson told me you and Susan plan to be married in June!"

His eyes widened, and an angry flush crept across his prominent cheekbones. "No doubt she was repeating what Susan had told her. Well, just for the record, I have no intention of marrying Susan in June or at any other time."

"Don't you think you should inform her of that?" Jenny shot back.

He made a sardonic sound. "Oh, I have! But Susan is a woman who doesn't listen to what she doesn't want to hear. I'll make her listen this time, though. There will be no further misunderstanding, believe me."

"Susan can hardly be blamed for misunderstanding," Jenny said. "When—when you pay a woman extravagant compliments, saying she looks ravishing, she is bound to jump to the conclusion you feel something for her."

Abruptly, his grip on her arms loosened, although he still held her immobile, and a maddening grin curved his wide mouth. "Why, Jenny Curtiss, I do believe you're jealous."

"Jealous!" she sputtered. "Oh, you are—you are the most—"

But she didn't finish, for he pulled her against his body, and his mouth came down on hers in a harsh, demanding kiss that took the words away, along with her breath, and left her defenseless and terribly frightened by her own shattering response. She seemed to have lost all control of her body, for her mouth under his was returning the kiss hungrily, and the strong hands moving over her back sent a pleasurable thrill through her that she wanted to go on and on. Then his hand strayed to the front of her blouse and rested warmly on her breast, sending such a warm surge of weakness over her that she would have fallen if he hadn't been holding her. Dizzied and horrified, she manged to gather the few remaing shreds of common sense left to her and turned her face away from his ravaging kiss.

Abruptly, he let her go. She staggered and steadied herself by grasping the edge of the desk. The dark eyes looking into hers were still liquid with desire, but the black brows were drawn together in an angry scowl.

"What are you afraid of, Jenny?"

She turned away, staring blindly through the window into the dark night. She drew a steadying breath. "I will not be another of your throw-aways, like Mary Steed."

He whirled her roughly to face him again, but whatever softness had been in his eyes a moment before was gone now. "Listen to me. Mary Steed was nothing to me—less than nothing. I was not the father of her child. I never even touched her."

She wanted desperately to believe him, but if Luke had been the child's father, he could not be expected to admit it, could he? And there had been no other man in Mary's life.

He must have read the doubt in her face, for he cursed furiously. "Why should you believe me?" he said and stalked out of the room.

Alone in the study, Jenny felt a fleeting regret over the loss of the placid life she had led before Luke's return to Pine Valley. These days she hardly recognized herself. The conflicting emotions he aroused in her were new to her experience and beyond her understanding. Always there was this feeling of being pulled in opposite directions where he was concerned. Several minutes passed before she felt calm enough to rejoin the party.

Returning to the dining room, she stood hesitantly near the door, looking for her parents. Lately she was often ill at ease when she was with people outside her own family. The anonymous note, the sheriff's warning not to go out alone, the confusion over her feelings where Luke was concerned—all combined to leave her on edge and uncertain. It seemed hardly credible that only a few weeks earlier she had felt safe and contented in this town.

She saw Susan Nelson across the room, and then the dark-haired girl made her way to Jenny's side.

"I thought I would give you some advice," Susan said abruptly. "I wouldn't want you getting the wrong idea about that bracelet the Highbridges gave you. Luke had nothing to do with it, you know."

Jenny had a sudden desire to see Susan's smug smile disappear. "Has he told you that?"

Susan laughed. "Surely you don't think he picked it out himself—just for you. Aren't you taking a casual skiing date a bit too seriously?"

So Tammy had told her about seeing Luke and Jenny at the ski lodge. "I wasn't aware that it was a date," Jenny retorted. "Thank you for enlightening me."

Susan's blue eyes narrowed, and there was venom in her tone. "You are out of your league, Jenny. Luke enjoys his conquests, but he becomes bored very quickly. I'm going to marry him, and if I were you, I'd think seriously before getting involved in a relationship that can't possibly last more than a few weeks. I have no intention of tolerating Luke's little flirtations after we are married."

Jenny felt her cheeks flaming. "I don't think we have anything more to say to each other." She turned her back on Susan and walked to the punch bowl, helping herself to a cup of punch that she didn't want. She was aware, after a moment, that Susan had left the room and, her hand trembling, Jenny set the full cup down on the lace tablecloth and walked away from it, going back to a place near the door. As she stood there, the conversation of two women who were helping themselves from one of the buffet tables reached her.

"Mrs. Nelson says that Susan is taking several months' leave from her job to be near Luke. I must say he wasn't acting like a bridgegroom-to-be earlier this evening. Susan kept losing him."

The second woman's words were lightly mocking. "Perhaps Luke is up to his old tricks. A few more wild oats before the wedding."

"From what his mother says, he's been too busy at the office to have much time for that sort of thing. And, besides, he's with Susan now. I just saw them together in the hall, and from what I observed, he's being as attentive as any girl could want. In fact, he was pulling her along after him in search of a private spot, I imagine."

The second woman laughed. "Well, if any woman can tame him, Susan Nelson can." They moved off together to have their champagne glasses refilled.

Jenny left the dining room quickly to find an empty corner in the den where she could stand unobtrusively looking at the other guests. The surge of anger that swept through her was surprising. Luke had left her in the study to go in search of Susan. So much for his insistence that Susan had the wrong impression about their relationship. While making a play for Jenny in the study, he had been planning how to keep Susan satisfied, as well. Jenny had not known that anything could stir her to such furious jealousy. For just an instant she had to restrain herself lest she set out to find Luke and unleash her indignation on him. It would do no good to make a scene.

Very soon Shirley found her. "Why are you over here in this corner alone? I've been looking for you. Oh, isn't this a fantastic party?"

"I've been circulating," Jenny said, "but I knew if I stopped here for a minute, you'd show up." She changed the subject quickly. "You look marvelous in that dress! Red is definitely your color."

Shirley beamed. "That's what Kent says."

"Where is he, by the way?"

Shirley glanced around idly. "Oh, I saw him talking to Tom and Mazie a while ago." Turning back to Jenny, she added in low tones, "Hey, what about *that* twosome? Have you and Tom had a fight?"

"No," Jenny said. "I guess we just don't enjoy each other's company as much as we once did. It's best that we both find other interests. Mazie is a nice person. I hope the two of them see more of each other."

Shirley's dark brows lifted. "You really mean it, don't you? But I still think Tom's crazy about you."

Before Jenny could think of a suitably noncommittal reply, Gerald joined them. "We're ready to go home," he said to Jenny. "Are you?"

"Kent and I could drop you off later," Shirley offered.

"No. I'll go with Mother and Dad," Jenny said, relieved because an ordeal was almost over.

She found Sarah and offered her thanks for the evening, then left with her parents. The drive home was a silent one. Upon reaching the house, Doreen pleaded a headache and went directly to bed. Gerald went to sit in front of the den fireplace, and since he did not seem to want company Jenny bid him good night and retired to her room.

Beast greeted her from her bed with a quick, indifferent glance, then promptly went back to sleep. She un-dressed hastily and turned out the light, shifting the cat to one side so that she could crawl beneath the covers. She lay thinking about the evening, trying to sort out her reactions to all that had happened. Every time she was near Luke Highbridge, she was more drawn to him, on the one hand, and more frightened of him, on the other. If only there were someone she could talk to about her growing confusion, someone she could trust. But *who?* Shirley, whose emotions were simple and straight-forward, would never understand. Jenny shrank from going to her mother because Doreen had more than enough to deal with at the moment. And she felt more and more that she could not go to her father, either. Lately the complete trust she had always had in him was beginning to crack. She did not know how seriously he was involved with Sarah Highbridge or whether he was as innocent in his knowledge of the whereabouts of the missing revolver as he pretended.

It appeared she must keep her own counsel. Grad-ually weariness began to have its way, and she dropped into a heavy sleep in which there were no dreams.

Sixteen

Christmas day appeared festive on the surface, but Jenny was aware of the strain underlying the exchange of gifts and the lavish meal that followed, causing all three of the Curtisses to be somewhat subdued, even though each tried to hide it from the others.

She regretted her decision to keep the library closed until the 27th, wanting to get out of the house and back to work. On the day after Christmas, which fell on Monday, Gerald worked at the newspaper until noon, then returned to the house for lunch with Doreen and Jenny. There wasn't much going on along Main Street, Gerald told them as they sat down to a turkey casserole, but the street crew was clearing the main thoroughfares, and no snow was forecast for the next few days.

They were just finishing a fruit dessert when the doorbell chimed. Gerald went to answer and admitted Sheriff Turpin. Jenny and Doreen, hearing Turpin's voice, went into the den, where the sheriff was removing his overcoat.

"Hello, Jenny, Doreen." Turpin whipped off his stocking cap and tossed it atop his coat, then warmed his hands at the log fire. After a moment he turned his back to the fireplace and said, "I have some news for you, Gerald. Your gun was found this morning."

Gerald lowered himself slowly into an armchair and looked at the sheriff expectantly. "Well, that's a big help to you, isn't it?" The words sounded sincere, but Jenny knew from what he had said to her that he had mixed feelings about the gun's turning up.

She was sitting beside Doreen on the divan, and now she glanced at her mother to see how she was taking the news. Doreen's hazel eyes regarded the sheriff with something like relief in them. It seemed clear to Jenny that her mother hoped the gun's reappearance would clear Gerald of whatever suspicions the sheriff might have been entertaining about him. "Where did you find it?" she asked.

Turpin scratched his bald pate. "Luke Highbridge brought it to my office."

At this information, Gerald seemed to sag against his chair cushion. "Oh, my God . . ." he murmured.

Jenny had an urge to leave the room so she wouldn't have to hear any more. The wrench of fear in the area of her heart was very painful.

"You mean he confessed to the murders?" Doreen asked, incredulous.

Turpin gazed from one face to the other, shaking his head. "All nice and neat like? Far from it. Luke claims he found it in a bureau drawer in his bedroom and has no idea how it got there."

Doreen's gasp was disbelieving, but no less than Gerald's stricken expression. Perhaps he was thinking of what this would do to Sarah.

"This," Jenny ventured, "doesn't prove that gun was the murder weapon."

The sheriff said, "We just finished the ballistics and firing tests. It's the murder weapon, all right."

Gerald's hand passed over his eyes.

Turpin said musingly, "If Luke Highbridge killed those people and then turned in the murder weapon from the third killing, he is either very clever or very stupid. I only wish I knew which."

"Well, he's not stupid," Doreen said. "You can be assured of that."

Turpin seemed to shake himself from reverie. "No, I didn't really think he was." He picked up his coat and hat and put them on. "I'll be in touch, Gerald." He looked about the room, and there was the hint of reined-in excitement in his manner. "Things are coming to a head now. I have a feeling we've got the killer on the run, and that is the time when he is most likely to make a mistake."

He left the den, dismissing Gerald's offer to see him out. When Turpin was gone, Doreen said, "Maybe he got tired of the deception. A guilty conscience can be a terrible thing to live with. It must be a relief to confess after months of covering up."

"Luke hasn't confessed to anything," Gerald muttered, but his attempt to defend Luke seemed halfhearted to Jenny.

"Sometimes," Doreen said, "people who do things like that—take human lives—can't bring themselves to confess openly, so they provide clues that will lead to their capture. Subconsciously, they *want* to be caught." She sighed unhappily. "I don't suppose they will be able to keep this from Harold. It could cause a relapse in his condition, I'm afraid."

"Sarah will try to protect him," Gerald said, his brow wrinkling.

"I'm sorry for the Highbridges," Doreen said, "but if this leads to an arrest, at least the rest of the town can sleep easier."

Suddenly, Jenny could not bear her parents' seeming certainty that the discovery of the gun in Luke's belongings meant he was the killer. She got to her feet. "Excuse me. I'm going out for a while."

"Going out!" Doreen sounded alarmed. "Where?"

"For a short walk," Jenny said. "It's broad daylight, and I won't be gone long." Before either of her parents could protest further, she left the den, put on her coat and fur-lined boots and let herself out the front door.

Outside, she picked her way through the deep snow on the sidewalk and thought about the small lake at the foot of the mountain that rose behind the Tamaracks. The lake was not on Highbridge property but was on open land between the back of the Fir Street lots and the Tamaracks' grounds. It was in full view of several houses and, with school being out for the Christmas holidays, there would in all likelihood be children ice-skating on its frozen surface. Jenny decided to walk in that direction.

She pulled on her gloves, drew her hood up against the cold. Fortunately, even though the temperature was well below freezing, there was no wind and the sky was clear, the winter sun shining, reflecting brilliantly on the snow. As she walked, making fresh tracks in the snow, she was only half aware of the cold powder that sifted over her boot tops from time to time, wetting her jeans. She wondered if her parents were right about Luke. This possibility, which once she had been able to consider without a qualm, now seemed almost too painful to be borne. Perhaps that was why she was finding it so difficult to accept. If Luke were the killer, would he be so daring as to turn in the murder weapon? Without the gun, the case against him was really quite flimsy. And, as her mother had said, Luke wasn't stupid. Had he decided that producing the gun voluntarily would rebound to his seeming innocence more than disposing of it where it could not be found?

As Jenny had expected, several children were ice-skating on the lake. She found a spot near the lake's edge where she could watch them and at the same time be somewhat sheltered from their view by a clump of wild-growing shrubbery.

Most of the children were pre-teens, brightly clad and exuberant in spite of their less than expert skating ability. They were having glorious fun, and, watching them, Jenny almost forgot for a few moments her own pyramiding worries.

She was so engrossed in watching the skaters that she did not hear anyone approach, and she jumped involuntarily when a voice spoke behind her. "Were you too restless to stay indoors, too?"

Luke Highbridge had come upon her from the trees surrounding the Tamaracks. She could see his footsteps clearly marked in the snow behind him.

"Yes," she admitted. "The cold air seems to have a clearing effect on the brain." She was remembering what had happened in the study during the open house, and she felt warmth creeping into her face. She looked toward the lake again. "It would be nice to be able to forget one-self so totally in play like those children out there. Some-how we seem to leave that ability behind as we grow older."

Beside her, Luke said quietly, "Wordsworth had an explanation for that. Children are closer to the celestial realm from which we all come. They are still trailing clouds of glory, or so Wordsworth believed."

She glanced at his angular face. Somehow he did not seem the sort of man to quote romantic English poets. Would he always surprise her?

Aware of her scrutiny, Luke smiled half-apologetically. "As for me, I think things just pile in on us."

She might have been frightened being this close to him,

but surprisingly she felt no fear at all. What could harm her on this sunny winter day with so many witnesses around? "And," she said after a while, "it's much more difficult to lose ourselves in activity." She felt, his eyes upon her, but she didn't turn to meet his gaze.

"Why should you want to lose yourself, Jenny, I wonder?" She didn't reply, and after a pause he went on. "I saw the sheriff's car at your house earlier. Did he tell you about the gun I found in my bureau drawer early this morning?"

"Yes," Jenny said, still not meeting his gaze.

"I didn't know until I turned it in that Gerald's gun was missing. Turpin came to the Tamaracks after leaving your house to tell me they'd checked the serial number and the gun I found was Gerald's. And they're certain now it's the gun that killed Brubaker."

Jenny drew a deep breath and looked at him. "The sheriff said you had no idea how the gun came to be in your bedroom."

His gaze was direct, unwavering. "That's right. I found it as I was looking for a box of tie tacks I'd placed in that drawer two days before Christmas. Jenny, that gun wasn't there on the evening of the 23rd, and I found it today, the 26th. No one outside the family, Beau and Beth was at the Tamaracks yesterday. Clearly, the gun was put there during the open house, on the 24th."

"But why?"

He laughed without humor. "Isn't that obvious? Someone is trying to frame me for Marty Brubaker's murder."

"Not just anyone," Jenny said, stunned. "What you are saying is that a family friend or an employee of the Highbridge Corporation is trying to frame you."

He stared out over the lake. "I couldn't have put it better myself."

Jenny shivered. "Of course, Beau Gleason could have done it yesterday."

His eyes narrowed as he glanced at her. "Or Beth, for that matter. Even Dad's nurse or one of my parents, if you want to talk about possibilities. Naturally, I don't believe my parents would do that to me. And the nurse is from Helena. Furthermore, I'm just as certain about Beau's and Beth's innocence in the matter."

"Which brings you back to the day of the open house."

"Not that that's much help. There were hundreds of employees in the house during the afternoon and over a hundred guests that evening. But whoever put the gun in my drawer didn't think I'd find it so quickly and turn it over to the police. He intended for it to be found there by somebody else, preferably the police."

What he was saying sounded reasonable, and there was an earnestness in the words. Jenny wanted to believe him.

"If only we knew who wanted Brubaker out of the way, we'd have the killer. You knew Marty, Jenny. Who had it in for him?"

"I can't imagine anyone having it in for Marty. Oh, I know he kept the fact that he was Gideon Garfield a secret, but from things I've been able to piece together, that must have been Leah's idea."

"Why would Leah have wanted to keep it a secret?" Luke's tone was sharply interested, and Jenny could not help feeling that he, like his father, was grasping at straws.

"My parents would not have approved of her seeing him if they'd known."

Luke was shaking his head. "No, I don't buy that. Leah was thirty-six years old, and she did pretty much as she pleased. No, there had to be more to it than that. Brubaker must have talked to you about Leah. Did he say anything that—"

Jenny cut him off. "I've gone over and over it, Luke," she said tiredly. "Marty was definitely looking for something, some information about Leah. He questioned me one day at the library. I know that he'd been entertaining various theories about her murder, but he didn't elaborate on them. Not to me, anyway. I just don't know what was on his mind."

"He must have had a line on the killer," Luke said. "Why else was he murdered?"

"I don't know. He seemed only to want to know about Leah's breakdown years ago. He asked about Garfield, and now I can see he was probably suffering from guilt feelings over her illness, thinking his leaving was the cause of it. Which it was, of course. You know, it's hard for me to connect Marty, as I knew him, with the actor who took Leah from her home and abandoned her in New York. Marty seemed to care about people. I always thought that's why he chose to work in the health field. Of course, the job at the hospital may have been the only one available to him when he came here—to find Leah, we now know. But that day, when he came to talk to me at the library, he did seem anxious about something. I remember that he kept gripping his knees so hard with his hands the fingers were white."

Luke's expression was speculative. "Jenny, try to remember everything he said. It could be important."

Not that she thought it would help, but to satisfy him, she went over the entire conversation between her and Marty as she recalled it, just as she had recounted it for Sheriff Turpin earlier. When she told him about Marty's suspicion that Leah had been involved, perhaps romantically, with someone at the Tamaracks, his expression hardened, and she hurried on, even relating what Marty had said about her blood test.

He gazed out over the lake to where a young boy was trying awkwardly to execute a figure eight. "Tell me about the other times—at the hospital when he did the blood tests."

All at once, Jenny wanted only to go home. "Oh, Luke, what does that have to do with anything?"

"Please, Jenny, humor me." He continued to stare out over the lake.

She sighed heavily and began, "The day of your father's stroke, Dad and I went to the hospital to give blood. It was the first time for me, although Dad has been doing it regularly for as long as I can remember. I'd never gone before because I was anemic as a child and I just assumed I was probably still on the borderline. But, as it turned out, my blood count was high, and Marty seemed especially happy because I have a rare blood type, AB-negative."

"OK," he said after a moment, "so he said you had a rare blood type and took your blood. Anything else?"

"Nothing significant. He did mention that Dad's type was the same as Harold's and said that would be handy if Harold needed a transfusion."

For an instant the voices of the skaters died away and the stillness seemed heavy, almost ominous. Luke turned from perusing the skaters to look at her directly. He seemed oddly puzzled. "Are you sure about that?"

She nodded. "I've told you everything as I remember it."

He frowned. "And you're sure Brubaker said Gerald and Dad have the same blood type?"

Perplexed, she nodded again.

For a moment he seemed lost in thought. Then he said, "A minute ago I asked you to humor me. Do you think you could keep it up for a while longer?"

"I suppose—" She had no idea what he was getting at, but something in his manner told her he was utterly serious.

"I want you to come to the hospital with me."

She could not have been more surprised if he had asked her to walk barefoot through the snow. Harold was at home now, unless— "Luke! Has your father had a relapse?"

"No, although I think Mom's taking him to the hospital today for a physical-therapy treatment. But this has nothing to do with Dad's condition."

She was totally confused. "Why, then?"

"There's something I have to do. I have a wild idea, but I don't want to say anything until I'm certain. You said you would humor me. Please?"

A wild idea. Marty had said something like that. *Don't pay any attention to my wild middle-of-the-night ideas.* But this was midday, and something she had said was causing Luke to look suddenly tense, as if a spring inside him had been wound tightly.

"If you're afraid to come with me," he was saying, "you can take your own car and meet me there."

Afraid? Well, perhaps she was a little afraid of him, for more than one reason. Yet it was ridiculous to refuse to ride in his car in broad daylight. "All right," she relented. "I'll go with you."

He seemed to relax. "Good." He took her arm. "My car's parked on Fir Street. I'd started to the office when I saw you and decided to see if you wanted company."

Walking beside him, she glanced at his profile furtively.

Their meeting had not been accidental, as she had thought. He had come deliberately to talk to her. Why? she wondered. Did he hope to continue what he'd started in the study on Christmas eve? Had he wanted to know the reason behind Sheriff Turpin's visit to her house? Had he expected to read something in her reaction to learning he'd turned Gerald's gun over to the police? She didn't understand any of it, and she realized forlornly that perhaps she was afraid to understand.

Seventeen

Luke sat behind the wheel of the car, his eyes hooded, fixed on the road ahead, as if he listened to something Jenny could not hear, something inside his own head. When they reached the hospital, he pulled into an empty parking space and sat for a moment without moving.

Then he roused himself. "Can't put it off, I guess," he said and got out of the car to come around and open Jenny's door. As she stepped out, he looked down at her and said, "We're going to the lab. Let me do all the talking. OK?"

Jenny nodded wordlessly, thinking this was like a dream in which she was lost and was being hurtled headlong toward an unknown, and somehow dreaded, destination. She was going along blindly, not knowing what Luke wanted here. She recalled her earlier feeling that he was grasping at straws. Was she a fool to have come with him? she wondered unhappily. She could read nothing in Luke's expression. He had learned to hide his secrets well behind the hard lines of his face. Only once had she glimpsed a gentleness in him—that afternoon at the ski lodge—and she had softened toward him then. At this moment that afternoon with Luke seemed like another lifetime.

They walked up the broad steps and into the lobby, where all the seats were occupied. But Luke did not even glance around as he continued across the lobby, looking back once to see if she was following, past the business offices, and through the swinging doors into the central core of the patient section of the hospital.

The young nurse on duty at the nurse's station looked up as they approached. "Your father is back in physical therapy, Mr. Highbridge."

"Thanks." Luke flashed a smile, which was returned by the nurse, who did not even look at Jenny.

But when they were around the corner, out of sight of the nurse's station, Luke did not take the hall that led to the physical-therapy department. Instead, he headed down another hall toward the lab.

"With Brubaker gone, I'm counting on their being short-handed," he said softly to Jenny, who nodded as if she understood, although she was feeling more confused by the minute.

As they approached the open door leading to the laboratory, they heard female voices. Luke caught her arm, and they stopped in the hallway short of the door. Then two young women in white uniforms came out of the lab, one of them carrying a small mesh basket containing needles, syringes, and blood-sample tubes. They looked at Luke and Jenny curiously as they passed, and Luke turned his back on them, bending over Jenny as if they were engrossed in conversation. As soon as the two technicians turned a corner in the hallway, Luke grabbed her hand and pulled her toward the laboratory door.

She held back. "Luke, what are you doing?"

"I'll explain later," he hissed and, still holding her hand, led the way into the lab. No one was there. Luke went straight to a row of filing cabinets against one wall and began opening drawers, looking at the contents and closing them again.

"Stand at the door," he told Jenny. "If you see anyone coming, warn me."

Dazed, Jenny did as she was told. Behind her she could hear the drawers opening and closing. Once Luke asked, "Was your mother ever admitted to this hospital?"

The thought crossed Jenny's mind that perhaps the strain of being investigated in a murder case was too much for him. She wondered fearfully what would happen to them if they were caught going through confidential medical records.

Behind her Luke exclaimed in a hoarse whisper. "Here we are!" Jenny looked around and saw him bending over a bottom drawer in one of the cabinets. He glanced at her. "Did you hear what I asked about your mother?"

"Yes," she said, watching him, while the desire rose in her to run. "Mother was here several years ago. She had gall-bladder surgery." This seemed to satisfy him, and he turned back to the file drawer, pulling out folders and scanning the contents hurriedly before shoving the folder back into place again.

"Please hurry!" Jenny pleaded desperately. She looked in both directions in the hallway and saw no one. But someone was certain to come along any minute—a nurse or those two technicians they had seen leaving the lab.

Luke muttered something that she did not understand, and she checked the hallway again. After several minutes, which seemed to Jenny to stretch on and on, Luke said, "Come here. I want to show you something."

Giving the hallway another quick look, she reluctantly moved into the lab. Luke had pulled several folders up in the file so that they extended above the others in the drawer. He opened these folders one by one while she looked over his shoulder. "This is your file," he said, "and here's your blood type, AB-negative." Going to another folder, he said, "This is Doreen's folder. Blood type A-positive. And Gerald's—O-positive."

Jenny was staring at him. He did not appear to be irrational, but what he was saying had no meaning for her.

He shoved the folders back into place and closed the file drawer, straightening his tall frame. "I wanted you to see for yourself."

Before she could think of an answer, the young technician carrying the wire basket strode into the lab. She started visibly at the sight of them but recovered quickly. "Oh, hello. May I help you?"

Luke flashed another of his winning smiles, but Jenny thought its falseness must be obvious to anyone. "I hope so, miss," she said with just the right degree of puzzlement in his voice. "We're looking for the snack bar."

"Oh, well, you're going in the right direction," The technician said helpfully. "You just turned left when you should have turned right." She stepped to the door. "Go down there to the next door across the hall."

"Thanks a lot." Luke took Jenny's cold hand and hurried out of the lab. Because the technician was standing in the doorway watching them, they entered the snack bar, which, mercifully, was deserted. When Jenny started to sit down at one of the small tables, Luke said, "Come on. She's not looking now."

Half running to keep up with him, Jenny slipped past the open lab door, glancing nervously inside, where the technician, her back to the door, was looking into a microscope. Just before they reached the nurse's station, Luke muttered, "I hope we don't run into my parents."

Jenny hoped not, too. She hoped they ran into no one until she could get back home and get away from Luke, who was acting so strange.

The young nurse saw them and said brightly, "Did you find your father?"

"Yes, thank you," Luke said and pushed Jenny through the swinging doors into the lobby.

In the car again, they left the hospital behind. Jenny drew a shaky breath, the full impact of what they had done finally hitting her. "We would have been in trouble," she said with sudden irritation, "if we'd been caught."

Luke considered her, his dark eyes appraising. "That's why Brubaker wanted to take another blood test. He wanted to check your blood type again to make sure he'd got it right."

Jenny glanced at him uncomfortably. "He said he'd changed the test solutions. He wanted to be able to call on me whenever AB-negative was needed, but he had to make sure my count was high enough."

Luke shook his head. "That may be what he said, but it was your blood type he was interested in." He frowned. "I'm surprised he didn't ask to recheck Gerald and Doreen."

"Dad gives blood regularly. He didn't need to recheck him," Jenny said. "He did say that he'd asked Mother to give a pint of blood and she refused."

Luke nodded. "So he did ask, although he must have been fairly certain by then."

"Certain of what?" Jenny's irritation and confusion had risen to the point where she was near tears. "I don't understand what you're talking about. Why should our blood types be so important?"

He acted as if he hadn't heard. He was quiet for a time, his eyes on the road. With one hand he absent-mindedly reached up to smooth his dark hair. "Wait," he said. "I'll tell you when we get to the Tamaracks."

Jenny heard him in disbelief. "The Tamaracks! I'm

not going there with you." A chill of fear went through her.

They were turning onto Fir Street, ascending the steep lane that led past the Curtiss house. He gave her a side-long glance. "I have to explain this to you. We can have some privacy there, although Beth will be in the house, of course—and Beau's at home." When she did not respond, he added, "We won't actually be alone." His tone was as cool and detached as if this conversation were of no consequence. Yet the grimness of his expression belied that. She studied him. He knew she was afraid to be alone with him; yet he did not seem angry. He seemed morose somehow, even sad. And the tenseness she had noted earlier was still there, as if he had to do something he did not want to do.

He met her gaze. "I'll take you back home after we've talked." For the remainder of the drive, she continued to watch him uneasily, although she did not know what it was she tried to read in his face. Something stirred vaguely in the dim recesses of her memory, but it was gone again before she could grasp it.

Luke brought the car to a stop in front of the Tamaracks. He got out and opened her door, taking her arm to help her up the broad steps. In the foyer he took her coat, hanging it in the guest closet.

"We'll go back to the den," he said, leading the way. "I'll tell Beth to bring some coffee."

In the den Jenny sat on the sofa and stared into the blazing fireplace. Luke joined her shortly, carrying a tray bearing a carafe of coffee and two mugs. She watched him, feeling somehow detached, as he poured the coffee. Then he went to the bar against one wall and returned with a bottle of brandy with which he laced the coffee in their mugs.

He handed Jenny her drink, then sat beside her, watching her silently as she sipped.

When he spoke, she was prepared, she thought, for almost anything—except that what he said seemed totally unrelated to what had been said at the hospital and in the car.

"Do you remember much of your freshman biology course at the university?" What could he be getting at?

she wondered. And then something came back to her—
the biology book that had disappeared and reappeared
with several pages missing, pages about inheritable traits,
a section about human blood types. She discovered that
her hands were trembling. Carefully she set the mug down
on the glass-topped table and covered her face with her
hands, swaying a little.

"Are you all right?" Luke touched her shoulder, steadying her.

Something frightening, something shattering had almost
been grasped, but now it receded. "It's nothing," she said.
"To answer your question, I remember very little. I never
liked science classes, so I was never very good in them.
Why? Where is this leading? Please, just tell me, Luke."

"I had to check the lab records to be absolutely sure
you had understood Marty correctly when he said Gerald had the same blood type as Dad. I knew Dad was
O-positive. And I wanted you to see the records with
your own eyes so you would know I'm telling the truth.
You are AB-negative. Gerald is O-positive. There is no
way you can be his daughter. You can check that out in
any biology textbook."

She felt the blood leave her face. "I don't believe you!"

"Look it up, then," he said quietly. He got up abruptly
and found a sheet of paper and a ball-point pen in the
desk in one corner of the room. Returning, he said, "Let
me show you." He placed the sheet of paper on the table
in front of them and looked at her, his pen poised to
write. "Forget the negative factor for now. It is possible
for two positive parents with negative recessive genes to
have a child with a negative blood factor." He began to
write letter combinations joined by plus signs in a row,
one beneath the other: $AB + AB$; $AB + A$; $AB + B$;
$A + B$. "These are the only blood-type combinations
that can produce a child with type AB."

She stared at what he had written, comprehending at
last. "You're saying my mother became pregnant by another man, aren't you?"

"No."

"Oh, of course you are! You—"

He took both of her hands in his. "Jenny, these tests

don't prove Doreen is your mother, only that she could be."

She said almost feverishly, "Why are you telling me this? Why do you want to hurt me?"

He answered in a constrained voice. "I wouldn't have, Jenny, please believe me, except that I think it had something to do with Brubaker's murder."

Jenny drew in her breath with a quick, shocked gasp. She had known he was grasping at straws, but now she knew he was desperate enough to suggest that someone had killed Marty to keep her from learning that her parents had adopted her. Because she realized now, of course, that that is what must have happened. Somehow Doreen had found her in New York and brought her back to Pine Valley as her and Gerald's child. Marty had stumbled onto the knowledge by accident when he typed her blood, but surely that could not have been the cause of his death. Wasn't it unethical for medical personnel to disclose information such as that? And even if Marty had told, who besides Jenny herself would have been hurt? Only her parents, and Luke knew this very well. So what he was suggesting was that Gerald had wanted to shut Marty up, had wanted it enough to . . .

He was looking at her searchingly. "Jenny, I'm sorry. I didn't want to hurt you. Let me help you now."

She did not believe him. She could not believe now that he would stop at anything to implicate her father to save his own neck. When he tried to take her in his arms, she pulled away. "Don't bother!"

The pines outside the bow window cut off most of the declining sun. In the suffused glow from the log fire, his face with its distinct planes of cheekbones and jaw looked closed, unreadable. And Jenny was suddenly frightened. He had said Beth was in the house, but Jenny hadn't seen the housekeeper with her own eyes.

She got to her feet nervously. "I have to go."

A muscle leaped along his jaw. "I'll get your coat."

She felt such an urgent need to get away from him, away from this house, that her hands, hanging at her sides, twitched. He seemed about to say something more, but then he only turned and left the den. She followed him into the foyer, where he had already taken her coat

from the guest closet. Wordlessly, he helped her into it;
then he reached into the closet for his own.

"No!" Jenny said. "You needn't drive me. I want to go
alone."

His brief smile did not warm his eyes. "I can't let you
do that."

She reached the door in quick strides. "I won't go with
you!" And then she opened the door and was outside on
the porch before he could reply.

Clumsy with agitation, she clambered down the wide
steps and slipped on the bottom one. Her feet flew out
from under her, and she banged her elbow against the
sharp edge of concrete as she fell. But she was on her
feet at once, elbow smarting painfully.

Behind her, she heard Luke's angry voice. "Jenny,
come back here!"

She started to run. She knew that she couldn't go home
and face her parents yet, and so she veered from the
path that led to Fir Street and ran in the only direction
that offered privacy, toward the mountain behind the
Tamaracks.

The air was cold and exhilarating, and the earlier calm
had lifted. A wind was rising. Jenny could hear it seethe
through the tall pines, and she found herself wishing it
would increase to a loud gale and drive the painful sense
of betrayal from her mind.

She was running between the close-growing trees, stum-
bling over rocks that were made deceptively smooth by
the snow. The ground beneath her feet was climbing
now, and the rocks grew larger, crouching like silent white
beasts between the trees, eerie in the fading light.

And then, just as abruptly as she had begun her flight,
she halted, remembering the teacherous crevices and
sheer cliffs that were scattered across the face of this
mountain, cliffs like the one from which an early-day
Highbridge ancestor had plunged to his death. The drop-
offs would be even more dangerous now because of the
snow that drifted into the low places and filled the cracks,
presenting the illusion of safe, level ground to the unwary.

Some yards behind her, lower down the slope beneath
an ancient spruce, she saw a boulder that had been sheltered from the snow by thick interweaving boughs. Re-

tracing her steps, she veered from her previous course and sat down on the boulder, pulling her coat close about her and huddling against the tree.

Above her the spruce creaked in the wind like some elderly arthritic, but the sound did not shut out the questions drumming in her thoughts. Why had Luke insisted upon telling her that her parents were not her parents at all? Something to do with Marty's murder, he had said. But how could that be? The police, everyone, seemed convinced that Marty's murder was somehow linked to Leah's and Mary Steed's. And what did her being adopted have to do with the two women?

She shivered and drew her coat more closely about her. With the action, the golden Demeter charm dangled before her eyes.

She took the charm in her other hand. FOR JENNY, MAIDEN ALL LOVELY. Had she been wrong in feeling (hoping, perhaps?) that Luke had meant the words in a personal sense? Going to the trouble of looking up Homer's words would be out of character for the Luke Highbridge the world knew—aloof, proud, even arrogant. But she had seen another Luke, who quoted Wordsworth and touched her with gentleness, a Luke who enjoyed reading Demeter's story over a glass of mulled wine.

She turned the charm over, holding it at an angle in the murky light so that she could see the crowned head. The engraver had done a good job. The fragile lines of the goddess's profile suggested unhappiness—unhappiness over the loss of her daughter, Persephone. *We are a lot alike, Demeter and I,* Leah had said. Like the tragic goddess, Leah had been moody, melancholy at times, but had she meant something more by the statement?

This was the question Jenny had been holding at bay. And in that moment a number of things fell into place: Leah's reluctance to leave the Curtiss house, Marty's intense interest in Jenny's blood type, the subconscious spark in herself that had always responded to Leah on some essential level of feeling, even the meaning of Leah's complaint to Sarah about dreams coming true too late to do anybody any good.

Leah was her mother.

She tried to reject the knowledge, but it was too intuitive to be denied, and she felt an odd tingling of all her nerves. She was so engrossed in her stunning discovery that she didn't hear Luke's approach. His voice calling her name was so close to her hiding place that she jerked violently at the sound of it.

She heard his muffled footsteps as he passed near where she was sitting, following the route she had taken earlier, although it must be almost too dark now for him to see her footprints in the snow.

She was torn between a desire to stay hidden, nursing her shattering discovery, and an impulse to rush after him, throw herself into his arms and sob out her thoughts against his chest. She hesitated and heard him, above her now, still calling her name.

What stopped her going to him was the sudden realization that he must have suspected all along. Why else would he have said, "Jenny, those tests don't prove Doreen is your mother, only that she could be." He *knew* and had been trying to prepare her for this final revelation.

And then she heard another voice, higher-pitched, more frantic-sounding. "Jenny! Where are you? Jenny!"

It was Doreen some distance to Jenny's left and higher up—Doreen whose anxiety had been palpable of late, Doreen the woman who she had believed for twenty years was her mother. Both of her parents had been trying, she realized now, to shield her from this knowledge.

And now that she knew, other things began to fall into place. The day the biology book had disappeared from her desk, Doreen had been in the library checking out books. Jenny could almost see Doreen's eyes falling on the book title and then the almost inevitable jumping to the conclusion that Jenny had been reading about blood types and how they were inherited. And she could see the immediate reaction of Doreen's hand grabbing the book and slipping it into the shopping bag she carried. Later, Doreen must have torn out the offending pages and then, not wanting the book to be found in her possession, had dropped it into the trash barrel behind the furniture store, just a few steps from the back door of the newspaper building.

Jenny had little doubt that one of her parents had sent the anonymous message, too, suggesting that she leave town. Doreen probably, since it was she who had suggested the same thing earlier. No wonder Jenny had puzzled over the wording of that message. It had not been a threat, but a desperate plea. And later, the night after Luke changed her flat tire and she'd left her wet coat in the kitchen, Doreen had retrieved the note and burned it.

But through the blood tests Marty had stumbled onto the truth. *Leah loved someone else more,* Marty had said. And it was true. She had loved her daughter. And his daughter. Marty must have threatened to come to Jenny with his discovery, and Gerald's gun had killed him.

Gerald's gun.

Luke, Sarah, Beau Gleason, Doreen, the newspaper employees and dozens of other people had passed through Gerald's office in the days before the murder, but only Gerald and Tom had known of the gun's existence. And only Gerald had known where the gun was hidden.

Oh, Dad, how could you? she cried silently.

She heard Luke calling to Doreen then, heard him clambering through the dark trees toward her. Reluctantly, Jenny left her hiding place and, feeling her way step by step, headed toward Luke and Doreen, toward the inevitable confrontation.

As she drew near the spot where they had met, she heard angry voices—Doreen's high-pitched and too incoherent for Jenny to understand, then Luke's voice raised in anger.

". . . living a lie! You had no right, no right at all!" he was saying.

After a pause, Doreen's reply sounded calmer, more reasonable, but the words were too low for Jenny to hear.

Luke's next words trembled with rage. "It's already too late!" And then some more words she couldn't hear.

She wanted to cover her ears with her hands and scream at them to stop fighting over her. And she might have done just that, but Doreen cried, "Don't Luke! Please, don't!" and then there was a loud scrambling sound followed by an anguished shriek that ended in a gradually diminishing cry.

With a strangled moan, Jenny stumbled forward. Luke was standing near the edge of a cliff, and when he saw Jenny, he stood unmoving for a moment, as if he were dazed, and then he took a step toward her.

"Jenny . . ."

Jenny looked about wildly. "What happened? Where is Mother?"

She was close enough to him to see the naked pain in his face. "She—she fell. . . ."

He tried to take her arm, but she shook him off and moved to peer down over the cliff. In the fragile evening light, she could make out a dark form marring the whiteness of the ledge below.

Panic drummed in her ears as she whirled to face Luke.

"Be careful, Jenny." His voice was tense.

Crouching at the edge of the cliff, she forced words between lips that were numb with cold and fear. "Stay away from me! Murderer! Murderer!"

Peering up at him, she began to sob helplessly.

"I'll go for help," he said then. "Stay with her. Don't move or you will lose your way, and there are crevices all around here. I'll be back as soon as I can." He turned and disappeared into the trees.

Jenny looked down at the ledge again, trying to stop crying. Doreen lay perhaps twenty-five feet below her, her body at an odd angle, as if . . .

"Mother," she called brokenly. "We're getting help. It won't be long."

"Jenny?" Doreen's voice was a frail sound in the rising wind.

Jenny went weak with relief. Doreen was alive! "Yes, Mother. Lie still until we can get to you."

"My back . . ." There was anguish in the words. "I—I can't move."

Jenny was thinking, *If I hadn't come here, she wouldn't have come after me. She wouldn't be lying there now.* "It's my fault, Mother. I—I didn't want to face you."

"Oh, Jenny, I didn't want you to know."

"It's all right, Mother. Luke had no right to tell me,

but since he has, it's all right. He—he has other things to answer for now."

"No"—Doreen's voice from below rose, cutting Jenny off—"Luke didn't push me. You mustn't think that. I fell —my heart—"

"Luke's gone after Dad," Jenny called to her mother, but she was afraid it wasn't true. Would he leave town again? How long should she wait before going for help herself?

"You mustn't blame your father, Jenny. That—that girl bewitched him."

Jenny thought that Doreen was confused, her mind drifting, but before she could reply, Doreen went on. "It only happened once, Jenny. Don't blame your father. He never even knew about the child."

What Doreen was saying hit Jenny like a blow to the stomach. Gerald and Mary Steed! Gerald had been the father of Mary's child! That was why Mary left the Curtiss house without notice. That was what Leah must have discovered. But surely Doreen was wrong. Gerald must have known. Leah must have told him. That is why he had killed them. She was hardly aware of the anguished moan that escaped her.

"I begged that girl to go away. I offered to pay her. But she went to Leah . . ." Doreen's voice trailed away.

Peering down, Jenny saw that her mother's form was barely discernible now. "Don't try to talk anymore," she pleaded.

But Doreen seemed not to hear her. "Leah threatened to tell you. . . ."

Jenny said, "That I was her daughter, hers and Marty's."

The silence that followed was broken only by the grieving of the wind. And then Doreen said, "She didn't want you when you were born. She said she didn't want anything that reminded her of that actor. She agreed that Gerald and I could raise you as our daughter. She used my name in the hospital. And all these years she kept the secret, until—"

"But she wasn't responsible," Jenny couldn't help protesting. "She was too ill to make a decision like that."

"She said that later, too, after we had come back home. But she kept her bargain until that Steed girl came into our lives. I didn't want to do it, Jenny. You must believe that. But they left me no choice. Afterwards, I wanted to die, too, but I thought that you needed me, you and Gerald."

A dawning horror tightened Jenny's chest. "You—it was you!"

"I waited for that girl on the mountain path and killed her. But Leah saw what I'd done. She came to me and accused me, and that's when she threatened to tell you that she was your mother. She said that your father wanted her back and she was going to tell both of you. I—I said I'd tell you, but she had to keep quiet about Mary until I did. I convinced her she owed me that much, and I—I followed her along the mountain path—"

"You killed her!" Jenny's cry was wrenched from her. "But Marty began to suspect, didn't he? When he saw my blood type, he started to ask questions."

"He said you had to know he was your father."

When had he confronted Doreen, told her who he was? It must have been that cold day when Doreen had gone to see Harold and had come home white-faced and weak, frightening Jenny into going to the Tamaracks in search of Gerald.

Doreen's thin voice rose suddenly. "He had no claim on you! He deserted Leah before he even knew she was pregnant. He—he called and asked for you that night. I said you weren't home yet. I said you'd have to call him. But when you came home, I put a sedative in your chocolate, and I went to his apartment. He was leaving—to come to you."

Jenny's grief for the father she had never known was a twisting pain in her chest, and she remembered the anguished words penned in the mythology book: *Leah, my darling, I'm so sorry.* Sorry he had deserted her, sorry he had not known all those years that they had a daughter. He had suspected before, but the story of Demeter and her lost daughter must have convinced him once and for all.

The high keening noise had gone on for several seconds before Jenny realized it was coming from her own throat. Then, blessedly, she passed into a numbness in which she merely sat and waited for Luke to return.

Eighteen

"Jenny?"

Awareness returned slowly. With momentary puzzlement, she looked into Luke's face illuminated by the glow from the lantern he carried. Behind him, in the murkey light, several men were standing at the edge of the cliff.

She heard Beau Gleason's voice. "I'll go down. Just make sure you hang on to the rope."

Jenny struggled to stand, her legs numb with the cold. "Mother . . ."

Then she heard Gerald's voice, thick with fear. "Doreen! Doreen, can you hear me?" There was no answer.

Luke helped Jenny to her feet, supporting her with an arm about her waist. "They'll get her out. I came as fast as I could. I stopped at Beau's apartment, and he went with me to get Gerald and some others."

Jenny shivered, glancing at the huddle of men. In the lantern light she saw Beau Gleason's stocking-capped head disappearing below the cliff. "I'm fine. Mother's back may be broken. She said she couldn't move."

"We brought a litter," Luke said. "We'll take her to the hospital in the Bronco." He looked into Jenny's eyes. "Do you still think I pushed her?"

Jenny shook her head. "Forgive me, Luke. Mother said she fell. Evidently she had a spell with her heart. It's just that when I heard her begging you not to do something, and then she fell—I'm afraid I jumped to the wrong conclusion."

"She was pleading with me not to tell you of your true parentage. I was trying to tell her you already knew when she fell."

"Why did she come out here?" Jenny asked.

"When you didn't return home, she became worried and went looking for you. She must have gone to the Tamaracks and learned from Beth that you'd left. She probably was able to follow your footprints around the house because of the yard lamps. And then, when we ran into each other, I was so worried about you and where you'd gone that I lost my temper and accused her of lying to you all your life. She became hysterical. In a way, I *am* to blame for her fall."

Jenny shook her head again. "No." Her throat tightened then, and she couldn't go on. She moved to the edge of the cliff. Beside her, she could feel Gerald's shock-filled eyes boring into her, but she could not meet his gaze. Below, the litter had been lowered, and Beau Gleason, with his enormous strength, lifted Doreen onto it, securing the ropes on either end of the metal frame. Then he took off his down-filled jacket and tucked it around Doreen's motionless form. He looked up, his face in dark shadow. "OK, Raise her, but be careful!"

With three men on either rope, they raised the litter slowly until they could grasp the frame and lower Doreen carefully to the ground and untie the ropes, one of which was flung down to Beau Gleason. As the men brought Gleason up, Jenny and Gerald crouched over Doreen.

"She's so cold." Gerald's voice quavered.

"Mother, can you hear me?" Jenny said urgently, but there was no response. She tucked the jacket closer about Doreen's neck and shoulders and, pulling off a glove, laid a hand on her forehead. It was difficult to tell how cold Doreen was, since Jenny's own hand was numb with cold, but she could make out a fragile, speeding pulse at the temple.

Beau Gleason, holding a lantern high, led the way because he knew the mountain and was more familiar with its dangers than the others. Their descent was slow, but finally they came out at the back of the Tamaracks. Luke hurried ahead and backed the Bronco from its stall in the garage. The men slid the litter into the back of the vehicle, and Jenny and Gerald got in front with Luke.

At the hospital Doc Weaver was waiting. Beth Denton had called to tell him that they were bringing Doreen. The doctor and a small crew of hospital personnel took charge of the injured woman, transferring her to an examining room, where the doors swung shut behind them.

Luke, Gerald and Jenny were kindly but firmly banished to the waiting room.

Mercifully, they had the room to themselves. Perhaps feeling as if he were intruding, Luke excused himself to go to the snack bar for coffee.

Jenny sat down on one of the vinyl-covered couches, and Gerald sat beside her. He leaned forward, elbows on his knees, and buried his face in his hands. Jenny touched his arm lightly, but he did not seem to notice.

Finally he spoke, his voice muffled by his hands. "You know, don't you?"

To what, Jenny wondered, was he referring? Her parentage? His relationship with Mary Steed? Or did he know of Doreen's guilt? She knew there was no point in postponing the inevitable, and, taking a shaky breath, she said, "I know that Leah and Marty were my parents. And Mother—Mother confessed to killing them, and Mary Steed, too. I can't help thinking she had some kind of mental breakdown."

Gerald was silent for so long that Jenny wondered if he had comprehended what she said. Then he said, "I was almost sure. She has been too jumpy recently. And when she learned you had given blood, she practically went into hysterics in our bedroom. We had an awful row. She accused me of wanting you to find out that we weren't your parents. Until she brought it up, I hadn't even thought about the blood types and the possibility that yours might prove you weren't our child. I've grown so used to thinking of you as my daughter."

That was the night when she'd found Gerald outside, the night he had drunk too much and talked so enigmatically. Pity for this man who was the only father she had ever known welled up in her. No matter what he had done, he would always be her father in her heart.

"Doreen was adamant," he went on, "that you should never know. She was always possessive where you and I were concerned, more than was healthy, I thought." Jenny recalled his telling her once before that one person can't own another. She hadn't understood what he meant at the time. "Periodically, through the years," Gerald went on, "Doreen accused me of having an affair with Sarah, even though there has been nothing but friendship between Sarah and me since her marriage. I've always wanted to believe that Harold took Sarah away from me by some kind of trickery, some terrible lie he made her believe. I know now she simply fell in love with him. But Doreen has always been obsessed with jealousy. She couldn't seem to let it go. Once she told me that she would never allow anything or anyone to break up our family. But I've never seen her as hysterical as she was that night after you'd given blood. That's when I began to wonder if she'd killed Leah to keep her from telling you the truth. And then when Marty was killed and we learned he was actually Gideon Garfield, things began to fit together. Doreen must have found my gun by accident on one of her visits to the office."

"I'm sure she never thought about the fact that it could be traced. And when it was, she tried to make Luke look guilty," Jenny said sadly.

Gerald sighed. "He was the most likely suspect, and Doreen must have been slightly unhinged by that time."

"We'll have to tell the police, won't we?"

"Yes." Gerald lifted his head and looked at her with pain in his eyes. "How did Mary Steed come into it?"

"I think when Marty came back and asked Leah to marry him, Leah must have considered telling me the truth about my birth. She said something to Sarah that made me think she was trying to make a difficult decision just before Mary was killed. She must have dreaded leaving the house because of me, and maybe she thought she could draw us closer together by telling me the truth. Then Mary Steed discovered she was carrying your child, and she told Leah. Leah made the mistake of going to Mother with it."

"Oh, my God!" The cry was wrung from him. "And Doreen felt she had to shut them up, both of them."

"Maybe," Jenny said tiredly, "Leah rationalized that your behavior somehow released her from her promise to keep my parentage a secret. She must have been looking for an excuse to tell me, anyway. If she married

Marty, she wanted me to be able to visit them as their daughter."

"It was a little late for that," Gerald said bitterly.

"Leah said something like that to Sarah. She said that sometimes dreams come true too late to do anybody any good. All those years she must have dreamed of what it would have been like if she and Marty and I could have been a family. She never stopped loving him. I'm convinced of that now."

"Jenny, there was nothing between Mary and me. It was only one moment of weakness, my weakness. She was too young and naive to be at fault. She was lonely without her family, and from what she said, her father was a cold, undemonstrative man. She had little defense against the first older man who was kind to her. I'm sure it's no secret to you that our marriage—Doreen's and mine—hasn't been on very solid ground for some time. And then one night I had too much to drink . . ." His voice broke, and he buried his face in his hands again.

"Dad, don't," Jenny pleaded.

"I was so ashamed the next day," he said. "I was relieved when Mary decided to leave us. I talked Sarah into taking her at the Tamaracks so she could go immediately. I never knew. . . . She never told me. . . ."

"I know that," Jenny said, "and so does Mother."

He took a heavy breath. "When the rumors started about Mary and Luke, I suppose I wanted to believe them. It let me off the hook."

At that moment Jenny heard the swinging doors open. A heavy tread approached them. She looked up into Dr. Weaver's weary face, and she read everything in his eyes before he said a word.

"I'm sorry, Gerald, Jenny," the doctor said. "She's gone. Her back was broken. but that isn't what killed her. Her heart just stopped. We did everything we could —injections, heart massage. Nothing helped."

Gerald sobbed softly into his hands, but at that moment Jenny was unable to cry. She felt numb. She looked into Dr. Weaver's kind eyes as he took her hand.

"She didn't want to live," she said.

Nineteen

Two days after her mother's funeral, Jenny packed a suitcase. It was January 1, the first day of a new year, and she had received permission from the library board to take a three-week leave of absence. She hoped that would be enough time to decide what she intended to do with her life. She had almost decided to leave Pine Valley, at least for the time being, but she wanted to be alone to think about it. Although Gerald had not tried to dissuade her, she knew he hoped she would decide to stay at home.

The news of Doreen's guilt had burst upon the town only hours after Gerald and Jenny told the sheriff of Doreen's confession. Friends, particularly Tom and Shirley and Kent, had been solicitous, but it was impossible for Jenny to avoid the curious stare of the townspeople wherever she went. She wanted to get away from that, too. If it was a cowardly reaction, she didn't care.

From the bed, Beast watched intently as Jenny moved from closet to bureau, deciding what to take on her trip. She'd been able to save most of her salary since she had started working at the library, and now she would be able to pay for this much-needed vacation without any help from Gerald. She and Gerald had talked things out, and she had told him she didn't blame him for what had happened, or for what Doreen had done, even though he still was inclined to blame himself. And she truly did not blame him, but there was a strain between them that she hoped the three weeks apart would help to banish.

She was lifting a nightgown from the bureau drawer when she heard footsteps in the hall outside her door. There was a soft rapping, and Luke's voice called, "Jenny?"

Her heart thudded, and she went to the door and opened it. He stood there, not smiling. "Gerald said you were up here in your room."

She tried to cover her surprise. "Come in." As he followed her into the bedroom, she added, "I'm packing, as you can see."

He stood near the dormer window and then, at Jenny's invitation, sat down on the window seat. She began to fold shirts and slacks and place them in the suitcase.

"I didn't know you were taking a trip. Gerald didn't mention it when he let me in just now."

She smiled briefly. "He's probably hoping I'll change my mind at the last minute. But I won't. I have to get away for a while."

"How long will you be gone?"

"Three weeks—for now." She shivered slightly, thinking that she hadn't been really warm since that horrible moment on the mountain when Doreen had fallen. "I want to go someplace warm. I thought Mexico or maybe the Caribbean. I'm taking a plane from Missoula to Denver tomorrow."

He said, "And after that?"

She looked at him. "I don't know, Luke. I may leave Pine Valley for good. There are so many memories here."

"You have to face them sometime," he said curtly. He got to his feet and moved toward the bed and stood looking down at her. "I didn't think you were one to run away from trouble."

He had every right to criticize her, she thought sadly. But she was too tired to fight anymore, and she felt so terribly alone. If only he would look at her tenderly instead of in that aloof way. Aloud she said, "There comes a time when running is the only thing a person is capable of. I thought you would understand that."

Abruptly, the cool, detached look in his eyes faded and gave way to a strangely intense expression, a kind of naked pleading. "A vacation will be good for you, but after that I want you to come back here to stay."

After a moment she managed to say, "You make me feel ashamed."

"Why?"

"After everything my mother did to make you look guilty of the murders, and the things I thought about you —I know I'm taking the coward's way out. The gossip has been dreadful. Having the whole town know of Mother's guilt is awful, and it will be even worse when word gets around about Dad's being the father of Mary Steed's child."

"Why should it get around?"

She looked at him, unable to speak for a moment. "I —I assumed you and your parents would want your name cleared. It's only natural—"

"What?" He managed a jaunty smile. "And spoil my reputation as a rake?"

She said, bewildered, "You mean you would let everyone go on thinking—"

"What people think doesn't concern me much."

"Thank you," she said simply. And then, "Beau knew —about Dad and Mary, didn't he?"

"He suspected," Luke admitted. "He came upon Mary crying in the kitchen one day, and when he asked what was wrong, she blurted out that she wished she'd never heard of the Curtisses. Beau says he suspected she was pregnant even then. He says she had that expectant look." He smiled. "When I tried to pin him down on that, he said it's something about the eyes. Anyway, he put two and two together. After Beth discovered Mary's pregnancy, she let something slip to Beau that made him think Mary was trying to put the blame on me. And, realizing that Mary had probably confided in Leah, he thought Leah was urging her to take that way out, to protect Gerald. After Mary's death, when her pregnancy was confirmed, Beau was more sure than ever that he was right. It wasn't any kind of proof, though, so he never mentioned it to anyone."

Jenny sighed. "When I think of how I accused Beau . . ." His hostility toward her made sense now. He had thought she knew the truth about her father and, like Leah, was trying to place the blame on Luke to protect Gerald.

"Don't worry about that," Luke said. "Beau's a tough old bird." Luke paused. "Will you come back to stay? Maybe I have no right to ask you, but I want us to have a chance."

"Us?" she repeated, confused.

"I think we could come to love each other. Although

I might as well admit it—I love you already. I want you to come back and let me prove I'm not quite as unprincipled as a lot of people think."

"But what about Susan and you?" It was all she could think of to say.

"There is no Susan and I," he said wryly. "We settled that at the open house on Christmas Eve, after I talked to you in the study." So that is why he had taken Susan into the study that night, to convince her he did not intend to marry her. "She's going back to New York in a few days."

"Oh."

"Well?" he said in a strained voice. "Anything else you want cleared up?"

"No. I'm beginning to see things clearly—for the first time in a long time, I guess."

"Then, you'll come back to stay? You'll give us a chance?"

Come back! She didn't even want to go away from him for three weeks now. But she would, to give herself time to think about things alone. Not about Luke and her—she had never felt more right about anything. But about Gerald and Doreen, and Marty and Leah. Being in a different environment would give her a new perspective. She had to let go of any remnants of resentment and strive for understanding. Only then could her life go on happily.

She saw hope glowing in Luke's dark eyes, the eyes that used to seem so cold and remote. She remembered the afternoon at the ski lodge when she had first glimpsed the man beneath the proud veneer. And the evening of the open house when he had kissed her with a blend of anger and desire. And she knew that, no matter how she had denied it to herself, she had loved him from the moment he walked into the Copper Kettle, back into town and into her life.

Almost awkwardly, he took her into his arms then, enveloping her in the warmth and security of his presence. Beast stared at them with his yellow eyes, looking wise and superior, as if he had known all along that they belonged together.

"I wish I had a pomegranate seed," he murmured

softly into her hair, "so I could be certain you'd come back to me."

"Oh, Luke," she said with the first contentment she had felt in weeks, "I'll come back. I promise."